Capturing
the lost woman

Also by Anna Buckley

AWAKENING the lost woman
(book one of the lost woman trilogy)

FINDING the lost woman
(book three of the lost woman trilogy)

Capturing
the lost woman

(book two of the lost woman trilogy)

august
XXIX

Anna Buckley

Published by august XXIX, an imprint of August Twentynine pty. ltd.
mail@august29.com.au

First published 2014.

1-2-1.00

National Library of Australia Cataloguing-in-Publication entry: (paperback)

Author: Buckley, Anna, author.

Title: Capturing the lost woman / Anna Buckley.

ISBN: 978 0 9924781 1 7 (paperback)

Series: Buckley, Anna. Lost woman; no. 2.

Subjects: Women-Fiction, Women-Conduct of life-Fiction, Erotic stories.

Dewey Number: A823.4

ACKNOWLEDGEMENTS

Thank you to the group of people who read the first manuscript. Your feedback and encouragement was invaluable in the writing of the second book.

Special thanks to Karyn, my editor, for her untiring work and to Karlene for her continuing support.

ABOUT THE AUTHOR

Anna Buckley is an author based in Melbourne, Australia. Her previous career was in design.

Her aim is to write books about women taking control of their lives, financially, emotionally and sexually. Her books are set across the world and feature art, architecture, design, fashion, food and wine.

Anna Buckley has a blog where she posts stories and pictures behind her books. Visit it at <u>annabuckley.com</u>

Contents

Part 1   1

America and it all gets Bigger......................................1
Los Angeles...4
Weekend with Dan..19
The Power of One Woman...45
Wise Aura..50
The Price of Fame..53
New York...60

Part 2   79

Back to Business..79
Christmas...84
Coffee and Newspapers..91
Boxing Day lunch..94
Brotherly Love...102
Trampoline in the Bedroom......................................108
Meeting with Kate..111
Work, Work, Work...117
First Approach...121
Building...123
A really Great Man...130
Farewell Beautiful Lovers...139
Temporarily Homeless..144

Part 3   151

Tasmania...151
Lands End Lagoon...158
Rescue..166

Let's Eat...181

Settled..183

Joe..186

Domestic Goddess...190

A Cold Day In..193

Muse...197

Anniversary...199

The Bridge..206

Hunter Gatherer..214

Part 4 231

Captive..231

Lost and Found..234

Joe and Bob...236

The Cellar..237

Searching for Tina..241

Wild Goose Chase..243

Missing Presumed Dead..245

Prisoner...246

My Eyes Opened..249

Seduction..252

Upstairs...257

Feeding Moses Smith...266

Discovering Moses...284

Confused...296

The Pact..303

Trip to Town..310

Part 1

America and it all gets Bigger

I tossed and turned fitfully. The sleeping tablet didn't last long. Los Angeles was going to be a very drawn out fifteen hour flight.

My mind was still trying to process what had just happened. All that intensity, words of love and then abandonment. Who was I kidding? How could I have even considered a relationship with Adam? Would I have been his dirty little secret? Kept hidden from the brother who seemed to have an emotional stranglehold over him.

It would never work. I got out my computer and wrote.

Adam,

A life with you would require you to choose your brother or me. I can't and won't ask you to do this

Please understand that we can never see each other again, the hurt would be too much to bear.

Don't try to contact me, it will just make things harder.

Tina.

Short, sharp and brutal. This was the only way.

I'd been given this taste of what love could be, then had it ripped so mercilessly away. It hurt so much. And then I wept. Into the pillow, muffled, uncontrolled sobs.

I was interrupted by a polite knock.

'Everything ok, Mrs Brown? May I come in?' said James, the steward, with a concerned look on his face.

'Not really, but come in anyway. Stupid girl stuff,' I blurted out.

'Anything you want to talk about?'

It all came tumbling out, it was freeing. I was surprised at how easily my confession was made to someone I barely knew.

'There, there, I know it hurts now, but you've done the right thing,' said James, taking my hand.

Almost immediately I started to feel some relief.

'Now, let me do my job and get something to cheer you up.'

He returned with a tray of food. Steamed salmon and green beans, chocolate fondant, French brie and a glass of champagne. He turned on the TV and showed me the movie menu. I was quite hungry and pleased to be distracted by some mindless thing on the screen. The food and wine did its job and this time I slept like a baby.

When I woke a few hours later I felt slightly better, but still needed to get my mind off the events of the last day. I had promised to put together this week's editorial on the flight and, with a few more hours in the air, knew that writing would keep my mind occupied. 'Choices' was what I really wanted to write about, but realised this would not be the diversion I needed. Instead I decided to finish an article I had been writing about the difficulties we Australians have in the Southern Hemisphere doing business with Europe and America in the Northern Hemisphere. A bit of a nothing story, a mindless distraction. Perfect for the last few hours of the trip. It started with a humorous line about what it's like to live upside down on the bottom of the globe. Australia sleeps when the rest of the world works. Designing clothes in a hot Australian summer when the north is blanketed in winter snow. Dealing with the massive distance between us and the northern trade centres. I remember listening to a New Yorker complaining about jet lag after the eight hour trip to Paris. In Australia that would only get me to Singapore, with Paris still at least another 14 hours away. I fantasised about the idea of being able to leave in the morning for a Paris dinner date that same night!

I also wanted to mention other more trivial things. Australians drive on the left hand side of the road. I remember my first trip to America, trying to cross the road, checking for oncoming traffic, when I nearly stepped into the path of a truck. I just instinctively looked the wrong way! We design our houses to face north to capture the sun. We don't know what a 'stick' of butter is when we are cooking from an American cookbook. And as for buying shoes and clothes online, who the hell knows what the sizes are?

The writing was a great panacea and, in all honesty, this flight was no ordeal. Far from it, the suite I was given was more like a private luxurious cabin. Cindy had mentioned to the airline that I would be travelling with them and might include a story about the experience. That's why I was upgraded. She was a very shrewd operator and as usual, I was extremely grateful. There were many perks to being a high profile blogger. James returned to tell me I could have a shower if I wished. What a great idea. I would be ready to hit the ground running.

Los Angeles

The first thing I did was send the email to Adam. A chauffeur was waiting for me. An electric window separated us. I had privacy, relieved I didn't have to engage in polite conversation with a stranger. I was not feeling that approachable just yet. Then I turned on my phone. A message.

'Tina, I'm so sorry. We need to talk, Adam.'

Too late, my email had said it all. I pressed delete. Dragging this out would only make it harder. I feared that hearing his voice would weaken my resolve and I'd succumb to a remorseful lover's persuasion. The temptation would be too great. I had to be strong. The emotional barriers needed to be back in place. No more vulnerability or love struck blindsiding. I could handle this. I took a deep breath, then rang Cindy.

'Hi Cindy. Had a great flight. Brilliant upgrade! How are things back at the office?'

'Where are you now?' she said hurriedly.

'On my way to the hotel. Why?'

'You'll be going straight to the TV studio. Shauna, your publicist, will meet you there.'

'Fuck! Did you say TV? When, how?'

'Soon, within the next hour or so. You'll be going out live.'

Cindy told me what had happened. One of the largest syndicated 'News' talk shows on American TV was doing a show on the new media. One of the panellists, a blogger, had gone into labour and couldn't make it. They needed someone to fill the gap. It was Shauna who suggested me. Cindy told me I was heading straight to the studio, my driver had all the details.

'Hey, I've also had Adam on the phone. He wants you to call him. He won't let up. What's going on? What do you want me to do?'

'It's complicated. Tell him I'm unavailable. I don't want to speak to him. I'll explain when I get home.'

'Sure..... and good luck!' said Cindy, slightly bewildered.

All went as planned. I was met by Shauna at the studio door, rushed into wardrobe and make-up and introduced briefly to the host. Before I knew it I found myself on set, at a desk in the studio, bright lights shining and a guy counting down. No time to meet the other commentators sitting either side of me. The host, Dan, introduced us.

'And our third guest today, Ladies and Gentlemen, all the way from Melbourne, Australia, Mrs Chris Brown, Mommy Blogger, over here to promote her new book 'Escape Money'.'

The studio audience politely applauded.

It was the term 'Mommy Blogger' that got me going, my blood started to boil. Somewhere in my addled brain I let rip at the presenter, saying I resented the term 'Mommy Blogger'. I barely paused to draw breath. I thought the phrase was a derogatory term thrown at women who were not considered real players. I quoted a few statistics about followers and responses to product promotion and said that people like me and my fellow bloggers were having success rates that the dinosaur media operators could only dream about. This term was misogynistic and women like me were getting sick of it, and so was our audience. Spontaneous applause. This then lead the discussion. I had set the terms. I thrived. After what seemed like no time at all, it was over. We shook hands and were escorted off set.

'You were amazing!' said Shauna, as she followed me back to the dressing room.

'Thanks.'

'Yes, you were great.'

I looked around and it was the host, Dan.

'Ah, thanks,' I responded.

'What are you ladies doing now? Can I take you out for a late lunch?'

I grimaced at Shauna, but she ignored my signals.

'Love to Dan. Where do you have in mind?' asked Shauna.

I didn't catch what he said, but Shauna seemed to know what he was talking about.

'Meet you there in 45 minutes,' said Shauna

'Yeah, see you soon.'

I removed the makeup and changed into something suitable for LA. The car was waiting, Shauna was already inside.

'Sorry about that, but having Dan Raven on your side is a good thing in this city. Nobody knocks back a lunch invitation from him.'

'I get it, but I feel so jet lagged. I don't think I'd make a good dining companion.'

'After your performance on the show! I don't believe a word you say about jet lag. Your mind was sharp, you had them eating out of your hands.'

Shauna's phone rang.

'Hey, yep, yep, yeah. How many? Shit! I'll pass that on. Bye.'

'Chris Brown, they're going crazy. The website, the retailers, all of them are being swamped with requests for your book, they love you. You're the talk of the town.'

'Wow! That's amazing! Things certainly happen fast around here. And Shauna, please call me Tina, Tina Maxwell. My real name, the one my friends use.'

'Well, buckle up Tina Maxwell, you're in for one hell of a ride,' she said.

We pulled up in front of a white walled restaurant, potted green topiary in dark glazed pots framed the entrance, the concierge opened the car door. The room looked masculine, the kind of place where the powerful men of Hollywood gathered, old school. It's interior, understated elegance, white linen, dark leather chairs, a glass wine wall. The entire space lit by a massive skylight, lifting what could have been a rather sombre interior, giving it a bright, fresh feel. The handsome maitre'd escorted us to a table in the centre of the room.

'This way, Mrs. Brown,' he said, with a knowing efficiency. This was, after all, Beverly Hills.

Dan stood to greet us, a double kiss for me, a perfunctory handshake to Shauna. He smelled of expensive aftershave, his skin smooth. He gestured for us to sit.

'Welcome ladies, would you like something to drink?'

'Ah yes. What would you recommend, Dan?' I asked.

'I think Champagne is in order today. A Krug, 98 Rose Brut, thanks,' said Dan to the sommelier.

'You certainly made an impression, Mrs Brown. Everyone's talking about you. The blogosphere is going nuts. That comment about misogyny has gone viral.'

'Well, we all know a put down when we hear one, don't we Shauna? However, I've got to say, I think my publishers might be a bit pissed off that I didn't mention the book enough.'

'Quite the contrary. That comment is what's started all the interest. Now it appears people are dying to read what else you have to say.'

'It's interesting that 'Escape Money' could almost become a subversive text, arming women for financial freedom,' said Dan.

'Yeah, I thought about that. It's why I included stories of women who run multinational companies applying those same thrift principals. Women have always been good at this sort of thing, but often don't think they can apply the same knowledge to business. Sometimes the language of business confounds women. It's not really what I say that's subversive, it's the fact I can.'

The champagne arrived, the sommelier said it was compliments of the men at table five, pointing in their direction. Dan looked across the room, smiled and nodded, acknowledging the gesture. The suited men smiled back, looked my way, and silently applauded. This is how business was done, networking, knowing who has the power. Sometimes I just loved America, this would never happen back home.

As time passed, Shauna was being more distracted by her phone.

'Listen guys, I'm afraid I have to get back to the office. Things are going crazy. Here are the details of your accommodation. Just call the driver when you're ready to leave,' she said, handing me a folder.

'Sure,' I replied.

'Get a good night's sleep. I'll be around early tomorrow morning, it's all on your schedule,' said Shauna, efficiently.

'Ok, no problems,' I responded.

'Bye Dan. See you tomorrow, Tina.'

'No worries, see you around,' he said, standing politely as she left the restaurant.

'She called you Tina, I don't understand.'

I explained the whole name thing, that my friends call me by my real name, Christina, Tina. How it helps to give me an identity away from the public persona, Chris Brown, the woman with the blog.

'I understand,' he said knowingly.

Of course he did, his celebrity was so much greater than mine. He was, after all, one of the most influential media men on the West Coast. And, after the general madness of the last few hours had calmed, I could see he was handsome and charismatic as well. He was tall, intense blue eyes, fair hair, immaculately dressed in a fine tailored suit, cuff links, manicured hands, flawless skin, not a hair out of place.

Dan told me he had found out a bit about me before I came on set, enough to get a basic profile.

'I read your blog, Googled your name, but it wasn't until we finished the interview that I wanted to know more about you. You've achieved so much in such a short space of time,' he said admiringly.

God these Americans were so polite.

'Well, I'd wasted so many years and there's still so much I want to do.'

I told him about the dress project in Cambodia.

'My Dad always used to speak about the atrocities in that country,' said Dan.

'Your father was there?'

'He was a Vietnam veteran. Spent a lot of time near the Cambodian, Vietnamese border. Saw the destruction caused by the carpet bombing of Cambodia. Hated the way this supposedly neutral country was being screwed over.'

'Always look behind the headline, he would say. It was his interest in the truth that got me into journalism in the first place.'

I had made the assumption that Dan was just a talking head, a pretty boy media presenter. I was wrong. He had studied journalism and was first posted to Kuwait during the Gulf War.

'I was just a kid, twenty one and on the front lines sending back stories every night. I am embarrassed to say I was fuelled by the rush it gave me. It was addictive. I went to every troubled hot spot for the next fifteen years, to feed my addiction.'

'Afghanistan was where it all fell apart. My dad said we were in an impossible situation, that it was just like Vietnam, we would never win. I became overwhelmed by the futility of it all. Had a bit of a meltdown. Came home.'

'What did you do?'

'I just dropped out. The network gave me time off. I bought a van and went surfing. I left a boy and returned a thirty five year old man with nothing to show for it but a fucked up head full of images I couldn't erase.'

He told me that eventually he decided to take a softer role, anchoring news and current affairs. He liked to ask the questions now.

He was fascinating.

It was getting late, the staff were beginning to prepare the restaurant for that night's dinner service.

'I think it's time we were getting out of here. Do you want to go somewhere for a drink, it's only five o'clock?' he said.

'Dan, I've had a really lovely time, but my body clock is completely thrown. I need to get some sleep.'

'How long are you in LA?' he asked.

'Till Monday morning,' I replied.

'Can I give you a call?' he said, handing me his card.

'Yeah, sure,' and I scribbled down my number.

'I've got the weekend off, maybe you could show me the sights?' I joked.

'I've got the weekend off, too. Maybe I just could,' he responded, with a twinkle in his eye.

I called the driver. He was waiting for me as we stepped outside.

'Bye Chris, it's been great to meet you.'

'Bye Dan, it's been really nice to meet you too. Thanks for a lovely lunch, and by the way, you can call me Tina.'

As he shook my hand he leant forward and kissed me, lingering for just a second. The driver held the door open, I got inside. Dan took the keys of his white soft top Merc. and drove off. What an interesting and unexpected start to the tour.

I woke early and saw the sun rise. The clock said six am, I had slept for twelve hours. To my surprise the driver had taken me to a house rather than an hotel. Last night I'd crawled into bed, barely noticing my surroundings, it had been dark and I was ridiculously tired. The house, a mid century modern, was stylishly fitted out, very luxuriously appointed. It was as if I had stepped onto the set of 'Mad Men'. I walked out to the terrace and saw that this steep site overlooked a lake. I had pictured Los Angeles as a flat, dry urban city. I was pleasantly surprised to see lush green gardens, quiet winding streets and a clear bright sunny day. This would be a nice place to return home to, Cindy must have spoken to my publicist. The fridge was full of food. I was starving, hadn't eaten since yesterday. I remembered now, it had been lunch, not dinner. Lunch with Dan, in Beverly Hills. I was in America.

I gave Cindy a call, it was late afternoon in Australia. She told me the site had gone ballistic and book sales were through the roof. The traffic to the dress site caused it to melt down and our tech guy had been working on it all day.

'You've made front page of today's paper. Your rant about misogyny has hit a nerve here as well.'

'Wow! News travels.'

'Hey, I nearly forgot, thanks for finding the house, it's gorgeous.'

'Knew you'd like it. Shauna recommended it. Couldn't see you holed up in a hotel for five nights. You'll have enough of hotel rooms for the rest of the tour, although I'm sure whatever Shauna chooses will be good, she seems to be really on the ball. You should Google it, the suburb you're in, Silver Lake, is full of those houses.'

We talked about my schedule for the next few days, then said goodbye.

The next task was more onerous. I deleted all the texts from Adam, not bothering to read a single word. It was the only way. I cried again, the pain still real.

Thursday was crazy with more interviews and book signings. Shauna had filled my schedule to bursting point. That night a dinner was held for me at a small but fashionable Peruvian restaurant. Not knowing what to expect, I chose to wear a dark chocolate coloured dress and wedges, something sexy but safe. Unlike lunch, the room was filled mainly with women. A casual, more friendly vibe. We could easily have been in Fitzroy. The small shared plates were a delicious mix of South American, Spanish, and weirdly, Japanese fusion food.

'Tina let me introduce you to my partner, Nancy,' said Shauna.

'Hi Tina, pleased to meet you,' said the gorgeous, dark haired, woman on Shauna's arm.

'I've heard a lot about you.'

Nancy looked nothing like the cliché. Her pant suit was fitted and feminine, a jacket cut low to reveal the gentle curve of her small breasts. She wore Jimmy Choo heels and exuded a predatory sexual energy. Even the lesbians looked immaculate in Hollywood. We chatted about the interest my comments had generated. She told me how much harder women needed to work in this town to earn respect. I could well imagine. I discovered Nancy was a film producer.

'Do you have any plans for tomorrow night?' she enquired.

'No, why do you ask?'

'We're having a few people over for drinks and would love it if you could join us?'

'That would be great. I'd love to.'

I sensed that Nancy had wanted to check me out before she allowed Shauna to invite me to their house. Obviously I had met with her approval.

Friday was more of the same, only this time Shauna had given me some time off in the afternoon. Not that I could go home and curl up with a good book. She had scheduled me in for a bit of pampering at her favorite spa. I was groomed to within an inch of my life, skin smooth, no follicle untouched and I left the salon with an Audrey chignon, looking and feeling a million dollars. This time I wore a taupe backless number and, again, the almost regulation killer heels. I twisted a long strand of pearls three times around my neck. I was having fun doing business.

I had no idea what to expect of tonight. We drove up a steep, winding road and through a gate. In front of me was a sleek, long curved building, interrupted only by a wooden door. I rang the bell, Shauna opened the door. I was surprised it was her and not some black and white attired maid.

'Tina, lovely to see you, welcome to our house.'

House was an understatement. It was a massive white space. A wall of glass doors opened onto a beautifully manicured lawn terrace with spectacular views of the valley. The sun was setting into a dusky pink sky and the lights below were just starting to twinkle. Nancy was obviously not making Indie movies!

'This is spectacular!' I exclaimed.

'Yes, we've only just finished it. My sister designed it, she's an architect. We really love it. We thought we'd have a little house warming with just a few friends.'

Luckily I had brought a gift of hand stitched table linens. Something I'd purchased on Rodeo Drive, next to the spa. Not too overstated, just tasteful and elegant.

Nancy came up and greeted me.

'Tina, you look magnificent. Shauna tells me she sent you to our spa for some well deserved pampering. And that dress, where did you get it? It's stunning, like you,' she said admiringly.

'Thank you, it's one of my own creations.'

'Shauna honey, you didn't tell me your Tina was a dress designer as well as a bestselling author.'

'I don't back losers, babe,' responded Shauna, cheekily.

'Come with me, I'll introduce you to some people,' said Nancy, intimately taking my hand. I had never fancied another woman, but tonight seeing this beautiful couple together, I became slightly curious and wondered what actually happened in their bed.

We walked into the main body of the room where about twenty guests stood, mingling, drinking. The pleasant hum of quiet conversation, music playing in the background. All the guests looked stylish, I had dressed appropriately. I thought how surreal this seemed and how unlikely this would have been just one year ago. Much to my surprise the people here were very warm and welcoming. This was a party of friends. Not hustlers looking to do the next big deal.

We drank Californian wine and the appetisers reminded me of the food we had eaten the night before. Shauna must have hired the same team to do the catering.

There were a few recognisable faces, actors who looked so ordinary when not on the screen. I had no trouble chatting. People were interested in my misogyny comment and curious about Australia. The conversation flowed.

After about an hour we were ushered to the dining space where a long table was set. I felt a hand firmly touch the small of my naked back, guiding me to a seat.

'I do believe we are sitting together tonight,' said the familiar deep voice.

I turned and looked into those brilliant blue eyes, it was Dan. I felt a strange rush of warmth as we greeted each other like good friends.

'What brings you here?' I said, smiling curiously.

'You,' he said flirtatiously.

I was glad to be sitting next to someone familiar. I was keen to pick up on the conversations we'd started at lunch. The first course of sashimi was served. Appropriate for these beautiful bodies. I was very aware of him next to me. The brush of a sleeve against my bare arm, a foot accidentally touching. Dan Raven was sending out signals and I liked it. We talked to each other, to guests either side and across the table, pretending nothing was going on. Upping the ante ever so slightly as the discrete game became more daring. A hand lingering near my thigh, the sides of our bodies touching, breast rising as my breath quickened.

I felt the sudden weight of the pearls as they tumbled into my lap. A temperamental hook! I picked them up, fumbling with the catch as I tried to put them on.

'Here, let me,' said Dan.

He brushed away the stray wisps of hair and I felt his fingers run down the nape of my neck after he snapped the clasp shut. A barely perceptible arch of my back in response to his provocative touch. By dessert this subtle dance had let my mind wander. The touching had been electric, my body craved more. Some guests were starting to leave, the night was ending.

'Call your driver, tell him you won't be needing him. I'll take you home,' he whispered, as we stood to say our goodbyes.

I did as he requested and was intrigued as to where this was heading. We walked across the gravel drive to his car. The top was up, it was early December, the night air cold. He pulled up in front of my house and switched off the motor. He turned, took my face in his hands, staring intently with those deep blue eyes and then slowly kissed me.

'Would you like to come in?' I said breathlessly.

'I can't stay,' he whispered.

I pulled away, confused.

'I have an article to write, can I see you tomorrow?' he breathed.

'Yes,' I stammered, slightly disappointed.

He got out of the car and like a true gentleman opened my door. He kissed me again and I felt his hardness as he pulled me close. He walked me to the front door.

'What time tomorrow?' I asked, still bewildered.

'Early, very early,' he replied and walked away.

I went to bed baffled by his behaviour and shocked at how readily I was prepared to take another man into my bed.

Weekend with Dan

The bell rang, it was 7:00 am. I stumbled out of bed, grabbed a flimsy cotton top, pulling it on, aware it barely covered my body.

'You are early, didn't you go to bed?'

'Look outside, it's a beautiful day,' he said like an eager kid.

He looked different. He wore jeans and a tee shirt, his hair was messy and he hadn't shaved. Gone was the formally attired, well groomed person I was familiar with. The man standing in front of me looked fresh, relaxed and casual, unkempt. I barely recognised him.

'You look so different.'

'It takes a lot of effort to achieve neat,' he said grinning.

'There's a great farmers' market just up the road on West Sunset Boulevard. Saw it as I drove past. Thought we'd get a few things then head up the coast.'

'Sounds great, but I need a coffee.'

'You take a shower, get ready and I'll make some,' he said, already grabbing the cups.

Still half asleep, and a little bit hungover, I let the shower do its work.

I plodded out to the kitchen to see that he had made coffee and set the table for breakfast.

'Yum! You're domesticated,' I commented, as he pulled out a chair.

'Here sit. I thought you might need something more substantial than coffee.'

'God, you're right. I didn't think I drank that much last night, but my head is telling me something different.'

I was just collecting my thoughts about what actually did happen last night, when I remembered the awkward farewell. Digging through my post alcohol dulled brain, I tried to recall if I'd done anything to embarrass myself. I think I was ok, just a little taken aback by his rejection.

The eggs, bacon and coffee helped restore my body, clear my head.

'So what's the plan?' I asked.

'I thought we'd go for a drive along the Pacific Coast Highway. Stop at the beach, have a picnic, maybe a surf?' he said.

'Sounds great, but I can't surf.'

'You can't surf? I thought all Aussies could surf? Beaches everywhere,' he commented, sounding truly surprised.

'I live in Melbourne, more urban, more like New York. Sydney has the beaches.'

'Sydney, yeah, did a show from there a couple of years ago. Opera House and Bridge. Surf beaches close to the city, funny sounding names, Bondi, Coogee.'

'That's it, and you're right, there are lots of surf beaches, all around Australia, just not in Melbourne where I live.'

'Makes no difference, it's still a great day to sit, eat and watch the waves roll in.'

I grabbed my bag and we headed out the door, not too sure of what this day would offer.

'Where's your car?' I asked looking to the street, expecting to see the white soft top.

'Here,' he said, opening the door to a beaten up old van.

'I don't understand.'

'It's my escape vehicle, the one I hit the road with when I had my meltdown,' he said.

'It also means I can travel without being noticed. The white car is all for show. In this one nobody recognises me.'

He held the door open and I climbed up into the seat.

'Here,' he said, handing me a cap, 'Do you have sunglasses?'

'Why?'

'Travelling incognito. Today I want us to disappear. I'm leaving public Dan in town,' he said, donning a dodgy, old hat and uncool shades.

I understood his need for privacy.

We gathered together a feast of delicious produce, enough to feed a small army. He had wandered past the market stalls freely and was pleased that nobody recognised him, his disguise had worked.

We drove past the million dollar homes of Malibu and the white surf beaches, hugging the coastal road. The old van struggling at times. Dan told me we were heading to Santa Barbara, about a 2 hour drive north. I remembered seeing the movie 'Sideways', set in Santa Barbara, about two guys who spend a weekend touring the wineries, eating and having a last fling before one of them got married.

As we drove into town, he pointed out the mission style architecture, quite unique to this part of the world and yet there was a strange familiarity. The Californian bungalow houses, the eucalyptus trees, the dry, fire scorched hills. We could be near Melbourne and the highway reminded me of the Great Ocean Road back home in Australia. I had to remind myself that we were in California and that Australia was a 15 hour flight away.

Dan said he had a place he wanted to show me. We travelled past acres of vineyards till eventually the landscape changed. No more grapes or wineries, just remote wilderness miles from any town. We drove through a set of imposing ranch gates, along a dusty road and past scrubby coastal vegetation. I was awestruck by the rugged beauty before me. Coastal dunes, a broad stretch of beach, rocky cliffs, bright blue water, waves rolling in. Not a house or a soul to be seen.

'What do you think?' said Dan.

'It's amazing! How did you know this place existed?'

'My grandfather bought it years ago, before the developers snapped up all the available land. It sits next to a national park. My dad put a caveat on the title so that no new buildings could be erected or the land divided. It's where I go to get away from it all. We used to come camping here when I was a kid,' he said, smiling.

We pulled up under a stand of tortured old pines, a small patch of grass, a green oasis amidst the wild surroundings. Some sheets of iron on the ground sat sticking out from under a few fallen branches.

'You hungry?' he asked

'I'm starving!' I replied.

It was two in the afternoon. Dan grabbed a blanket and I collected the bags of food. We walked down a sandy path, through the dunes, to the beach. It was a magnificent day, cooler than I had expected, clear bright sunlit sky, rich azure sea. We ate, gorging ourselves, talking with our mouths full. Relaxed, chatting as if we'd known each other for years.

He took me for a walk along the beach, said he wanted to show me something, as we headed to the cliffs.

'This is where I'd come as a child and pretend to be a pirate, looking for hidden treasure,' he said as we entered a shallow cave.

I could imagine him as an angelic little fair haired kid and liked that he was revealing something private, personal. We seemed to connect.

'So how often do you get here?' I asked.

'Not often enough! The highway gets pretty busy in summer, weekends are a nightmare. I prefer the cooler months and anyway the surf's better in winter.'

'You said you surfed? Why didn't you bring your gear?'

'I did. Come with me.'

I followed him back to the camp site. He removed the old dead branches and lifted the rusty metal sheet, to expose a set of concrete stairs down to a padlocked iron door. I followed him in to a pristine bunker kitted out with supplies and camping equipment.

'Wow, you have everything here. No one would ever know.'

Dan told me his grandfather had been obsessed by the Russian Communist threat during the Cold War. He had it built to cope with the impending nuclear disaster he thought would most certainly hit the world. He was an eccentric man who used this bunker as his prototype and then made a small fortune building them all along the west coast. It seemed that many Americans held similar fears. Then Dan spoke about his father.

23

'Dad went to fight because he believed China was behind the Vietnamese conflict. Saw China as a bigger threat than the Russians. He continued this almost obsessive idea of impending doom, sure the Chinese would take over and wipe out all that we Americans held dear. Take away our property, our businesses, our freedom. He thought we could escape to this place, miles away from anywhere, sure no one would ever find us. Whenever he came back from active service he would insist we come to the bunker and go through a series of drills that, once rehearsed, we would seamlessly put into action if America was invaded. He would send letters to my mother insisting she kept everything well maintained, ready.'

'What happened when the war finished?' I asked.

'Well, Dad became increasingly disillusioned.'

Dan explained that his father felt the need to hang onto the idea of impending doom and when the Chinese didn't land he found a new threat. He started to obsess about climate change. He thought the earth would reap a savage vengeance on our mistreatment of the planet. Nature had usurped China. The bunker would save his family from the fires and extreme weather events he predicted would wipe out southern California.

'And your father, does he still come here?'

'No, not anymore. He shot himself, committed suicide a few years ago. He went mad, nothing could stop the voices in his head. His obsession, the things he saw in Vietnam, fucked him up.'

'God, I'm sorry. How did your mother cope?'

'I think she was quite relieved when it was over. In the end there was nothing she could do to reassure him, he lived a hermit's existence out here. She remarried last year and moved back to New York. I don't see much of her now. She has rediscovered her Jewish faith. She never really fitted in here.'

The not fitting in, that was something I really did understand.

'And so now it's my escape, not many people know of its existence. I can come here and be truly alone, at peace. I fixed it up when I took that year off, got sick of hauling all my stuff. It means I can get away more easily.'

I looked around as he showed me the surfing gear hanging neatly in racks, near the entrance. This was the first of a series of underground concrete rooms.

'My Grandfather designed these modules so they could be interlinked, rooms that provided a semblance of normalcy if the family was trapped underground for any length of time.'

I was surprised the rooms didn't smell musty or damp and asked Dan about it.

'That was a big problem. I had an engineer look at the place and he designed a ventilation system that allowed air to circulate. There are a series of pipes that channel air from the cliff near the beach, away from any threat of smoke in the event of a fire.'

He continued to show me around. A completely stocked kitchen, cupboards filled with canned goods, dried food and bottled water. The next chamber was a spacious bedroom furnished with a double bed.

'Wow, this is hardly spartan,' I said, as we walked through.

It was painted white. A large mirror and framed black and white photos showing outdoor panoramas gave the illusion of windows. A cupboard to one side was filled with sealed, plastic wrapped linens, towels and clothing.

'Looks like you have a touch of that family obsession?'

He laughed and told me that's how it comes back from the laundry, ironed, folded and sealed in plastic. I could see the cleaner's receipts inside. Perhaps he wasn't quite as obsessed as his forebears.

Next we walked through to another bedroom with two single beds and finally into a bathroom.

'Look hot water!' he said, turning on a tap.

I ran my hand under the slightly sulphurous smelling water and felt its warmth.

'How on earth did you do that?'

'We were trying to tap into the underground aquifer, to find a permanent water supply. This is what came up. It's drinkable, but it comes out warm.'

I looked up and noticed natural light streaming through reflective sky lit tubes in the ceiling.

'You really have thought of everything,' I said pointing to the source of the brightness.

'Well, I guess it does become quite obsessive after a while. When I fixed it up I kept thinking of how much Dad would love it. How he would love all this innovative technology.'

I marvelled at this strange, surreal place. I felt like I really had met the Omega Man. On our way out he grabbed a wetsuit and board.

'Want a suit? I have one that would fit you.'

'No thanks, I'm happy to sit on the beach. I have some writing to do.'

I sat watching him surf and imagined the release this must have given him after seeing the horrors of war. I thought about what Dan had shown me, about the lure of a safe haven. I could begin to understand this preoccupation with Armageddon. I'd read that a number of people in America shared this obsession. Many early settlers had escaped religious persecution in Europe or the poverty of a newly industrialised England, fleeing their own doomed existences, to come to America to find sanctuary. Perhaps it was hard wired into the American psyche?

I needed to write an editorial. I wrote a piece called 'Escape money, where would you go?'

It was getting late in the day. Dan emerged from the surf.

'I guess we should think about getting back. I don't really want to do that drive in the dark.'

'Yeah, I'm glad it's you driving, some of those bends were a little scary,' I commented.

'Could you give me a hand?' he said, struggling to remove his wet suit.

He unzipped the back, but couldn't seem to release his shoulders. I got up and as I started to yank down the black rubber, I was shocked by the horrific scarring I saw all over his torso. His eyes were closed, his face raised skyward, grimacing. I left the suit hanging at his hips.

'What happened?' I whispered.

He sat down, covering himself with a towel.

'Afghanistan,' he replied quietly.

We sat silently until he was ready to talk.

'I was embedded with some troops.'

He paused, then proceeded to tell me his story.

'It started out as a fairly routine patrol of the neighborhood in an armoured vehicle. We saw a young woman being beaten by a group of men and got out to investigate. It was a trap, the soldiers were shot and I was taken hostage. I was kept blindfolded for many days and had no idea of what the demands of my kidnappers were. Eventually I was taken to a room where I was videotaped and told to read from a script, basically saying that to secure my release the American government would have to find one million dollars. After a few weeks I discovered the government wouldn't pay, but negotiations had started with my employer. This became a game between negotiators from both sides. It turned out that I had been captured by a warlord just wanting money. If it had been a politically motivated kidnapping my chances of survival would have been much less.'

'Anyway this went on for months. Occasionally a guard would let me know that my employers were being stubborn and no agreement could be reached. It was frustrating, not knowing how long this process would take. I lived in fear that my captors would kill me in anger at having to wait for so long for the ransom to be paid.'

'The treatment I received was brutal. Daily beatings, isolation from people, thirst and hunger. The kidnappers had taken me to a remote, barren location, some type of outpost. My captors were holed up in a run-down mud brick dwelling. I was kept outside, exposed, in what looked like a stone animal pen, with just a canvas canopy in one corner for protection. The heat in summer was brutal, the cold of winter relentless. Most days my feet were shackled to a very short chain.'

'Finally one night, I heard the sound of a low flying plane and then within minutes the whole place was bombed. I cowered against the wall for protection, saw a white flash of light, felt intense burning and then nothing. I woke up in hospital, I had been rescued.'

Now I knew why Dan got out. I sat closer to him and put my arm around his waist.

As the sun began to set we packed up and walked back to the van.

'Fuck!' sighed Dan, a pained expression on his face.

I could see the dimly fading headlights.

'I must've knocked the switch.'

He got inside and turned the ignition. The dull dying whir of the engine told me the battery was dead.

'Fuck, fuck, fuck!' he said thumping the dash.

He got out and looked at me.

'Do you have to be anywhere this evening?' he asked.

'No, I planned on having a quiet night in. What about you?'

'No, nothing.'

'Is there any way we can fix this?' I asked sheepishly.

We tried push starting it, but the road was too uneven for us to get any speed.

'I'll see if I can give someone a call,' he said wandering up the track to get a signal.

He returned after a few minutes, his anger dissipated.

'My mechanic will bring a new battery.'

'Great, I guess he'll be a couple of hours away?'

'Not quite, he can't make it till tomorrow. Family commitments. Looks like we're stuck here for the night.'

'Lucky we have so much food left,' I said trying to sound cheery.

'We've got enough to survive for months,' he replied in a slightly self deprecating manner, grinning, not taking himself too seriously.

We gathered wood and lit a camp-fire. It was pleasant sitting there, poking the coals, staring into the flames, something I hadn't done since I was a kid. I talked about what had happened in the last year, filled in some of the gaps not written about in the blog.

'And you, are you married?' I asked.

'Separated, have been for awhile.'

'What happened?'

'We just grew apart. When I came home she couldn't deal with me being around all the time. Our relationship had always been long distance,' he said wistfully.

'Any kids?'

'No. Timing was always wrong and the antidepressants I used to take screwed with my body.'

'How?'

'I couldn't fuck my wife. My cock couldn't get hard,' he answered with brutal honesty.

'That is one of the reasons I disappeared for a whole year. I wanted to see if I could get off the meds.'

'And did it work?' I asked, surprised at his candour.

'It did, but the marriage didn't. I guess we'll get divorced someday. We're still good friends.'

Our conversation was cut short by a sudden cold gust of wind signalling the arrival of a heavy down pour.

'I guess sleeping under the stars is out of the question?' he yelled, as we ran for shelter.

I grabbed my bag and the remaining food and followed him underground. Dan lit a gas lamp and I followed him to the kitchen.

'Here, pick something. I'm going to have a shower, wash off the salt,' Dan said, pointing to a well stocked wine cupboard.

Santa Barbara was a wine growing region, but the labels were unfamiliar. I picked a syrah, that would be safe. I caught my reflection in the mirror. I looked a bedraggled mess, my clothes were damp and I smelled of smoke. He came back into the room, towelling his wet hair, wearing only jeans. The muted light obscured his scars. He obviously felt comfortable around me.

'How rude of me, would you like a shower?'

'I'd love one, but I didn't bring a change of clothes. I didn't think we'd be away for the night.'

'Well, if you don't mind some of my stuff, I've got tee shirts and boxers that might fit. Here, come and have a look.'

We went to the cupboard in the bedroom and he showed me the selection of clothes. He ripped open the plastic and held them up for me.

'What do you think?'

'A bit big, but anything's better than what I've got on now.'

He handed me a towel and I went to the shower.

It seemed incongruous I was here, underground, taking a hot shower, washing myself with exquisite soaps and shampoo. Miles away from Australia, stuck in the middle of nowhere with a slightly fucked up rich journo. This seemed strange, even for Hollywood!

I dried myself off and put on the boxers first, white, pure cotton, they fitted well. The tee shirt was huge and suitably covered my body. I noticed that the beds had been made. The single in the second bedroom answered the question in my head about what the sleeping arrangements would be.

'Better?'

'Much, thanks.'

He poured me a drink and got out some bread and cheese. We talked for a little while until I started to feel sleepy.

'I think I might go to bed,' I said, drowsy from the long day and the wine.

'You can take my bed, I don't mind the single,' he offered politely.

I looked at his huge frame and laughed.

'Dan, I don't think you'd fit. But thanks for the offer. I'm a better size for that bed and I don't mind. It will be cosy.'

'Goodnight Tina.'

'Goodnight Dan. Thanks for a great day.'

I curled up in the crisp white cotton sheets and pulled the duvet over my shoulders. It occurred to me that this was the third time I was farewelling Dan, returning to an empty bed.

I was jolted awake by the sounds of screaming, deep guttural animal noises. It took awhile to get my bearings. I was underground in Dan's bunker. It was Dan I could hear. My instincts took over, I grabbed a torch and went to his room to see if he was ok.

He was tossing in bed, sheets strewn about the floor. I picked them up attempting to cover him, but the fitful thrashing continued. I sat down on the bed to comfort him, holding him tightly till the nightmare abated. His body slowly stopped trembling and I cradled his head in my lap, stroking his forehead until he was peaceful again. When I could hear the gentle rhythm of his breathing I placed his head on the pillow and crawled in next to him, pulling the blankets back over us, and wrapped myself against his back, holding him tight.

The dawn light woke both of us, he rolled over and looked at me, puzzled, wondering what I was doing in his bed.

'Nightmare, last night,' I whispered.

He stared with urgent eyes and held me. I felt his strong arms move firmly up my back, lifting the tee shirt, running his fingers down my spine, pulling me towards him and kissing me deeply. I responded with eager intensity and wrapped my legs around his body, feeling his awakening cock against my eager cunt. Our breathing quickened, his kisses more demanding. I reached down desperate for his body, I wanted him inside me. I grasped his cock, rubbing it against my damp sex, he stiffened to attention. He rolled me forcefully onto my back, and wrenched down my boxers. I writhed under him freeing my legs, to open up, and then, with a forceful brutality he rammed himself into me. I thrust forward, hungry for him. We fucked with ferocity. I felt pain, transposed with intense pleasure. We both grunted and yelled as we greedily hunted for that build up of sensation before finally erupting in waves of cataclysmic pleasure.

We lay still, I could feel his heart pounding against my breast. I could smell his animal sweat and feel the heat radiating from his spent body. I had not had enough and lay there, my cunt throbbing for more. He had been taunting me, flirting outrageously over the last few days. I had built up a hunger that was far from sated. He eased himself off me and lay to one side, but I had not finished. I moved down the bed, placed his soft cock in my mouth and tasted the salty mix of his cum and my juices. I then began to swallow him deeply, taking his full length easily in its flaccid state. I sucked with a vengeance, desperate to bring him back to full rigid life. Quickly his cock lengthened, thickened and when I could no longer eat without choking I mounted his body and rode him hard. He knew I had found that sweet spot and grabbed my ass, forcing me even more deliberately upon him and again we fucked furiously until I exploded, an intense satisfaction spreading through every part of my body. This time I was done. Wordlessly he embraced me, my back cocooned against his firm, strong chest. It was still very early, we went back to sleep.

I woke in an empty bed. My watch said 11.30 I could smell coffee and followed my nose. Dan was in the kitchen preparing breakfast.

'Good morning. Coffee, juice, champagne?'

'Coffee please'

'Mmm... thanks. Have you heard from your mechanic?' I asked.

'Yeah, thinks he can get here sometime late this afternoon.'

'Well, I guess you've got plenty of time for a surf.'

'I don't think the raging weather outside will allow that. It's even worse than last night. We'll be stuck inside all day. Come and have a look.'

I went up to the entrance and saw it was pouring rain and blowing a gale. Not even a chance of a walk on the beach.

'God, it's shocking out there,' I said, slamming the door.

'What on earth are we going to do to kill time?'

'Well, we're not going to run out of food and we've barely touched the wine cellar. I propose we have a feast, and I could think of other interesting things to do if you get too bored,' he said with a suggestive smile.

'Mmm, I wonder what you have in mind?' I responded curiously.

'You'll just have to wait and see!'

He chose a wine and we sat down to eat.

'Dan, I don't understand why you come here. After what you went through in Afghanistan. Don't you feel confined, captive?"

'Quite the opposite. I feel safe, secure, in control. When I was being held, I would be left for days with barely enough food or water to live, isolated and exposed outside. This was a complete mind fuck for someone like me whose father and grandfather had an almost morbid fascination with Armageddon. They knew what was needed, they meticulously planned and prepared for survival. Their end of the world looked nothing like my imprisonment in Afghanistan. However I was no fool and was not prepared to sit down and die. I caught insects, lizards, ate anything that wouldn't kill me. Dug holes in the earth to catch water when it rained. Prolonged my chances of staying alive.'

We continued to eat, drink and talk.

'I get it. I understand your need to create this safe place, but quite frankly I feel a bit strange. I don't know how long I could stay down here, it's a bit claustrophobic,' I said, looking around this bizarre, alien environment. No big windows or open air spaces like the architecture I was so fascinated with.

I told him about the farm, the road and that different form of incarceration.

'I actually feel quite trapped.'

'But you shouldn't, you have everything here you need, and you are free to go.'

'Well, not right now.'

'So you don't fancy being my prisoner? I would look after you,' he said with a devilish grin.

'Dan, I couldn't think of a nicer person to hold me captive, but aren't we treading on dangerous territory here. Doesn't even the mention of capture scare you?'

'Actually I have this pretty fucked up fantasy about being here in a post apocalyptic world,' he said.

'No kidding?' I said wryly.

'I've often wondered how I'd cope being here on my own. I fantasise about the idea of finding another survivor, a woman and what that'd be like. Would she stay, how would I establish trust?'

'And hoping that 'survival woman' wasn't some barren, toothless old hag?' I said, smiling, bringing him back to earth.

'Well, it is my fantasy and, of course, she would be beautiful, nubile and desirous. She might be someone just like you?' he replied smiling, his stunning blue eyes twinkling with the thought.

'Might she just?' I said flirtatiously, the wine loosening my tongue.

I was becoming quite intrigued by the picture he was painting. We had a whole afternoon to kill and I began to think of how I could make the next few hours a bit more interesting. I casually walked up to the door, slid the bolt and opened it. The storm had become more violent. I leaned heavily against the door, closing it, briefly shutting out the noise.

'One thing that you would have to remember, Mr. Raven, is to lock your captive in!' I yelled back as I yanked the door open, escaping outside and running as fast as I could.

I headed for the nearest cluster of bushes and watched as he emerged from the bunker and ran toward the beach. When he was out of sight, I left my cover and sprinted for the sand dunes, where I would be slightly more sheltered from the rain. I saw him briefly come up from the beach and scout around, but still he could not find me. My heart was beating not only from the physical exertion, but also from the shot of adrenalin this game of adult hide and seek was giving me. He came close and I shrank even further behind the undergrowth, almost too scared to breath, aware that any movement might tip him off.

He went past, more deeply into the dunes and out of sight. I had eluded him, but needed to find somewhere more protected from the driving wind and rain. I remembered the cave we had walked to, it was not far and Dan was headed the other way.

At last, some shelter. I was freezing and began to realise what an idiot I had been coming out wearing only a tee shirt and boxers. I wouldn't last long in this cold, somehow I had to get back to the bunker without being caught. I kept my eyes out for Dan, but could see no trace of him. He must have gone to the other end of the beach. I was ready for my next sprint. Cautiously I started to climb back up the dune, the coast was clear. Suddenly I felt a rope, lassoing me from behind, bringing me to an abrupt halt. My arms were trapped tightly against my body. A rough blanket was tossed over me and I could feel more rope binding me. I was completely encased. I screamed at him, demanding he let me go. He ignored my pleas and tossed me over his shoulder. He was rough, I was freezing cold and pissed off that he had won. The door slammed, silence, we were back inside.

I felt him dump me across the table, take off the outer ropes and pull away the blanket.

'Untie me you fucking bastard!' I shrieked as I writhed, trying to disentangle myself from the clutches of the lasso cutting into my skin.

'We can't have this noise Madam, you will need to learn to be quiet!' he said harshly, pulling off his tee shirt, ripping it apart to form a gag and tying it around my mouth. His broad chest heaved from exertion. He ran the back of his hand across his forehead, wiping the sweat, combing away the hair falling over his eyes, looking at me lustily.

My heartbeat quickened. I could feel the growing warmth between my legs and liked this twist to our game very much. Before he released the lasso he bound my feet and tied my hands. I was still his captive. My desire grew.

'You are cold, I must get you out of these wet clothes,' he said.

My body shivered, nipples erect.

He produced a pair of scissors. First he cut through the front of my tee shirt and wrenched back the wet cloth, exposing my breasts. I felt his warm mouth engulf one, then the other, sucking hard. I let out a stifled groan. He cut the boxers, ripping them away, leaving me naked and exposed. The gag remained. I could barely take in enough oxygen, panting with desire, wondering what he would do next. I watched as he stripped off his wet clothing and again he tossed me, effortlessly, over his shoulder and headed to the shower.

A blast of steaming hot water poured over my back, warming me up, matching the heat building deep within my belly. His hands running along my spine, between my ass, slipping easily inside my willing sex, hot and wet, so very hungry to be fucked hard. I felt his weight shift, one strong arm tucked under my buttocks holding me firmly against his chest, the other hand withdrawn, running down my thigh to my ankles, pulling at the rope, unbinding my feet, till eventually my legs were free. Instinctively I opened them, wrapping my legs around his body, sliding down his torso, while he held me firmly against him. I felt the nuzzling of his huge thick cock. Swiftly he responded, pulling me down, impaling me on his rigid phallus, groaning at the sheer audacity of his action. Almost completely immobilised I communicated by squeezing my vaginal muscles firmly around him. He let out a deep moan, and reciprocated by violently pounding into me, forcing himself deeper and harder inside. He thrust until I could take no more. My back arched as my body gave in to the overwhelming sensations of this most savage euphoria. He drove hard against my womb, until he, too, came violently. We were both panting and breathless. Exhausted, we collapsed to the floor, hot water still running over our bodies.

We sat like this for what seemed like ages, until I felt the delicious sensation of his cock coming back to life, wakening deep inside me. Still mounted on him, he struggled to his feet and carried me into the bedroom. The thrust of each step, pushing against my cervix, building a new level of arousal.

He deftly lifted me off him and tossed me onto the bed. I watched as he gathered the pillows, one on top of the other, then lifted me so I lay face down, my buttocks mounted high. He knelt on the bed, behind me. I felt him part my legs, open and wide. His hand stroked my gaping, exposed sex and spread my wet juices all over the tender folds. With my hands still tied hard against my back, he grabbed my wrists, linking his fingers through the ropes, and, without warning he rammed into me, entering from behind, pulling my bindings toward him like a bronco rider, fucking me hard, brutally. I had never felt such exhilaration and arched my spine driving my buttocks back at him with equal fervour. He let out a cry with each thrust, quicker and harder until he howled with ecstasy and we came together with shattering ferocity. He collapsed on top of me, panting, exhausted.

Slowly he lifted himself away from me and I heard the sound of his bare feet slapping on the concrete. He returned and cut the ties from my wrists, licking and sucking the delicate skin. He then removed the pillows and with ease rolled my limp body over. He cut the gag and slowly kissed my lips. I opened my mouth, our tongues hungrily connecting.

The sex had been fast and aggressive. I realised I had a lot of pent up anger, it seemed we both did.

'I've never taken a woman here, like that, before,' he spoke breathlessly.

And I'd never had such brutal sex, shocked by how exhilarated I felt by his capture and my submission. We fell asleep, exhausted.

Eventually the light changed, the sun was out, the storm had passed, we could leave our private chamber. I wanted to stay. I turned to look at him as he slept. His fiery scars were in full view. I traced my fingers along the damaged, imperfect skin and he reacted by covering his torso, grimacing with a remembered pain. Gently I took his hand and lifted it away, placing it back down on the sheet. I lay my cheek on his chest and listened to his beating heart. He put a protective arm around me. I continued to touch and noticed his heartbeat changing, and as it quickened I looked down seeing his cock faintly stir.

'I want to see your cock rise,' I whispered in his ear.

'Think about me fucking you, riding you hard deep inside me,' I continued, breathlessly.

I was entranced. Slowly it began to raise itself from its soft cushion, nestled against his balls and move to one side as it began to grow. The head emerged, shiny as the velvety skin became engorged and pulled away. I took his hand and placed it between my legs, letting him feel the wetness of my arousal. His penis lifted from his firm flattened stomach and stretched and thickened exposing the skin seam. The thick vein underneath formed a distinct separate ridge, and I knew he was now ready. I lifted my hips over his torso and then smoothly slid straight down on his rigid cock and gently began to rock, until he was so deep inside me that I could barely stand the intense pressure. And I couldn't stop. I needed the ferocity of a hard fucking. Again he grabbed me, forcing his way deeper until I screamed out and felt the familiar pulsation of his cock, shooting cum deep inside me.

His phone rang. He hastily withdrew. It had come to an end. The mechanic was waiting at the gate. Dan told me to wait inside, the battery would be exchanged and we could get back to LA. I got dressed, cleaned up and after an hour or so we were ready to leave.

The evening fog made for a difficult trip. Dan seemed to be in deep thought, glancing over at me only occasionally. Neither of us spoke. I was wondering about tonight, tomorrow, knowing we had connected at a very deep level. It was a long drive home.

We pulled up in front of the house. He got out and, in that gentlemanly American style, opened my door. His piercing blue eyes looked at me longingly as we stood on the pavement and I kissed him passionately.

'Please, Dan, stay with me,' I whispered.

He couldn't, mumbled he had commitments. Our unexpected weekend had left us both a day behind. Something wasn't right.

I entered the house feeling truly alone. My computer gave me the answers. Dan Raven wasn't separated from his wife. The article spoke of the deep affection between the couple who defied Hollywood odds by staying happily married all these years. Photos showed him celebrating a birthday, a kid's party last Friday night. That night at dinner he had arrived late because he had been hosting his son's tenth birthday. No wonder he couldn't stay.

'Fuck, fuck, fuck!'

What had I done?

I had spent the last nineteen years being someone's perfect little wife. Trying to fit in with a group of people who resented my very existence. Then, with Adam, I nearly walked straight back into that world, lured by the temptation of adoration and an unrealistic belief that love would conquer all.

And today, here in California, thinking I was free to start again, only to be caught up in another man's fucked up utopia, potentially at the expense of his family. I wondered how he would explain what he'd been doing all weekend, to the wife left at home coping with the reality of the everyday.

I felt disappointed in myself for being so willing to walk straight into another man's arms. Not stopping to think about what I might have to give up if I were to have another relationship and what sacrifices I would have to make.

Had I succumbed to the naive idea some women have of being rescued by a man? That all I would have to do is love this flawed Prince Charming and my world would be perfect. What did any of us really expect? What did Dan's wife expect? Did she feel less attractive, less interesting, less like the woman a man would want to come home to? A man who needed to take a lover, not his wife, to his place of sanctuary. Where was her place of sanctuary? Who knew of the compromises she had to make bringing up his child, juggling home, work, marriage, dealing with the complicated man who was Dan Raven. Her knight in shining armour had betrayed her and spent the weekend with me. How different the fairytale becomes when reality sets in.

Sometimes it's particularly difficult when we try to be all things to all people. The compromised wife, mother, lover, breadwinner, friend.

43

Stretched beyond capacity needing to fill other people's expectations of what a woman should be. Often so harshly judged when we fail in a world so heavily weighted against our success.

When we try to compete with our male colleagues who rarely have to race home before day care closes, or when we arrive late to an early morning breakfast meeting because we've been trying to get the kids off to school. Doing two jobs, exhausted at the end of the day, with a husband wondering why we are no longer interested in sex.

And if a woman decides to stay at home and raise the kids, the so called ideal, they are left in a state of financial servitude with nothing in their superannuation accounts and no financial autonomy. Often undervalued, with their partners questioning what is was that they actually did all day.

Then there are those mums without a partner, raising their kids on their own, who are considered to be damaging the well being of the fatherless generation. As if it's entirely the fault of the mother that the child's dad is not present. Or that the welfare dependent mother is the fiscal cancer eroding the very fabric of our society, not a woman just desperately trying to raise her kids in an almost impossible state of poverty.

Misogyny was endemic and my 'Escape Money' would give a new voice to a world that needed change. I was so angry at myself for pretending it was any other way. I didn't need rescuing or a man to make me whole.

Tomorrow I would be back. The tour would continue with me solely focused on publicising the book, building the brand that would protect and insulate me from the danger of dependency.

The Power of One Woman

Shauna arrived at seven the next morning. I had been up since dawn, looking over my schedule and shoved the timetable in her face before she could sit down.

'Looks a bit light on, I think we should make better use of the time. Lots of gaps I might as well fill while I'm in the States. Here, here and here. I have absolutely no need for down time and can catch up on sleep during the flight home,' I demanded, pointing to vacant spots on the planner.

'Wow, what's eating you?' said Shauna.

'Nineteen years of wasted time!'

'Jesus Tina, I'd been pushing you hard, I give you the weekend off, and you're more manic than when I left you. What's going on?'

'I've been such a fuckwit!'

'What do you mean? I thought you'd had a quiet weekend in? No reports of you in the papers. Paparazzi had nothing to show. In this town that means nothing happened.'

I blurted out the events of the last forty eight hours, relieved at being able to make my confession.

'There, there honey,' she said patting my hand, 'you're not the first person to fall for that story.'

'What, so the charming Mr Dan Raven isn't the man I read about in the press? Loving father, family man?'

'He probably is, and he might also be the man he told you he was, the one you spent the weekend with. But Tina, this is Hollywood, you can be whoever you want. And darling girl, as your publicist, it's my job to create the person we want the world to see. Nothing here is real.'

She was right. She sat me down and got us both a coffee.

'And the reason there are gaps in your schedule is that we have to be flexible and, if you'd let me get a word in, I'll tell you about the good news I received earlier this morning,' she said grinning like a Cheshire cat.

'Sorry, I didn't mean to dump that on you first thing. Guess I was feeling a bit guilty, a bit stupid. Thanks for listening. Now what's this news you have?'

'A particular someone wants you on her show this afternoon,' she replied rather cryptically.

'Who?'

'Aura Wainwright.'

'You're kidding! How did you pull that off? I thought it took weeks of negotiation to get on to her show?'

'Normally it does, but when you're the hottest ticket in town, even they find the time.'

Aura Wainwright had a daily show. It was watched by millions of people all over the world. She had become a kind of mother confessor to women everywhere. They would tune in everyday to hear her interview the most elusive, controversial and famous people on the planet. She had an uncanny ability to get people to open up to her. And unlike many celebrities was completely open about herself. We followed her battle with weight, with relationships. She was like a dear friend, had the same problems and insecurities we all faced. She was just like us. Except that she wasn't. She was Americas richest media star, had created an empire, her wealth measured in the billions, her influence worldwide.

'So what happens next? What do they want me to do, to talk about?'

'They've got their money expert on today. Want to do a show about empowering women. Getting them to understand how to liberate themselves from debt, how to build financial freedom. They want you to talk about your own journey. It will be taped this afternoon and go to air tomorrow.'

What Shauna was saying was quickly sinking in. I could pull off the interview easily. What was really amazing was the realisation at what this might mean for my business. The Chris Brown brand, the books, the blog, the dresses and little old me, were about to go global. I rang Cindy and she, for the very first time, was speechless.

'Cindy, are you there? Hello Cindy?'

'Sorry boss, just trying to get my head around what this will mean. You know we could go into meltdown if we're not prepared?'

'Yeah, I know. Ring Chenda, warn her about what might happen, get her to make sure the co-suppliers are ready. Make sure the I.T. team are geared up. Call in whoever you think we might need, spend as much as necessary. This is a once in a lifetime opportunity, we can't fuck it up.'

We wrote lists of who and what would be needed to make this work. Extra staff would have to be hired to take calls, follow up on enquiries. A sales team would have to let our advertisers know what was coming and we would need to send out press releases alerting the traditional media outlets of tomorrow's show.

Shauna rang the publishers. They would handle the extra demand on book sales, printed copies of 'Escape Money' were being dispatched across the country immediately. Copies for the Christmas rush would be sent out early. The printers were called, warned that the demand for the book, after the interview, might exceed all expectations and that they needed to get their presses rolling if they too wanted to cash in on the interview.

The 'Aura Effect' was the term used when a book, a movie, a charity, any product featured on her show. Real rags to riches stories were told of the people whose lives changed dramatically after an endorsement by Aura Wainwright. It would be tough going, but I trusted Cindy and knew she would rise to the challenge.

Shauna spent the next hour making calls and sending emails, rearranging things to fit this change of plans.

The interview was scheduled for four in the afternoon. It would be done in the Seattle studios, headquarters of Aura Wainwright Enterprises, or AWE as it was colloquially known. It would be the final taping for the day. I hoped we had enough time to put everything in place.

We had been working solidly for three hours. I looked at my watch, it was ten in the morning. I Googled flight times, Los Angeles to Seattle, and was shocked to see that the flight could sometimes take almost three hours, depending on the time of day, wind speeds, airport traffic. For some reason I thought it was only a short flight, maybe one hour away. A moment of panic ensued.

'Fuck, Shauna, we're running out of time. Seattle can be almost a three hour flight. By the time we get through the traffic, we'll barely have enough time for make-up,' I cried frantically.

'She of so little faith! I think we've both done about as much as we can do here. I noticed your bags were packed, I have a driver waiting. Trust me, we'll get there on time. Take a deep breath, pack up your computer and let's go.'

In her usual efficient manner Shauna had already called the driver, the car was running, the doors open. I didn't recognise the route, Shauna told me we would be leaving from Van Nuys, not LAX.

'How come?'

'You'll see.'

And see I did. Waiting on the tarmac was a private jet. Our bags were loaded and we climbed the stairs to be greeted by an impeccably groomed steward.

'Welcome aboard Mrs Brown, Shauna, my name is Jason and I'll be looking after you on this flight.'

Pale interior, soft leather seats. We sat down and Jason brought us a drink.

'I like your style Shauna!'

'I like yours even more Tina Maxwell, cheers!'

No long queues, no waiting at airports, not even sharing the flight. Shauna was right, she would get us there on time. How my life had changed.

Wise Aura

Being on set, in a television studio, was no longer daunting. I had spent the last week doing many interviews, none as surprising as the first and none more powerful than this.

Aura had come to my dressing room to welcome me personally. She talked about what she knew of my story and generally how the show would play out. I was pleasantly surprised, a co-producer had already been in, given me this information. I was touched that Aura had taken the time to make me feel at home. She was warm, sincere and quite playful. Aura knew the value of the audience, her people, and so did I. We clicked immediately. She was called to set. I sat waiting to go on and sent Cindy a text to tell her what had just happened. This time last year I, too, was one of her viewers and would religiously make time everyday watch her show. Today I was on it. Who would have thought!

She had such a presence and was clapped liked a rock star as she walked on set. Tickets to the Aura show were booked out months, sometimes years, in advance. The women in the audience were dressed up for this very special occasion. They seemed to have taken time to look good, possibly camera ready for an audience scene. The crowd needed to be told to sit, to quieten their applause, so that the show could begin. They watched her adoringly as she welcomed them to the studio and introduced her first guests.

The first half of the show was taken up with three members of the general public, all women with their own financial problems, giving their life stories, confessing in front of 'Mother' Aura. The financial guru then gave very specific advice and played the role of bad cop to Aura's hand squeezing, knowing nods, empathetic, good cop.

After a short break it was my turn. I was introduced as the Aussie who'd completely changed her life. A slide show of shots from the blog were screened along with a pre recorded commentary giving a short history of my life and what I did after the death of my husband. It was when Aura started quoting statistics such as hits to my blog, advertisers' comments, book sales and turnover of my company, that I did a bit of a double take. Hearing the figures out loud sounded so impressive and my ego did a little hop, skip and jump with pride, as if Aura's saying it made it so much more legitimate.

She then went on to talk about the dress business. When Aura mentioned how difficult it was to find the perfect dress and that I had found a way to make it possible, the audience cheered, hands raised as if bearing witness at a revival meeting. She finished with the story and pictures of the women and children at the Cambodian factory and the audience rose to their feet clapping, as if to acknowledge my now saintly endorsement. Once the people had settled, she asked me a series of questions and almost immediately I was under her thrall. The answers flowed, I held nothing back. We talked about shared issues, as if we had known each other for years. After a while she threw to the audience and I was delighted to answer their eager questions. Eventually time was up. She made a closing speech and the director counted down till finally the cameras were off.

But it didn't finish there. The director came up to Aura and requested if we would be happy to continue the questions with the audience a little bit longer. It would be recorded and shown later during one of the 'Behind the Scenes' specials. She knew we were onto to something, that the audience weren't ready to stop and we continued the Q and A for another thirty minutes. Eventually we were done. The audience were sent on their way happily swinging bags loaded with gifts and product samples. All of them buzzing with excitement after being in the same space as the woman they had come to worship.

I was sitting in my dressing room, removing the make-up, trying to come down off the high after such a monumental day, when there was a knock at the door. It was Aura, behind her was an assistant carrying a bottle of champagne and two glasses.

'Hey Chris, mind if I come in? Great show, thought we might celebrate.'

'Sure, come in, sit down, please,' I said confidently, as if we had been friends forever.

And for the next hour we debriefed, discussed some of the trickier questions, and most importantly what steps I had taken to deal with the inevitable publicity the show would generate. I told her I had a team back home trying to get ready, to second guess just how this would affect my business. She wanted the details, needed to know I'd be ready. She didn't take the 'Aura Effect' lightly. Eventually, when she was satisfied enough had been done, we just chatted away like old friends. After some time and a couple of glasses, she looked at her watch, it was getting late.

'So Chris, where are you staying tonight, what have you got planned?'

'I'm not sure really, a hotel downtown, probably order in, watch a movie. My publicist is travelling with me, she has the details.'

'Well, after a show like that I am wide awake, pumped, not ready to call it a day. I want to know more about the dress site, about you. I'm sure there are things that not even Chris Brown tells her readers,' she said cheekily.

'I have a really big house and an empty guest room. Would you like to come and stay?'

I was completely taken aback, the most famous woman in the western world was inviting me for a sleepover. I paused for a moment, taking in the absurdity of the situation, then answered.

'Sure I'd love to.'

'Give your publicist a call. My driver is waiting. I'm done for the night.'

Needless to say, Shauna was blown away by the offer and immediately agreed that I should stay.

The Price of Fame

We drove for a while, out of the city, past tall forests, glimpses of water, the lights of Seattle flickering behind us. We arrived at a fortress like wall, where a high, solid timber gate opened before us. The driver waved to the guard seated in the glass booth. We entered her vast estate overlooking the Puget Sound and drove up to the Gothic revival mansion. It was huge and made my former home in Toorak seem tiny by comparison. A butler greeted her warmly and took my luggage from the driver.

Our arrival was interrupted by the shrill barking of two small dogs. Aura stopped, reached down and lovingly patted her pets. They licked her excitedly as she tried to calm their enthusiasm, stroking them and talking to them the way a mother would greet a child.

'Yes, my babies, Mommy's home. Have you been good girls?' she spoke, baby talk.

'Sorry Chris, I've been downtown taping for the past few days. They've given me tomorrow off. Can't wait to put my feet up and unwind. Are you hungry?'

'Starving actually.'

'Follow me. I'll see what Clara has cooked for us tonight.'

I followed her down a long hallway, into an immaculately presented dining room. The table was set for two with gleaming silverware, fresh flowers and elegant candelabra. A large bay window looked out onto the moonlit water. A woman in a grey uniform and white apron greeted us. She pulled out a chair and gestured for me to sit.

'Welcome home, Miss Wainwright. Would you like something to drink with dinner?'

'Hi Clara, this is my friend Chris Brown and yes, a Pinot Gris would be good. Is that ok with you Chris?'

'Sounds perfect.'

Clara procured a bottle from one of three ice buckets sitting frostily on the sideboard and poured.

'Good evening Ma'am, would you care for a glass of wine?'

'Yes, thanks,' I replied

'I shouldn't really be drinking, my trainer has got me on a ridiculously strict diet at the moment. I'll be turning fifty in a few months time and want to look my best. We're doing an ongoing story on my weight loss and fitness regime. It's not just him I'm answerable to, my audience are expecting the miracle makeover as well.'

'I understand, it's a continuous battle!'

'But you, Chris, you look great, how do you do it?'

Before I could reply Clara placed in front of us a simple dish of steamed white fish and green salad.

'God, not more of this,' groaned Aura at the sight of the food.

'You know Chris, it's been a big week and I really couldn't face another plate of this. Clara could you please fry up some chicken, southern style. You know how I like it. Maybe some potato salad, collard greens and black eyed peas. Let's make Mrs Brown a true American feast.'

'But the diet? Won't you get into trouble? What will your trainer say?'

'Hang the diet, I'll work my butt off in the gym tomorrow. Let's go to the kitchen, much nicer in there. Clara can show you how real southern food is made.'

The kitchen was a large bright airy space. New England style, bespoke joinery, very Martha Stewart. We sat at a long bench and I watched as Clara prepared the meal.

'Now, where were we?' said Aura, as Clara efficiently went about her work.

'Yes, you, how do you keep your figure?'

'Do you have a computer?' I asked.

Aura got out her ipad, handed it to me and I Googled my blog, clicking back until I found those original postings. I handed it back to her. I watched as Aura's eyes lit up in wide eyed astonishment.

'Sweet Jesus, and I thought I opened up to my audience. God you're so brave, I could never reveal my body like this! With pictures like these it's no wonder you have such a huge following, I bet people were hooked right from the start. What made you do it?'

'It's a long story.'

'We've got all night,' said Aura, as Clara presented us with a generous plate of food and left the room.

I told her why I had begun my blog, about the hounding by the press. Then took a deep breath, started right from the very beginning and told her the whole pathetic truth. I had only just confronted this myself and had never told a single soul the real story of my life with Paul. To Aura I confessed.

'Wow, that's something I bet your readers have never been told. But hey honey, don't think you're the first woman to have endured such a marriage. And just think what you might have missed out on. You have a child, something I will never know the joy of.'

'You're right, I'm very grateful. Kate is brilliant, she is the someone I will always truly love. And you, did you ever want children?'

'Sadly, by the time I was ready I couldn't find a man. I wanted a real husband, not just a donor.'

'But surely Aura, they must be queuing up, you're rich, successful, beautiful...'

'Yeah and that's exactly why I'm still single. Men are intimidated by those things. No one wants to be Mr Aura Wainwright!'

I hadn't experienced this, but I understood what she meant.

'How about you Chris, have you found that special someone?'

'Please Aura, Tina. That's what my friends call me,' and I explained the whole name thing.

'So you really do have two lives, but you haven't answered my question.'

'Not really, there's no one special.'

'What's your excuse, you too are beautiful, successful and still a good ten years younger than me!'

I could feel another confession coming on and told her about my first date with Raphael.

'God, that was so brave, how did you cope with showing your naked body to a man other than your husband.'

'Raphael was very charming and cleverly treated me to a very indulgent day of pampering before he seduced me.'

I continued with the rest of the story, explaining what had happened during that day.

'Jesus, honey that sounds like the most brilliant foreplay ever!'

'It was, it gave me the confidence to start to think differently about my body.'

'And do you still see him?'

'Only as a friend, his sister and I are very close. Actually, I don't feel that way about him, it would complicate things.'

'And so you've lived like a nun since?' Aura questioned, filling my glass as she spoke.

'Not quite, in fact I've been on a bit of an adventure in the last nine months.'

'Pray tell, Miss Tina,' said Aura in her best Southern Belle accent.

The wine loosened my tongue. I gave her a full account of the men I'd been with, the things we'd done and what I'd discovered. Aura giggled conspiratorially, we were like two naughty schoolgirls sharing secrets.

'And you Aura, you may not have a husband, but surely you haven't reclaimed your virginity.'

'It's so difficult. I've had more than one ex write the tell tale account of life with me. It's almost impossible to find someone who doesn't want to sell his story to the highest bidder.'

'But you still haven't answered my question, no woman can live on bread alone.'

'Well, there is someone, a fuck buddy, I believe they are called.'

'How on earth do you keep him from telling the press?'

'He has just as much to lose as me. He's in politics, very high up, married.'

'You naughty, naughty girl.'

'It's fun, we only get together occasionally. You wouldn't believe the elaborate lies we have to tell to sneak off. Absolutely no one else knows, not my staff, not anyone. You are the first person I've told.'

'And how do you deal with the fact that he's married?'

'We were friends long before we became lovers. It's hard to explain. I don't love him in the traditional sense, we are just friends who have sex. Want nothing more. It doesn't feel like cheating, he still adores his wife.'

'But it's still cheating?'

Aura paused before she spoke.

'She knows.'

'Wow! And she lets him get away with it?'

'She has a degenerative disease, her body is crippled, she suffers great pain. She understands his need for physical comfort. And don't get me wrong, this isn't some kind of weird polygamous Utah type thing. They don't discuss it, but she knows what happens when he goes away on one of his secret trips. It's not her we have to be careful of, it's Washington. The power brokers would never understand. He uses his wife's illness as the reason for his occasional absences. They respect her need for privacy, it's the one time they're both left alone.'

'But that doesn't explain how you get away with it. You have one of the most recognisable faces in the world.'

'I have an Island in the Bahamas. My staff know to leave me alone, it's where I go to escape. They set it up before I arrive and return to pack up after I leave. They are none the wiser as to what really goes on while I'm there. He tells people that he and his wife are in the area for medical treatment. She stays at a very remote and exclusive spa nearby. He comes to me by boat when she's settled in.'

'Don't you get lonely?'

Auras eyes welled with tears.

'I get very lonely. It's hard to know who the real friends are. Most people just want something from me, takers, users. It's not just ex boyfriends who have sold their stories, it's former staff, friends even disgruntled members of my own family. Relatives who think that the money I give them is never enough. People think I'm one of the luckiest women in the world. They have no idea of the price I've paid to be me. Sometimes I feel like my closest companions are my audience.'

I put my arm around her shoulders and gave her a big hug. She patted my hand, took a deep breath and composed herself. It was getting late and we were both very tired. Before we went to bed she had one last thing to say,

'So Tina, I see you, already successful, on the verge of something even bigger. Be careful, find that special someone you can trust, who can share this journey with you. Don't do it alone. Remember to have a life.'

And thus ended the gospel of Aura.

New York

It had been almost a week since that night with Aura. I had been in continuous contact with Cindy, checking she was coping with the ridiculous increase in business. And as I would have expected, she was handling everything beautifully. She had delegated many of the jobs. People we trusted were promoted and we hired professionals, paying them handsomely to manage the quantum leap Aura's show had given us. She had even appointed Jane Smith as editor in chief. Funny how Jane's tongue in cheek request had become reality.

Chenda had also wisely been training more of the Cambodian women in other areas of the business. Moving women off the sewing machines and into management positions as U-Dress-U went into overdrive.

Shauna and I had criss-crossed the country, being interviewed, fronting cameras, until finally we landed in New York, the last stop on this monumental trip.

I had been quite vague about the night spent at Aura's place, not wanting to break the bond of trust we had formed. I had told Shauna it had been very pleasant and that Aura had given me some wise advice about the future.

One thing in particular about what Aura had said stuck with me, 'Don't do it alone.' The words haunted me. Kate no longer lived in Melbourne and was my daughter, not the someone special Aura had meant. Lola and Raphael, although good friends, now divided their time between Italy and Australia. They were creating new lives, probably finding their own someone special in the country of their parent's birth. Cindy and my paid employees would most definitely not fill that gap. I didn't have that someone special, someone to go on the journey with.

Or did I?

Adam had said he loved me, but could not break the stranglehold his fucked up brother had on him. A brother who hated me with such a passion that a relationship with Adam would be impossible... Or would it? Could we work something out? I'd deleted all of Adam's messages. I hadn't even read what he had to say, didn't know what he was offering in the way of an apology or a solution.

I had acted rashly. I knew now Adam was that 'someone special' and I too had loved him. I just hadn't told him. I needed to rethink things and cursed myself at my knee jerk reaction. I'd never really given him a chance. Maybe we could work something out.

Shauna was far too busy to be concerned about all this emotional upheaval. The Aura interview had sent book sales soaring, we were number one on the New York Times bestseller list, it was all she could do to keep up with requests for interviews. Houston, Chicago, Washington, it had all been a bit of a blur.

All I knew was that I was completely and utterly exhausted and looked forward to catching a few hours sleep before a gala dinner at the Guggenheim tonight. We would be guests of the owner of the parent company that had the US rights to the book. It was a charity fundraiser for literacy education in the poorer schools of the city. Shauna informed me it would be good to be seen at this event and quite frankly the invitation was an acknowledgement that I'd arrived, was a success in the eyes of the people who counted. More of the way business was done in the U.S.

We drove through the busy streets of New York, noise, movement, skyscrapers, people, traffic, an intense energy. I remembered Adam telling me he had a place here, probably another spectacular penthouse like the one in Melbourne. I wondered where it was. We arrived at our hotel, The Regal on Greenwich Street, Manhattan. The concierge greeted us by name, Shauna must have called when we landed. Or maybe it was his business to know? Americans took service to a whole new level.

I gasped as we stepped into the foyer. It was shockingly familiar. Raphael's furniture, his distinctive interiors, familiar colour palette.

'Are you ok Tina? You look like you've seen a ghost. Do you need to sit down, you're so pale? I'll handle the check in.'

She sat me down on one of the luxurious armchairs, exactly like the ones at The Imperial. I took a moment to take stock. Was this where he meant, his 'place in New York'?

We were taken to our rooms. I was in a gorgeous suite. Modern Australian paintings on the walls, separate bedroom, large bathroom and double doors onto a rooftop terrace. It felt so familiar. A door connected Shauna's room to mine. She came through after offloading her luggage.

'Feeling better?'

'Yeah, just a bit tired.'

'Do you like your room?'

'It's lovely, you have good taste. How did you know about this hotel?'

'Actually, we had a bit of a problem. My assistant had booked us into one of the bigger luxury hotels uptown and when we changed our schedule they couldn't honour the booking. Something to do with the President being here for a UN meeting, no available rooms. I rang Nancy and she recommended this place. She always stays here when she's in town. Said there was nothing quite like it, gorgeous interiors, best staff, great food.'

'Anyway I think you should have a rest. I've got nothing planned until the Gala tonight. I've organised some gowns to be delivered to your room, something appropriately 'New York Charity Dinner'. The assistant said she'd be up in a few minutes to make sure we find one that suits. Give me a knock when she arrives, I'm just going to freshen up.'

Shauna left through the connecting door and I noticed it had failed to close, the plush carpet stopping it. Or perhaps she felt it was friendlier to leave it slightly ajar. I closed it anyway, I needed a few minutes to myself.

I opened my ipad, googled The Regal and, sure enough, my suspicions were right. The hotel was owned by Adam, interiors by Raphael and artworks from Gabriella's gallery. No wonder it felt so familiar. Was this a sign? I grabbed a mineral water, needed a drink, needed to think. I stared vacantly out the window wondering what I should do. I should contact Adam. We needed to talk. I wondered where he was. He travelled extensively. Would he be available at that number? What would I say? Perhaps his movements were being reported in the papers? I Google his name. It only took seconds. The listings were in the thousands, one caught my eye, it was posted yesterday.

'NATIONAL GALLERY ANNOUNCES TIM NOLAN RETROSPECTIVE'

I had no idea what relevance this had to Adam, but I was delighted to see Tim's name and wanted to find out more details about the upcoming exhibition. It didn't take long, the article cut through me like a knife. Adam was contributing a painting to the exhibition and the gallery director was pleased to announce that after the show it was being placed on permanent loan, as part of the gallery's display of great twenty first century Australian artists.

'Fuck, now the whole city will see!' I snarled at the screen.

The painting was titled 'Finding Tina Maxwell', my real name. The name I used with friends, one that gave me some distance from the very public Chris Brown. Now they would not only see, but know. Thankfully, there was no photo of the actual painting. Luckily art didn't warrant the same level of investigative journalism that my husband's companies downfall had generated. Although I'm sure it wouldn't take too long for the hacks to find out just who Tina Maxwell was after the retrospective opened. The gutter press would have a field day. I felt so betrayed. Why did I feel like I was being punished by him? And although I had broken off the relationship, it was Adam who'd committed the original offence.

The article went on to quote Adam as saying he no longer had room for the painting. Although reluctant to give it up, he said it would be good for the people of Melbourne to have the opportunity to view what was considered Tim Nolan's finest work. There was a photo of him shaking the director's hand. A link at the bottom of the image directed me to more photos of the cocktail party held when the announcement was made. I clicked and what came next was worse. A photo of Adam standing next to a gorgeous blond woman, Georgina Snelling, Fiona's younger sister, or Sissy, as Fiona liked to call her.

'Fuck, fuck, fuck!' He didn't take long, the painting, me, out of his life. A new replacement, a somewhat younger woman on his arm. Someone of breeding age?

How could I have been so naive to think he would be pining like some lovesick schoolboy? Of course he'd moved on. His relationships were like the way he conducted his businesses, no room for sentimentality, get rid of the underperforming players.

The doorbell rang, the assistant had arrived with the dresses. I choose a Lanvin, low cut, red satin gown and killer heels. So not me, but so right for the event tonight. I really did need to move on. The dress might help.

Our driver dropped us off on Fifth Avenue, out front of the Guggenheim, the spectacular inverted ziggurat shaped building, designed by Frank Lloyd Wright, breathtaking in its exquisite geometry.

Cameras flashed as New York's wealthiest and most influential arrived. It wasn't only Hollywood where a paparazzi shot was needed to tell the world about who and what was going on.

'God Tina, you look sexy. This gown you've chosen, it seems out of character. Not your usual understated elegance.'

'Pleased you noticed. I took your advice and decided that tonight I would be whoever I wanted to be. This dress, this look, this is who I want to be tonight.'

'Bravo girl. Any chance you'd consider changing sides? I could introduce you to a whole new way of thinking,' said Shauna, flirtatiously pinching my bum as we entered the main gallery where the benefit was being held.

'Sorry, Shauna, have to refuse your offer. Girls just don't have that one thing unique to a man that I've grown rather fond of! However if I was thinking of changing, you'd be the first to know!' I replied flirting outrageously back.

The dress had given me a new level of confidence.

We walked into the body of the building. I looked up to see the skyward spiral, lit like a stairway to heaven, a long winding gallery housing one of the world's most impressive collections of modern art. The main hall, the Rotunda, was decorated tastefully, tall cylinders of green goddess lilies canopying each table. My favourite flowers, another sign? Or perhaps not. My first supposed sign today proved to be a red herring. Why was I thinking like this? I didn't believe in this type of superstition. Perhaps I was thinking too much about what Aura had said. Was looking too hard. But then again, maybe I should start to look somewhere else, maybe he was in this room? The dress would be a beacon perhaps, a gown that sent out signals no red blooded male could ignore.

The attendant directed us to a board showing the seating plan. We had been separated. I was at a table at the front of the room, seated right next to Henry Edelman, owner of the publishing company and an obscenely wealthy member of New York's establishment. Shauna was seated at the back of the room. I guess publicists didn't count quite as much.

'Welcome, my dear,' said a cultured voice behind me. I turned to see a tall, distinguished, Donald Sutherland like, man.

'Henry Edelman, and I believe you are Mrs Chris Brown, my partner tonight,' taking my hand, kissing it delicately. Very charming.

'Mr Edelman, a pleasure to meet you.'

'The pleasure is most certainly all mine,' he said, stepping back looking me up and down, smiling. Silver fox.

He crooked his elbow, I slipped my hand in and he escorted me to my seat. The table, his table, was in the prime position. He introduced me to the other guests and I recognised many of the names, old money, upper class New Yorkers. Henry introduced me as his new author. They seemed to be familiar with the book, the elegant, wisp thin wives most eager to talk. They were all polite, engaging me, seemed genuinely interested. I felt none of the rejection I'd experienced at similar functions with Paul's mother in Melbourne. Americans loved success.

A string quartet played and after the first course the conversation shifted.

'Apart from promoting your book, what are your plans during your stay in our fair city?' asked Henry.

'I hadn't really thought about it. Shauna is keeping me very busy. I only have a few hours late tomorrow afternoon, then I fly out the following day.'

'Two hours, hmm... there is quite a bit we could do in that time.'

'Are you offering to be my escort, Mr Edelman?'

'Yes I am, if you don't mind being seen on the arm of an elderly man, Mrs Brown.'

'Far from it. I would be honoured to be shown around the Big Apple on the arm of a... more experienced man,' I corrected cheekily.

He understood and looked at me slightly more teasingly.

'Well then, what would you like to do? What interests you? And please call me Henry.'

'It's hard to say... Henry. I work a lot, don't have time for much else. I liked to cook once, perhaps we could share a meal.'

'Everybody eats, there must be something more.'

I looked up, pondering his question. It was obvious, it took this building to remind me.

'I love mid century architecture, art. That's what I like.'

'Then we're in luck. I'm on the board at MOMA, the temple of modern art. Tomorrow I will take you on a personal tour.'

'Sounds wonderful, I couldn't think of a better guide. However I do have one request.'

'And what might that be?'

'That you call me Tina.'

The night was lovely, Henry took his role as partner very seriously. Never left my side, introduced me to many people and danced with me when the big band played.

As the evening progressed, he told Shauna she was free to leave, that I no longer needed babysitting. He would see to it personally that I got home safely. Shauna agreed and whispered that she wanted to check out a 'girls only' club in Soho. She didn't need to elaborate, I could just imagine what went on in one of those places. A straight woman would only cramp her style.

'So Tina, we need to be up around seven for a make-up call, I'll knock on your door at six.'

'Sure, you know me, I'll probably be awake anyway. Have a good night, see you tomorrow.'

'You too Tina, and hey... remember to have fun!'

'I think Shauna is reminding you Tina, that all work and no play makes for a very dull person.'

'And how would you rectify that Henry?'

'Let's start with another drink.'

Henry and I drank champagne, talked and danced until the gala was over. He remained true to his word and accompanied me home, even though his own residence was close to the Guggenheim, overlooking Central Park. His driver pulled up, opened the door, and Henry walked me to the entrance of The Regal.

'Thank you Henry for a marvellous evening, it was a lovely surprise.'

'Yes it was, Tina. Now hurry along, it's getting very cold', he said, looking down at my pert nipples pressing hard against the cool shiny fabric of my gown. I'll pick you up at four tomorrow.'

He took my hand and kissed it.

'Until tomorrow.'

'Until tomorrow, Henry. Goodnight.'

I felt like Eliza Doolittle, just home from the ball, but Henry was no Mr Higgins. He was rich, erudite and attractive. He looked good for his age. I was too wide awake to sleep and so decided on a bit of research before I went out with the charming Mr Edelman. I didn't want a repeat of the Dan mistake.

Turns out publishing is only one of his businesses. He made a fortune buying up property in the seventies, parts of New York considered dangerous and unsavoury slums. Whole blocks virtually given away, purchased when he was just a young man, now exclusive and very desirable locations. Art, it appeared, was his passion, his collection unrivalled by anything in the world. My God, an older version of Adam. The only difference, he was fifty nine years old and, as the Wikipedia entry went on to say, he'd been married and had six children. Henry had recently divorced his third wife. Tomorrow afternoon would be interesting.

Unlike the previous night, I dressed truer to my own style. I wore one of my own dresses from the winter range, some beautiful new suede boots and a gorgeous Helmut Lang coat. Very December in New York. Understated elegance had returned.

Henry arrived at three. We set off and attempted to fight our way through New York's notorious traffic. I looked at my watch, Henry sensed my anxiety.

'Don't worry Tina, I'm on the board. They'll keep the place open for us. My donations give me special privileges.'

'It's not just that. I'm supposed to be attending a farewell dinner tonight.'

'I know, I'm your host.'

What an idiot, of course he was. For some reason I thought it was only with the team who'd put the tour together. Their head office was in New York, that's why we were finishing here. I had no idea Henry would be such a hands-on proprietor.

'You look marvellous, no need to change, dinner will be a pretty informal affair.'

I was relieved we didn't have to rush. I wanted to spend much more time with my art heroes.

By seven my brain could take no more and we said goodbye to the Warhols, the Lichtensteins and the Rothkos. A security guard let us out and to my surprise there was no driver waiting. I had become complacent about this service.

'Let us walk,' said Henry, taking my hand. I didn't understand, the night was cold and a light rain had set in. A few doors down we stopped.

'I have an apartment in this building. Museum Tower, part of the redesign and expansion of MOMA. Cesar Pelli was the architect. He designed the Petronas Twin Towers in Kuala Lumpur,' said Henry proudly as we stepped into the foyer.'

I remembered seeing the gigantic buildings on a stopover to Cambodia. We rode the lift high up into the tower, walked along a corridor and entered a somewhat modest apartment.

'You look surprised,' said Henry.

'Sorry, I didn't mean to. It's stunning.'

The main room was decorated in a pared back minimalist style, sixties looking designer furniture. Not quite what I had expected.

'The apartment was formerly owned by the famous American architect, Philip Johnson. He founded the Department of Architecture at MOMA.'

'Didn't he design the famous 'Glasshouse' in Connecticut?'

'Yes, one of the most beautiful modernist houses ever built. Did you see the model on show in the museum?'

'Yes. I would love to live in a place like that one day, although I don't know how I would cope with its glass walls. Feeling so exposed.'

'I'm sure Australia has enough hidden locations where a house like that could be built. Somewhere for you to escape to.'

'I'm sure I could find somewhere. I just don't have the time to look,' I replied.

'You know with all this media attention you're getting, you might need it sooner than you think.'

'Find someone special. Find somewhere to escape to.' A personal 'to do' list, at the insistence of others, seemed to be evolving. I changed the subject.

'The furniture, tell me about it.'

'The interior I've had restored back to the original Philip Johnson design and the furniture is some of his most collectable pieces. It's been a little project of mine since my divorce.'

Was he letting me know he was available?

Henry gave me a tour of the remaining rooms.

'You still look puzzled.'

'Well... for a man of your wealth, your standing, I guess I just expected...'

'Something bigger,' he said, finishing my sentence.

'Yes, and didn't you mention your place overlooked Central Park?'

'So keenly observed Tina. I do have another place. Much bigger, far too big sometimes. I come here to get away from all that opulence and ostentation. And I let my art loving friends use it when they're in town. But follow me Tina and I'll show you another reason why I choose to come here.'

Again he took my hand and led me to the windows. I looked out and was utterly delighted to see that Henry's apartment looked directly down onto the beautiful sculpture gardens at MOMA. We both smiled. I could now truly see the appeal of this modest apartment. I was becoming very fond of Henry Edelman. Could he be that special someone?

A doorbell rang and our intimate moment was interrupted. Shauna had arrived with the small team of people who had worked tirelessly behind the scenes during the tour.

Dinner was a more intimate affair than the grand event of last night. A chef from the museum's restaurant had prepared a simple but delicious meal. The table for eight sat modestly in front of the windows affording a spectacular view of the New York skyline. A single waiter saw to it that none of us had to leave our seats.

It was good to catch up with the people who had worked so hard over the last two weeks. We were all pretty exhausted, and although the night was fun, we were running out of steam. Henry sensed this and made a farewell speech. We toasted the efforts of the people around the table. By ten Shauna and I were ready to depart. It had not turned out to be quite like I thought. Henry had remained very charming, no inappropriate propositions, just more of the elegant good manners of the night before. I guess he wasn't so stupid as to complicate things by fucking with the talent.

'It doesn't seem like long enough. We must have you back in New York soon. There's so much more I want to show you. Next time you could stay in the apartment,' said Henry, as he walked us through the foyer of the building.

'I'm sure there is Henry, but what little I saw was truly wonderful and meeting you was perhaps the highlight of my trip.'

His driver pulled up to the curb. Shauna got in. He stood holding my hand and spoke.

'Tina, if I was a much younger man, I would ask you to stay. You're not the kind of woman who only sees me for my money. You are intriguing, beautiful, successful in your own right.'

'Thank you, Henry. I'm flattered.'

'And please, remember to look beyond the madness of the everyday. Look for something that gives you real pleasure. Find a life outside your business, find something for yourself. Don't leave it too late.'

He hugged me warmly. I think I understood what he was trying to say. Sombrely I stepped into the car, shut the door and opened the window. He looked in.

'And one more thing, don't forget to have fun!'

He tapped the hood and the driver pulled away.

And the list just grew. Find someone special, find a life away from work, find a place to escape to, and have fun. Four commandments from Aura and Henry. I would have some work to do when I got home.

Shauna and I went back to my suite, kicked off our heels, stretched out on my bed and had one last drink. She wanted to stay up as Nancy was flying into New York later tonight. Shauna was keen to spend a few days away from LA with Nancy, so that the two of them could have some alone time. It had been a hectic two weeks and Shauna confided that she'd missed Nancy terribly. A little wave of sadness came over me, no one would miss me, no loving arms to welcome me home. We could kill some time together, watch a movie, have another drink.

I woke a little disorientated. I was still clothed, but the blankets had been draped over me. The screen was turned off, the room dark. I must have fallen asleep. A seam of light appeared at the door joining Shauna's room to mine. It was caught on the carpet again. I could hear faint noises. Nancy must have arrived. I got up to shut it, give them the privacy of a night together. The door was ajar enough that I had a full view of the bed. It was dark enough in my own room that I could not be seen. Their room was gently lit by candles, faint piano music played in the background. I couldn't help but be curious about what I saw, transfixed by the two beautiful women on the bed.

Nancy was still partly clad, lace boy leg panties and matching bra. Shauna was naked, stretched out on the bed revealing a lean hairless body, legs slightly parted. I could see Nancy was sucking on her nipples, pulling them taut, one then the other. Shauna writhed, then took Nancy's head, kissing her passionately then redirected it. Nancy kissed her way down Shauna's belly. Shauna spread her legs wide, inviting Nancy in. Nancy's tongue darted between the folds, sucking biting, pulling on the sensitive skin. Shauna arched her back, letting out a low groan. Nancy looked up adoringly, then reached out to her lover placing her finger in Shauna's mouth. After some time the glistening wet fingers were removed and Nancy crawled back down the bed, pushing Shauna's legs further apart. First she used her fingers to rub the clitoris, again another moan and then she slipped a finger in, the heel of her hand working the clitoris as she played. Shauna grabbed Nancy's hand, squeezed the fingers together and then deftly directed them into her. Nancy worked slowly, first three fingers, then more and more of her hand, forced deeper, further, pumped harder till Shauna could no longer contain the orgasm so obviously erupting through her body, writhing and moaning with exquisite pleasure.

I felt ashamed I had witnessed this most intimate moment. I had not intended to stay so long and quietly closed the door. I undressed and returned to my empty bed.

The flight was leaving early. I shared a delicious breakfast in my room with the pyjama clad women. I shed a tear when the porter arrived and we said our final goodbyes.

'Don't come down, go back to bed.'

'Thanks Tina, it's been so good getting to know you.'

'And you too, Shauna. I'm sure it won't be our last tour together. Bye Nancy and thanks for letting me take your girl away for so long.'

'No problems, Tina. Next time you should stay with us,' Nancy replied with a wry grin. I wondered if she had seen me last night?

I gave Shauna one last hug and left. It had been a brilliant trip. I was returning home to a flourishing business and a new resolve.

Anna Buckley

Part 2

Back to Business

Unlike previous trips, I specifically asked Cindy not to book a break after the tour. Christmas was in ten days time and I had so much work to do, I could ill afford to have another minute away from the office. Truth be told, work was a good distraction. We would close the office for two weeks. The staff had been working around the clock and needed some time off. Kate would only be home for a few days. I would deal with the alone time after she left. Cindy had run a seamless operation in my absence and I was looking forward to the year ahead.

'Well Tina, you've waved your magic wand and everything has turned to gold,' said Cindy, showing me the sales figures.

'Your books have been on the bestseller lists everywhere. Advertising revenue is through the roof, I've upped your appearance fees and Chenda can barely keep up with demand. Tina Maxwell, do you realise you have become a very wealthy woman?'

The numbers were staggering. The US trip, the Aura interview, had turned this small enterprise into a much bigger business. Book sales alone would easily fund the costs associated with the growth and expansion. We had come a very long way in a such short time. The thought of that once pathetic little creature, squirreling away the cash, made me cringe.

'And Cindy Winter, if I am a very wealthy woman, then so are you!' I responded, smiling at the thought of such a spectacular achievement.

Next I met with our new editor, Jane, and all the sub editors to make sure the blog was running smoothly. Back at my desk, I wrote an editorial piece on the subtlety of misogyny, asking my readers to give me examples. Within minutes the comments page nearly went into meltdown. I had opened a can of worms and realised I'd be up all night responding to the issues raised in this heated discussion.

Misogyny had struck a nerve.

We teleconferenced Chenda at midday who told us the clothing business was going crazy and she too gave glowing reports. The Aura interview saw our business grow tenfold. It was evident there was a massive demand for the perfect dress. Chenda had been busy getting suppliers and other manufacturers on board to keep up with demand. My lawyer, Ruth, had put together a code of conduct that all new manufacturers had to sign before they could be part of our supply chain. It was something she did before I left and was glad it was now ready to go. I liked Ruth, she had foresight.

We talked about wanting to get an app designed so that women could easily access the dress site from their phone. How often had I been out shopping, totally exasperated by the lack of choice? I could harness this frustration by making the site more readily accessible to all those other women just as disgruntled as me. This could redefine impulse buying. Chenda suggested we could turn it into a project for the tech savvy kids of the mums who worked in the factory. I agreed and was curious to see what those fresh young minds would come up with. But we both agreed to wait a while, let things calm down a bit, make sure we were handling this huge growth in business before we launched any new projects.

And as for the perfect dress, it wasn't just women my age feeling ignored by the retailers. Women of all ages, from eighteen to eighty, overwhelmingly responded that they too had trouble finding the perfect dress. I would need to broaden my horizons and find a team of designers who could produce a range of clothes to fit this massive demographic and most importantly, I would have to appoint someone to run this department. It looked like it was getting far too big for either Cindy or me. We had to be available to everyone and could no longer afford the luxury of concentrating on one project alone. Cindy agreed and we decided to put out a post with a very specific job description. Someone who could lead a team of designers, had experience dealing with offshore manufacturing, had been in retail and lastly understood the frustration of never being able to find that perfect dress. We were overwhelmed with applicants. Coming up with the short list was going to be a big job.

Before we had even started, I got a call from Ruth.

'Hi Tina, saw your job ad.'

'And you're thinking of giving up your brilliant legal career to design clothing?' I said jokingly.

'No way, far from it. I don't have a single creative bone in my body!'

'So why the call?'

'I think I might just have the perfect person.'

Ruth told me about a young woman she had just successfully won an unfair dismissal case for. The woman had been a rising star in fashion retail, had worked her way up to become a leading department head for one of Australia's biggest clothing chains. I remembered reading about the case in the papers. When she complained about the unwanted sexual attention she received from the son of the company's owner, she was unceremoniously fired. The gutter press had turned on her, suggesting she was a gold digger and I remembered thinking how hard it would be for her to get employment in the future.

'I took the liberty of giving her a call and she said she was more than interested,' said Ruth.

By late afternoon I had arranged to meet with Lana Cunningham. She didn't have all the experience needed, but had the kind of drive and determination I was looking for. And a recommendation from Ruth was almost endorsement enough. Cindy liked her, intuitively felt she'd fit in well and cheekily reminded me that taking a risk on a young, but enthusiastic woman had paid dividends before. By five o'clock we had welcomed Lana to the team.

At the end of the day I sat down with Cindy and opened a bottle of champagne. There was one nagging question she had avoided.

'So boss, what the fuck happened with you and Adam?' she said bluntly.

'He kept ringing the office and I told Joan to tell him I wasn't available. Thank God he eventually got the message and stopped calling.'

'Thanks Cindy. I knew I was a bit vague when I rang.'

'Well, I just didn't get it. The last time I saw you, you'd cancelled your work commitments and were skipping out the door on the arm of Mr. bloody Darcy, like a love struck adolescent.'

I told her what happened and the history of the relationship.

'Wow, that must've hurt. Do you know why his brother has so much control over him?'

'No idea. It's tribal, they stick together, look after each other.'

'Jesus Tina, wasn't that glaringly obvious right from the start?'

'It was, I know, and I'm furious at myself for thinking it could be any other way.'

We finished the bottle and the effects of the alcohol loosened my tongue.

'Since this has turned into a bit of a confessional, I have to tell you about this nutter I spent far too much time with in LA,' I said grinning conspiratorially. Confiding in Cindy about Dan would help me get over the sting of that little fuck up as well.

'What the... ? I can see I'm going to have to manage your love life as well. No more men until they get my approval!' she said, shaking her head in disbelief.

'No more men, no more distractions,' I concurred.

'Don't beat yourself up too much. You didn't know psycho Dan was married and we've all fallen victim to the tall, handsome, but troubled, bad boy at some time,' said Cindy, once again showing her sage like wisdom. She was so much more than just a paid employee.

The rest of the week went smoothly. Cindy introduced me to the people she had employed, the experts who she hired when the Aura interview went to air. Advertising and sales, IT, logistics, people good enough to keep on as part of the bigger team needed since the phenomenal growth of our business.

Christmas Eve arrived and after a small end of year celebration, I locked the office door and walked home, exhausted but content.

Christmas

This Christmas would be simple, unlike other years.

Kate was coming home tonight. We would have Christmas lunch with Margot, she had booked a table at the very grand old Victorian era, Buckingham Hotel. Then we would go to the Finestra's on Boxing Day, a real family get together.

What a change. Last Christmas I would have been cooking like a madwoman, preparing the house for a Christmas loaded with expectation, tradition and ritual. Margot, as usual, keeping a mental note of my performance, judging, finding fault. I wonder if she had any idea of what my life looked like now? I dreaded seeing her, but owed it to Kate to be there. Kate loved her dad and Margot was a link to that past.

I hadn't bothered to get a vehicle. I walked to most places and when I needed a car I used the services of an on call driver. Kate seemed quite embarrassed at stepping into the chauffeur driven limo. Our trip from the airport was filled with the usual inane chatter between two people who had not seen each other for quite a while. Until we reached home.

'Mum, have you thought about getting a car, a bigger place?' said Kate, as we walked through the front door.

'Well, I've got no real need for a bigger house and I walk to work.'

'Yeah, I know that, but when I come here, it doesn't seem like home. It feels temporary, it's missing something.'

'Like what?' I responded, slightly peeved at this hint of criticism.

'When we lived in the big house you used to always cook, make stuff. We'd have dinners for the family, my friends. I walk in here and it seems lonely. Do you still cook, have people over?'

Ouch, she'd hit a nerve, which was very out of character for my quiet, beautiful child.

'So much has happened in the last year and my life has been so busy. I haven't really thought about it.'

What she was really saying was that she came back to a bed, not a home. I put the question to the back of my mind.

'And anyway, there are so many great places to eat around here. There's no real need to cook anymore. Throw your bags in your room, let's head out to Gertrude Street and have dinner.'

Christmas Eve was the beginning of the end. A time when Melbourne's inner city bars and eateries closed, as most of its residents, their customers, headed for the beach. A summer exodus that saw towns along the coast fill to bursting point and the familiar streets of my neighborhood all but empty. I remember seeing the 'trading over Christmas' signs on the doors of restaurants and observing that it would actually be quite difficult to book a table anywhere in January. We bar hopped. A drink here, a small course of something yummy there, dropping in at several of the numerous places that had become favorites. Greetings to the staff who had become familiar faces, but not real friends.

'Night Mum,'

'Night darling,' I said, as we went to bed.

Wide awake, sleep miles away, my brain went into overdrive, in that way it does when you finally have time to stop and think. I thought about my life. Kate was right, this was not a home. I had few friends and the loneliness of my past was resurfacing. I had filled my life since Paul's death with work, fucked a few men, made a lot of money. I thought I had fallen in love with a man I had once loathed and then shared it all with a paid employee, as if she were an old friend.

I feared that the legacy of the last nineteen years, the impenetrable emotional barrier I'd built up around me, was being reassembled, layer by protective layer. On the surface I was a success. The reality was that I might just grow old lonely. In a fit of alcohol fuelled melancholy I began to think about Adam. Why did I pick him? Why was I drawn back to him? Why had he given up so easily and not fought to get me back. Why couldn't I get him out of my head? I tossed and turned, no answers came.

I opened my eyes reluctantly, sleep had been elusive. Outside was the shimmering blue of a typical hot Australian Christmas sky. I could just imagine the loathing many women felt as they rose to get the turkey in the oven and the air conditioners on, ready for the marathon effort required to get through this day.

Kate and I exchanged gifts quietly. She was sad that it was only the two of us, she missed her dad. Christmas was the one time Paul made an effort to be home.

'What could this be?' I said, trying to lighten the mood by playfully shaking the obviously concealed magazines.

Ripping off the wrappers, I found a selection of publications about houses, architecture and interior design.

'Is this a subtle hint?' I said, smiling.

'Yeah, I've bought you a few subscriptions to give you ideas, get you motivated.'

Over coffee and croissants we flicked through the pages of the slick glossy magazines, pointing out the bits we liked that might come together to form our ideal dream home.

Unlike previous Christmases, we both spent a leisurely morning getting ready until it was midday and time to join the matriarch.

Our driver dropped us in front of the imposing old Victorian edifice of the Buckingham Hotel. The liveried concierge opened the car doors, greeted us warmly and ushered us past the foyer, into the stately dining room. It was a space where a queen would feel quite at home. We were met by the sounds of a choir singing traditional carols. Holly garlands and velvet red lilies in tall glass vases decorated each formally laid table, crisp white linen and silverware sparkling for this big day. The walls were hung with the portraits of some of Melbourne's most notable founding fathers. On the antique dressers underneath, sat generous silver salvers overflowing with exotic fruits, pomegranates bursting with ruby jewels, red blushing pears, plump cherries. A cornucopia, like a William Hughes still life painting. The smell of the tall pine tree, adorned with the most exquisite hand blown glass baubles, perfectly finished the scene. This place had a sense of the past, of solidity and permanence.

We stood as she made her entrance.

Margot looked her usual elegant self, wearing one of her smartly tailored suits. The staff fawned over her, she only acknowledged the most senior maitre'd. Perfunctory kisses to us both and a clipped 'Merry Christmas' in her overly affected snooty voice, completed her arrival.

After we sat back down she declared she had something for us and handed us each an envelope. Inside was a printed card informing the recipient that we had each given a goat to a family in Africa. It was the right gift to give, with the perfect amount of coldness expected of the ice queen. But we had the last laugh. Kate had told me Margot had hinted that she was giving 'worthy' gifts this year. We decided to have some fun.

We, too, handed over our envelopes.

'Who would've thought we were so in tune?' I said, grinning as she ripped them open.

I had to bite my tongue to stop myself from giggling, when I saw her thin lipped smile as she read that we had also given two goats, as well as a more generous water filtration system. The new me had grown a set of balls.

Stilted conversations about nothing topics, like the oppressive heat and the price of real estate, accompanied the first courses.

Looking around the room, I was curious about the stories behind each table of guests and why they had chosen to be here, instead of home. I was touched by the extra attention given to a lone elderly woman diner. At another table, six women celebrated what looked like an 'orphans' Christmas' and I shuddered to think that either of these situations could be mine.

After a glass or two of champagne, Margot started to loosen up a bit, as did we all.

'I hear you are doing very well for yourself these days, Chris.'

Kate chimed in and listed a few vital statistics about the book sales and my media presence, giving me a warm sense of affection for my daughter, who was so openly proud of her mum. And then I bragged about Kate's internship in Canberra and her success at university.

'I would expect nothing less. Your father was academically brilliant, too. Can't understand why he got mixed up with that nasty character, Justin.'

'I think Paul was just a good loyal friend,' I said, surprised at my defensive comment.

'It's a shame he didn't go into business with the other brother, Adam. Now he's done really well for himself.'

I felt sick at the mention of Adam's name and was keen to change the topic, but Margot continued.

'I suppose with the way that pig of a father treated Justin, it came as no surprise.'

'What do you mean?' I asked.

Margot proceeded to tell me tales of the brutalisation of Justin by his father. Luckily, Adam was a bright, gifted child who lived up to his father's high standard. For the less intelligent twin, Justin, beatings and deprivation were the norm.

'I remember one weekend visit. The boys had made the three hour train journey home. They had been boarding at the country campus for a whole term, as part of an outward bound program. We were all waiting on the platform to greet the children. They looked adorable in their uniforms, carrying their bags and tennis racquets. All but Justin, who had left his racquet at school. Graham Darcy roared at his son, yelling at him for being so stupid, immediately bought him another ticket and put him straight back on the returning train. We all said that he was being too harsh, but Graham was adamant that the child needed to be taught a lesson. The boys were only 8 years old.'

The compassion in her voice surprised me.

'Whenever I saw the boys after that, I noticed that Adam would always defend and protect his brother. It wasn't until Justin got older and stronger, that he started to stand up for himself. Unfortunately he ended up an even bigger bully than his father. Sometimes I was reluctant to let the boys play together. Justin seemed to have such control over Paul. They were always getting into trouble. In the end, I would only let them spend time together if Adam was present.'

'It's hard to believe that twins could be so different,' I said, trying to keep the conversation going, my mind barely able to concentrate. The mention of Justin's name reminded me of the shocking disc I'd found hidden in Paul's desk. The images of gross brutalisation and threatened blackmail, reminded me just how despicable Justin was. And then the violent, early morning altercation in the car park at Adam's hotel, just a few weeks ago, just confirmed his heinous nature. A repulsive man to be avoided at all costs.

'And by the way, I think Justin's treatment of you after Paul died was deplorable. I was surprised to see you had the fight in you to stand up against him to save the house.'

Had I just heard right, was that praise? I nearly fell off my chair. Margot had let her guard down.

'I always knew you had it in you. Wondered why it took so long to come out!'

The cynic in me thought Margot considered a more amenable relationship would be advantageous to her charities' coffers. Perhaps the truth was that she hated the fake me as much as I did.

By dessert, a massive storm dropped a layer of white hail over the gardens outside. I started to hum 'White Christmas', except that this was an intense tropical storm, capping off a stifling hot Australian day. What a bizarre sight to end an even more bizarre day. What an unexpected lunch with the dragon lady.

Coffee and Newspapers

Kate was sleeping in and we weren't due at the Finestra's until one. I hadn't read a newspaper for weeks and thought it might be fun to spread out the paper, read the local stories and do the crossword. Despite being a defender of electronic media, I still loved to read a paper. The smell of the print, the luxury of the solitary indulgence it allowed without the constant distractions when staring at a screen, listening to the ping of every new email arriving, demanding my attention.

The streets were quiet as the holiday exodus had already begun. The corner store, however, seemed to never close. Probably because the Vietnamese owners couldn't get that excited about Christmas or perhaps it was just that the notion of holidays was completely foreign to them. I grabbed two papers, the broadsheet and the tabloid. The first a serious read, the second a guilty pleasure.

Sitting down with a coffee I started to look. Nothing surprising, ads for the sales, heart warming stories of feeding the homeless, abandoned pets and opinion pieces on the year that was. The tabloid was much the same on this slow news day, the only difference was the gossip pages, which I turned to see how the partying classes were faring. Page after page of photos of the beautiful people appearing to have a jolly old time at the usual locations.

'PIERS PARTY WITHOUT PEER' screamed the headline. That was the restaurant Adam had attempted to take me to on our first date. I couldn't help but read further. It said that the owner, Di, was famous for her Christmas Eve party and inferred that an invitation to this particular night was harder to come by than an invitation to a marquee on Melbourne Cup Day. Scanning the photos to see who these people were, I nearly choked when the very familiar face of Adam Darcy appeared, tolerating the photographer, as arrogant as ever, and on his arm, Sissy Snelling, looking like the cat that got the cream. Other photos showed Justin and Fiona. One big happy family. My eyes brimmed with tears. I was shocked at my response, thinking he was out of my head. The sadness turned to contempt, when I thought about how quickly and easily he had replaced me. But why wouldn't he? It was me who had rebuffed him, ignored his calls. What did I expect, of course Adam went back to the people he knew, his tribe? Had I been completely delusional to think this could ever work? I was angry with him for so publicly declaring his status and even more angry at myself for nearly walking straight back into that world.

It still hurt.

Screwing up the stupid papers and ramming them into the bin made me feel a little better. Redundant dinosaurs, I thought, at least I could choose what to read when I opened my computer!

'What's wrong?' asked Kate, as she emerged to witness my bin stuffing tantrum.

'Nothing, just pissed off that I spent my hard earned cash on this drivel!'

'Jesus Mum, a few dollars? You need to get a life!' she said, rolling her eyes questioningly.

And she was right, again. I did need to get a life. And some friends and a car and a house. I reflected on what Aura and Henry had said and knew I had not acted on any of their wise words. Quite the opposite. I hadn't found anyone to share the journey with, no place to escape to (this pathetic little flat was hardly that!), no life away from my business and was definitely not having that much fun! In my head I could justify my position. I loved work, what I did, what I'd achieved, surely that was enough? I avoided the issue by doing the transformation thing, shower, dress, make-up, shoes. Hopefully my disguise would at least fool the Finestras.

Boxing Day lunch

We pulled up to the Finestra's house. I thought about the imposition it must have been on Andy, my driver to work on Christmas Day.

'Thanks, Andy.'

'No problems, Ms Maxwell. When do you think you might need to be picked up?'

'Look, I'm not really sure? How about you take the night off, spend it with your family,' I said patronisingly.

'Thanks, but to be honest with you, it's my job. I don't celebrate Christmas and I get paid well over the holiday period. I've got bookings all day, yours is just one of many,' he replied nonchalantly.

'Sorry, of course. I'll give you a call, bye,' feeling slightly stupid and ever so slightly hurt by his rebuttal.

He was right, it was his job. I should stop trying to please people and just get on with my life. Margot had made that very evident at yesterday's lunch. This would become another thing I could add to the growing list of New Year's resolutions.

It had been awhile since we'd been to see the Finestras. Kate was lovingly welcomed back into the warm embrace of this beautiful family and at last I felt we could celebrate a more meaningful and relaxed Christmas. Lola and I saw each other rarely now, as she spent most of her time in Italy. I realised she had no idea of the recent disastrous mess I had gotten into with Adam. It would be good to catch up, and, if I drank enough, I might just tell her the more juicy bits of the last ten months. Massimo immediately took Kate on a tour of his garden and it brought back memories of when the lunches were a sanctuary from my once tedious and lonely existence. In the kitchen Gabriella was just putting the finishing touches to lunch.

'Is there anything I can do to help?' I asked, almost certain of the answer.

'No, no, you two go outside, sit together, have a drink. I'm sure you have much to catch up on.'

Lola grabbed a bottle of Prosecco.

'Good idea, Mama. Just call if you need me,' said Lola, taking me by the hand and leading me outside to the terrace.

The pergola was covered by a gnarled old grapevine and in stark contrast with yesterday, the table was set with a tasteful minimalism that belied this family's endless generosity. We sat in the shade and gossiped like two schoolgirls. Lola spoke in hushed tones about the life she was creating for herself in Italy, of the independence it allowed her, away from the watchful eye of her protective father.

'I have my own place there now, you must come over and see it,' she said.

Lola was my age, but had never married. I knew she led an almost secret life where men were concerned. She wasn't interested in kids or permanent relationships. She had many lovers, but dissuaded the more enthusiastic ones with the threat of an inquisition by her southern Italian father. In fact Massimo was no longer like he had been when Lola was a teenager. He would love nothing more than a pack of grandkids to nurture and would probably accept any man who could father these much longed for children. What had once been a disincentive for Lola, now became her excuse.

'And you, surely you are not living like a nun?' she asked.

'God, I've barely got time to sleep let alone 'not sleep' with someone in my bed at night.'

She rolled her eyes and gave me a look of disbelief.

'Well, I think I might just be able to do something about that,' said Lola.

'What do you mean?'

Before she could answer, I heard the familiar sound of Raphael's voice as he called out from the entrance hall. Lola got up to greet her brother and I stayed seated letting the siblings reunite privately. It would be good to see Raphael. He had done a brilliant job with the office. I allowed myself to think about the time Raphael had given me that liberating day of pampering and the unexpected treat of his body that night. The thought of it was arousing. I would like to show him my new body and some of the things I had learnt over the past few months. In fact a good hard fucking by the 'no strings attached' man, was exactly what I needed. Was Raphael the surprise Lola had in mind?

'Ciao bella,' I heard him from behind and rose to turn and greet him. To my absolute horror, Raphael had not arrived alone. Standing rigidly next to him was Adam.

'Christina, this is my friend Adam. I believe you know each other,' said Raphael

'Adam,' I responded coolly.

'Christina,' he replied, barely able to contain his animosity.

Adam would never have come if Raphael had told him she would be there. He'd contacted Raphael about work and that's when the lunch invitation had been made. He was sure that pity was the motivation.

He hated the 'festive' season, hated being with his family. He remembered taking on the responsibility of trying to juggle the emotions of his mother after his parent's divorce, of becoming almost like a surrogate husband to the needy woman. She was always particularly difficult at Christmas. He loathed the performances of his father's latest girlfriend trying her best to be mother on Christmas morning. Sometimes women not much older than him. And he could never predict his brother's behavior. For many years, when they were little boys, his father's favoritism was evident in the gifts chosen. A well thought out gift for Adam, a reward for being the anointed, clever one, and for his brother Justin some piece of shit, picked without care. Adam remembered his brother's face, desperately trying to hold back the tears of another disappointing Christmas. Adam dreaded his father's callous rebukes when Justin's tears turned to crying. Not only at Christmas, but all the time. A bad report card, a call to the principal's office, a less than spectacular performance on the rugby field, anything his father could add to the list of Justin's failings. He hated the power his bully father had over them and he hated the role of fixer he was forced to play. Justin and his mother had very cleverly learnt how to manipulate Adam's guilt. This year he wanted to avoid spending Christmas with them and had chosen to work instead.

He'd let his guard down, had accepted Raphael's invitation. Lunch with the Finestras was something he thought would be a good panacea for the emptiness he'd felt since losing Tina. The last thing he'd expected was to see her here today.

97

The awkwardness was broken when Massimo returned with Tina's daughter, Kate.

'Greetings Adamo, buon natale,' said Massimo, grabbing Adam and embracing him with a fatherly warmth.

'And to you, too,' replied Adam, not really comfortable with this effusive show of affection. Adam did not hug. Showing emotion made him vulnerable. Adam never let anyone see into his soul. Anyone except her.

Gabriella appeared next. She looked beautiful. She had a sharp business brain, an ability to bring the right people together, her painters, her customers. He had been charmed enough many a time to part with fistfuls of dollars at her recommendation, and she always got it right. Not one of his artworks had ever been a bad investment.

'Welcome to our home. I am so pleased you could come. I always thought you would enjoy speaking to Christina in a less formal environment. Openings are no place to really get to know someone.' Today, however, she had gotten it completely wrong. Her intuition had failed her. Adam resented this little game of matchmaking.

I didn't know how I was going to get through today. Gabriella seated Adam right next to me. Lunch was going to be a very uncomfortable affair. I tried not to let the Finestras see my darkened mood.

After the antipasto Massimo and Raphael left the table to remove the suckling pig from the oven. Gabriella, Lola and Kate returned to the kitchen to prepare for the next course. I knew I had been set up on a surprise date and this was their less than subtle attempt to leave us alone.

'What are you doing here?' I snapped.

'Raphael invited me.'

'How dare you come here. These are my friends, my family.'

'I wouldn't have accepted if I'd known you'd be present. In fact I hate Christmas with its false pretensions, illusions of some idealised notion of family.'

'You didn't look to be having such a bad time Christmas Eve?'

'What do you mean?'

'I've seen your photo in the papers. Didn't take you long to find someone to replace me. I knew I didn't stand a chance when your family, your friends, have such a hold on you. What an idiot I made of myself. I can just imagine the laughs you had at my expense with that fuckwit brother of yours. I saw his picture too.'

'You've got it so wrong. I tried to talk to you, but you ignored my calls.'

'What was there to say? That everything was ok? That it was acceptable to cop that tirade of violent verbal abuse from your brother? That you wouldn't defend me, that your PA would handle me every time your brother required your complete and utter attention? That morning I was taken straight back to the encounter in the bar, when we were students. I couldn't believe I'd let myself come so close to making the same mistake again, thinking we could be friends. It was as if it was ok to fuck me, but when your brother turned up it was easier if I just disappeared. I felt like your dirty little secret,' I fumed, taking a deep breath before continuing.

'You fobbed me off with Sam. Didn't ring before I boarded the plane. I felt so humiliated. And then in New York, staying in your hotel, I contemplated calling you. I began to think I'd acted too rashly and wondered whether we could patch things up. Luckily the internet gave me all the information I needed to stop me making a fool of myself once again. Don't you and Sissy Snelling make a lovely couple?' I spat facetiously.

'And you've been living like a nun? Don't be so self righteous, you two faced bitch.'

'I beg your pardon!'

He was silent for a time, his anger palpable, and then he hit me with the bombshell.

'I came to LA.'

'What do you mean?'

'You wouldn't talk to me, Cindy had closed ranks. I felt powerless. I got on a plane, wanted to talk to you face to face. I had your itinerary and knew you had nothing on that weekend. I arrived Sunday evening. You weren't home and so I waited. I had all but given up, when a van pulled into the drive, a man got out and opened your door. I saw that you, too, had gotten over me.'

I felt sick, he had seen me with Dan, seen the passionate embrace, the kiss. I could no longer take the moral high ground or play the victim. He'd called me a bitch. There could never a relationship with Adam Darcy. The hostility of the moment was broken by the return of Massimo and Raphael carrying the pig on a big wooden board, ready for carving. The women followed. They all looked smug. If only they knew.

A difficult afternoon ensued. Every time I accidentally brushed against Adam's side, I felt him bristle. I distracted myself by drinking Prosecco, flirting with Raphael, trying to ignore the man sitting next to me. The afternoon groaned on. Kate left early to catch up with schoolmates. She told me not to wait up.

'Actually, Mum. I might stay at Sarah's, she's having a party. I'll see you sometime tomorrow. Bye,' she said as she left in her friend's car.

'Thank you Gabriella, Massimo, I should get going too,' said Adam, relieved at the opportunity to make his exit.

Raphael saw him to his car, and Lola and I began the clean up. Gabriella and Massimo left soon after, they had a dinner to attend, a catch up with friends. With just the three of us standing at the kitchen sink, Lola was the first to speak.

'What the hell was that all about?' pleaded Lola.

Out came the whole messed up story and once again Lola was there to rescue me. I wept like a child and Raphael consoled me with a hug. I felt an enormous sense of relief.

'I'm so sorry for ruining what should've been a lovely day.'

'It's ok, we shouldn't have made the assumptions we did. No more matchmaking, unless we talk first.'

I looked at my watch, it was getting late in the evening.

'Raphael, could you please give Christina a ride? The two of you are almost neighbors.'

Raphael complied graciously. We said our goodbyes and drove back, quietly, into the city.

Brotherly Love

'Sorry about that dismal attempt at getting you and Adam together. What a fuckup,' exclaimed Raphael on the drive home.

'Not as much of a fuck up, as if we'd stayed together,' I responded.

'You kept that a well hidden secret. How long had it been going on?' he quizzed.

'Look Raphael, it barely started before it was over. I've put it down to experience. I've told you the whole pathetic story. Feel free to ask about it, you're like a brother to me, but please don't talk to Adam.'

'How can I not talk to him? We work on so many jobs together?'

'No, no, not never, just don't talk about this specific shitty mess.'

'Sure,' replied Raphael mendaciously, knowing full well that he wanted to hear Adam's side of the story. He seriously believed Tina was making a big mistake. He remembered seeing Adam at the time he must have been with Tina and wondered why his normally cool business associate seemed to have softened, lightened up. He had probed a little further and Adam had mentioned there was a woman. She was unlike the bimbos he'd fucked previously. This one, he said, was different. Now Raphael knew who this woman was.

We were at the intersection of our two streets.

'Your place or mine,' asked Raphael cheekily.

'Raphael, you're very naughty and didn't I just say you were like a brother!' I responded smiling.

'Ah bella, that may be your perception, but it is not mine. And honestly that was not my intention. I just wondered if you wanted some company, it's only 7pm.'

I was embarrassed by my assumption, but still invited him in. I would be glad of the company.

We entered my flat and Raphael looked bemused.

'What?' I asked.

'This is where you live?'

I'd forgotten that he'd never seen my place before. All our most recent meetings had been on site or at his office. It reminded me of how little contact I'd had with my close friends. No one to share with, no place to escape to.

'Well, yes, what about it?'

'It's not what I expected,' he replied.

'What do you mean? What did you expect?'

'It's nothing like the warehouse, your office. I thought the brief you gave me would be reflected in your home. This place, this room, it's ok, but it's not you. It has no soul.'

So he sees it too. Ouch again!

'Thanks! I think you've forgotten that I was homeless and facing a massive lawsuit not that long ago,' I responded defensively.

'But you've done so much since then, created a small empire. This shabby little flat is no reflection of you. Is this the place you really want to come home to? Why do you ask so little of yourself?'

'Because I don't really care.'

'I think you do. Come here,' he said, reaching for my hand and pulling me close.

'You care, because I have seen the transformation of that once dowdy housewife into a strong, beautiful, self assured woman. You need to give something back to you.'

He'd summed it up, all the resolutions in one sentence, and he was right.

'You are not that same person I made love to all those months ago. I want to see who you are now,' he said seductively, reaching for the top of my shirt.

Slowly he undid all the buttons revealing my sexy white bra, then effortlessly pushed the shirt off my shoulders, letting it fall to the ground.

I felt exposed and quickly covered myself, crossing my arms in front of my breasts.

'You can't hide from me,' he said, as he took my hand, kissing it gently, unfolding my arms.

Then he undressed me. First my bra, then my skirt, then lacy panties. He smiled appreciatively and stepped back to look at me completely naked.

'You are more beautiful now than I could possibly have imagined,' his voice husky with desire.

And with that he picked me up and took me to my bed. He undressed and crawled in beside me. He kissed me and then looked me in the eye.

'Tonight we will fuck for the last time. You desire me, but you will never love me. All I want from you tonight is to show me how much you have learned.'

I had learned so much and decided I was in need of a little bit of Raphael affection. He looked so gorgeous, so sexy lying there in my bed. And he was right, I had changed, was not that same dull, broken woman he'd taken a chance on last March. So tonight it was my turn to reward him for the gift he had given me. I would take charge and give him a night to remember. And so slowly I crawled down the bed, knelt between his legs and took his cock into my mouth, sucking it hard until I felt it begin to come to life. He groaned as he lay back and accepted my tongue. When he was too engorged for me to continue I took hold of his hand and placed it against my wet sex showing him I too, was ready. I took a condom from my bedside drawer and artfully ripped off the packet, then slid it over his thick, glistening penis. Slowly I moved on top of his lap sitting right over his rigid shaft and rubbed my cunt along its length until I felt its tip at my entrance. I used my hand to guide his cock into me and with a slight tilt of my hip, thrust down forcing him deep inside me. I leant forward and whispered in his ear.

'This is how much I've learnt,' then sat up and began to ride him, rhythmically at first, gently, till he grabbed my ass and pulled me down deeper. I rocked harder, faster till I watched his eyes close in blissful ecstasy and felt the throbbing pulsation of his cock explode inside me. I collapsed onto his chest and felt his heart pounding.

'What about you?' he said quietly, stroking my face, knowing I had not climaxed.

'Shh, this is my gift to you.'

I didn't sleep, but lay in bed quietly thinking about what just happened. I looked over at Raphael, calmly sleeping. I wondered how many women, or men, had watched, fascinated by his beauty? He woke and smiled seductively.

'What's the matter, you look worried?' he asked.

'What did you mean, when you said that I desire you, but don't love you.'

'Just what I said. You can only love one man and I think you are still in love with Adam. You just don't know how to deal with the complications of his relationship with his brother. So you abandon any chance of trying to work it out.'

'You're partly right, but I think that the problem of his brother is insurmountable.'

'Have you ever asked Adam about it?'

'Well, no. Our relationship, if you could call it that, had only just begun, and honestly I didn't know how to broach the subject.'

'Families are complex and their problems are not easily fixed. Adam is a good man. How do you know he wasn't already trying to work things out?'

'I don't.'

I thought about the truth, that he had touched upon, but felt slightly betrayed by his defence of Adam.

'Another thing I don't understand is, if you like him so much, why did you just sleep with me?'

'Sleep? What we just did was not sleeping!' he said with a sexy grin.

'Ha ha, I still don't understand?'

'It was about getting you back again. At lunch I was seeing flashes of the old Christina returning. Something about the way you were dressed, your demeanour. When I came into your house I saw signs of you retreating into that self loathing behavior. I had hoped that you becoming sexually confident again might just flick the switch. I remember how much you changed after that night we spent together, and I liked who you became.'

'Next I expect you'll put that Marvin Gaye album on and start miming Sexual Healing,' I said, cheekily calling a truce and lightening the mood.

He knew, I hadn't fooled him. I cherished our relationship. I liked that we could have sex without feeling the need to become partners. I liked how he made me feel. I did love him, but I was not in love with him. Could he be my 'fuck buddy'? Someone like Aura's special friend?

'You hungry?' I asked.

'Starving,' he replied.

As expected Gabriella had sent me home with a generous basket of food.

Trampoline in the Bedroom

I got up and cleared away the dishes from the night before. Raphael had not stayed, but we had talked until late into the night.

Looking around at the flat, I knew he was right. It was soulless. It had the depressing air of trying to capture something lost. I had put together a room with easily bought objects, it felt contrived. Whereas the Sydney Road flat felt like it had been lovingly crafted and filled with treasures, the only time I'd really put together a place of my own. I had little time to think about creating something new for myself, home was just a place to sleep in, too busy to care. I lived for work, my efforts had made me extremely rich. Now I could afford anything I wanted, I just didn't know what that was. I didn't know where to start.

The kitchen and dining room at the office didn't really work. My dreams of big friendly dinner parties would never eventuate. It had been hopeless, no one wanted to party with the woman who couldn't disengage from work. I started to think about the possibilities of creating a space I might want to come home to and maybe even share with friends.

If I were to hire an architect now, I wouldn't know what to ask for. The magazines on the coffee table beckoned and I began to rip out the pages showing things I liked. As the morning went on I realised I was just creating a big pile of paper, and I was getting nowhere. I needed to start with basics. I would write a list.

This dream house had to be in Fitzroy, because I loved living there and I liked walking to work.

How many rooms?

A bedroom for me and a bedroom for Kate and a guest room for overnight visitors. Bathrooms for each bedroom. A kitchen, a laundry, an office, a dining room, a lounge room. The house should face north to capture the sun, with a modest garden to sit and eat in and a deck on the roof where I could see the city skyline. That was a good start.

What needed to be in these rooms, I asked myself and was reminded of an essay I had done when I was twelve. Our teacher had asked us what would our dream home be like? I remember being ridiculed for letting my imagination wander. A bath the size of a swimming pool, a kitchen like a lolly shop and a trampoline in the bedroom. My other classmates had more pedestrian desires. The girls wanted a 'good room' and the boys needed a shed. My teacher read of my desires wistfully, she had recently married a local farmer and knew there would never be a trampoline in her bedroom.

What a luxury, to design a house where I could do anything I wanted, could afford anything I needed. Although money hadn't been the issue in Paul's' Toorak mansion, the fact that it was his meant it would never be mine. Now was my chance to create a home just for me.

So what would these rooms look like? My bedroom would be simply furnished, a place of sanctuary, although a TV might be fun and a well organised dressing room would be great to hide the clutter.

A long galley kitchen with the sink, huge oven and fridge all within reach. A walk in pantry at one end, with all the electrical appliances laid out and ready for use would be practical. No high overhead cupboards, just deep drawers, where things can be reached without unstacking half the space. I hate the way kitchens are fully open to dining guests with the chaos of the mess of preparation in full view. A slightly raised bench would hide the mess, whilst still allowing guests to sit and chat. Do the designers of modern kitchens actually cook?

The dining table should seat twenty and be right next to the kitchen. I'm planning on getting a social life!

When we lived in the old house, I was always fascinated by the size of the laundry. Big cupboards and folding benches against the walls where all the linen could be folded and stored in the same room. Space to leave an iron and board permanently set up with hanging lines for freshly pressed clothes. My sewing machine would always be set up ready to alter a hem or make an adjustment.

So in my head I was creating a practical paradise, the type of place I would've needed when I was a wife and mother. It was difficult for me to think in any other way. It made me wonder what would be some of the grown up luxuries I desired, rather than needed? I thought back to the encounters I'd had over the last few months and remembered how often I'd had sex in the bathroom. This would be a good place to start. I would have a functional bathroom next to my bedroom and then there would be a whole other place, a separate bathroom where I could completely indulge myself. Obviously there would be large windows looking out to a lush secret garden. Perhaps there could be doors that fully opened on hot summer days? There would be an indulgent long shower head that could easily accommodate two, and a separate shower outdoors just for the sheer hell of it. A giant bath with a view of the garden outside. I had no desire for a spa and could never understand the appeal of a noisy motor, droning away, churning up the water. I remembered the sensual oily rub down I'd been given on that first 'Raphael Day' and thought that a massage table would be good. Then I remembered what I would have liked to have been doing on it and realised it would have to be adjustable. Something more like a daybed, exquisitely upholstered in the finest leather.

Fucking on hard surfaces was uncomfortable.

Fucking Adam in this room was what I wanted to do.

Fucking Adam was driving this fantasy.

I was most definitely not over him and wondered how long it would take.

Meeting with Kate

Kate went back to university, to the new life she was making for herself and I went back to work. She chose to stay in Canberra all the time now, claiming that her internship and study was taking up her spare time. I had sensed a change in our relationship, a distance that was more than the usual eye rolling disregard a child has for a parent. She had developed an impatience for my words of advice. A contemptuousness of my opinions and what seemed a rejection of my ideals, pushing me away. She had moved into a share house. She disliked living in the cocooned environment of the boarding college, referring to the other occupants as inmates. She had hinted at a boy, someone with high ideals whose beliefs appeared to be reshaping her way of thinking.

A glib remark about manufacturing in third world countries, disguised as charity, was a hurtful dig at me. I felt quite resentful. I had sacrificed much in choosing to keep my baby. It was easy for her to take the moral high ground. She had led a privileged life. And after the fight I'd taken on with Justin Darcy to save the house, she was earning a very big income, not to mention the wealth she would gain, if she ever chose to sell. She championed the underdog, wanted to save the planet, scorned big business and derided the global economy. She was free to generously support the causes she talked about. I'm sure no one questioned the source of her donations. She could live a highly idealised life, though I wondered if maybe I would have been just a bit like my altruistic daughter had I chosen a different path. But probably not, I would've had to work, start from scratch, no inheritance to fall back on.

Rebellion against a parent was inevitable, I guess I was just shocked at how much it hurt. I needed to let it go. Eventually she would realise that the world is a complex place, where problems are not so easily solved. We chatted occasionally, with me always initiating the calls. I could hear the exasperation in the voice of this young woman who was growing to despise me and my business. She made many excuses for not coming home. We were growing apart.

It was Cindy who suggested I take a couple of days off, go to Canberra, try to reconnect with my daughter. Kate said we should meet at my hotel. I barely recognised her when she entered the lobby. She was dressed in a shabby pair of overalls and Doc Marten boots, hair shaved on one side, dreadlocks on the other. From private school preppy to post punk woman. The hint of a tattoo peeking from beneath a sleeve.

'Kate darling... how are you?' I said trying not to show how shocked I was by her change in appearance.

'Good Mum, and you? Great you could make the time to come up and see me,' she said with a hint of sarcasm in her voice.

The conversation hardly flowed and I wondered whether it would be easier to talk over a meal.

'Have you eaten?'

'Ah no, but I have plans,' she said haltingly.

'What do you mean 'plans'? I've come all this way and you're too busy to have lunch with me?'

'Well, I said I'd meet someone after I'd seen you. A good friend, a guy.'

'God darling give him a call. I'd love to meet your friend. Tell him it's my shout, I'd love to take the two of you out for lunch.'

'Umm... I don't know, that's a lot of pressure, meet the parents, I don't want to intimidate him. I don't know if it's that serious yet.'

'It must be pretty serious if you're choosing to abandon me in favour of him. Come on Kate, I won't do anything to upset you. I'm only here overnight, surely you're not so embarrassed by me that we couldn't share a meal.'

She relented and said they'd arranged to meet at a restaurant. She had her bike and wondered how I would get there. Was she that determined to keep me away? I suggested she go ahead, I would catch a cab.

I shouldn't have been surprised, I'd read about this type of restaurant. It was vegan. You nominated how much you wanted to pay and a percentage of the profits went to a charity. The interior was made up of recycled furniture. The food was set up on a rustic timber buffet and the patrons ate at shared tables. Kate looked anxiously around the room. He'd said he'd be there when we arrived. Her face lit up when she spotted him. He got up, she walked over quickly, into his outstretched arms and he passionately kissed her. As if in defiance of me, just letting me know how serious this actually was. I made my way to them.

'Mum, this is my friend Will. Will this is my Mum, Christina.'

'Pleased to meet you, Mrs Brown. Kate has told me a lot about you.'

'Hi Will, nice to meet you too,' I responded, shaking his hand.

Will looked similar to Kate, dressed in the same type of anti-establishment garb. It all felt a bit awkward. Kate suggested we eat. We wandered over to the buffet and helped ourselves to an interesting array of food. It was surprisingly delicious.

We had fairly predictable conversations about the cold weather, the cost of renting and the lack of reliable public transport in Canberra. It was interesting that none of this should really be a problem for Kate. She could well afford a heated apartment and a car. I guess she had chosen differently. I didn't know how much Will knew about her wealth and didn't want to make things awkward by openly questioning her.

'So Will, what are you studying?' I said, presuming they had met at university.

'Politics, Law. Kate and I sat next to each other in one of our lectures. Thought she was just another boring middle class Melbourne kid. Didn't really say much until I bumped into her at an asylum seeker protest. Was blown away by her knowledge of refugee rights. We pretty much hooked up on that day.'

I was surprised at how much he'd revealed and felt a little uneasy about his cocky self assuredness. Perhaps I just felt a little jealous that he was the one she now chose to be close to.

We ate quietly, Will spoke first.

'So babe, what you been up to this morning, you left so early?' he asked, looking fondly at Kate.

He'd said 'so early'. Were they sharing a house, a bed? I knew so little about the life my daughter led.

'Trying to finish that essay on international human rights law. Needed to do some research in the library. It's driving me crazy. The more I read, the madder I get. It's the poorest in the most oppressed countries who have no voice. It shits me that they have almost no access to the things we take for granted here. Indentured labour working sixteen hour days, seven days a week. A salary that barely covers the loans they've taken out to move to the cities where the work is. As if someone from a village in Bangladesh could afford a lawyer to speak on their behalf. One law for the rich, one law for the poor.'

'Yeah, and it's not getting any better. Big business shops around for the cheapest goods it can find. Small manufacturing businesses in third world countries compete for each contract, screwed to the bone on price. Cutting wages is the first thing they do.'

I didn't like where this conversation was heading, but now knew why Kate had shown such hostility to my own clothing business.

'So Mrs Brown, Christina, how do you resolve this issue. How do you sleep at night knowing you're contributing to this problem?'

'That's a little unfair. You know nothing of how I conduct my business.'

'Don't you get your clothes made in Cambodia? Do you realise that country has one of the most corrupt governments and exploited workforces in the world? Isn't clothing manufacture one of the worst industries of them all?'

I was completely taken aback by the attack and clumsily tried to defend what we were trying to do at our own factory in Phnom Penh. But he was having none of it. As far as he was concerned, the whole charity thing was just a smokescreen, a marketing tool used to fool consumers into buying more products. Feeding a bloated, debt ridden, materialistic culture with 'shit they don't really need' as he so poetically put it.

'Businesses like yours could never exist in countries like Australia, where we protect our workers with real wages, healthcare and human rights.'

'But none of us could compete if we were to set up here. I'd go broke before we got our first range out.'

'And by having that attitude you've effectively made a whole generation of skilled workers redundant, unemployed'

'But it's the consumer who votes with their wallet. They are the ones demanding cheaper goods'

The conversation was spiralling into an ideologically driven fight, neither of us prepared to give ground on this chicken and egg argument. Eventually Kate broke the slanging match by telling me she had to go to a lecture. I got up and paid the bill as she said goodbye to Will. We parted coolly and arranged to meet for dinner later that night. I went back to my hotel room, furious that this shit of a boy could ruin the time with my daughter.

I was relieved when she turned up alone that night. I had ordered room service and hoped we could just talk. Little did I know it would get worse. First she was unhappy with the menu, pissed off that there were no vegan options. Then she told me how upset she was that I had fought with Will and lastly she confirmed my biggest suspicion and said that they were in fact living together.

Again she said she couldn't stay long, Will had organised for them to go to a lecture, something about a new world order. I hugged her and told her how much I loved her and hoped she would come home soon. She pulled away and told me she had plans for the upcoming mid-term break and didn't know when she'd be able to make it back. She had become the kind of ideologue I imagined I might have been, had my life taken a different path. If I hadn't given up everything to become a mother and the perfect wife. I resented her attitude towards me. My life now should be complete. Money could buy me anything. A table at the finest restaurant, first class travel, real estate. But it didn't fill the emptiness. I was lonely. I had no one to share it with, no one to love and no one to love me back.

The door had barely shut before I burst into tears. The closeness of our relationship seemed to have ended, she was growing up, becoming a woman, choosing her own life. She was not my someone special.

Work, Work, Work

As usual I immersed myself in work. It was a good way to forget my disastrous time with Kate.

The business continued to grow at an extraordinary rate.

My publishers wanted a second instalment of 'Escape Money' with a greater emphasis on rags to riches stories of successful businesswomen around the world. The idea of this becoming a tailored franchise to places like India and China held endless possibilities, their growing middle classes were a massive potential new market.

Under Jane's capable leadership the blog had grown and was posted daily. We were getting millions of hits. I now had a sales team drumming up business with companies prepared to pay a premium to advertise on my site.

And naturally enough with all this fame and success, my speaking engagements increased, as did the fees.

The dress business, too, was unstoppable. Lana was hiring more designers, both young and older women, to broaden the demographic and keep the designs fresh. It wasn't just middle aged women looking for that perfect dress.

The phone app 'U-Dress-U' was launched in May and became an instant hit. Now women could order up a dress anywhere, anytime, usually after a frustrating day not finding that perfect dress in the shops or online.

Chenda was doing a brilliant job in Cambodia and was completely unfazed by the massive amount of business we were generating for the 'Beautiful Sisters'. As the business grew, we established higher paying positions and appointed Cambodian women, prepared to take on greater responsibility, giving them the chance to build a career pathway beyond just working at a sewing machine. I also loved seeing what financial autonomy was able to give them. Some were able to move out of the accommodation and buy their first apartment. Others were able to send their kids to more elite schools, all of them were good providers for the many people they called family.

My trips to that country were frequent and tiring, even the first class travel was beginning to lose its shine. However, reconnecting with the women in Cambodia made up for all the exhaustion of constant travel. These women were truly inspiring, what they had been through put my feeble complaints into perspective.

Kate was so wrong in her perceptions of what we were doing.

By June we had expanded to such an extent that the small ground floor space was no longer adequate, we were bursting at the seams. Luckily the warehouse next door came up for sale and, with a bit of reshuffling, moved our existing tenants into the new building. We stayed and took over the top floor. The demand for the type of office space we were providing seemed to be growing and it would be easy to fill all three storeys with new occupants.

Providing an office space wasn't enough. I'd learnt much from the misogyny comments on the blog. It was the juggling act that was a woman's life that was the major hurdle. The kids, the household, health, finance to name a few of the things that appeared to be obstacles stopping women from reaching their maximum potential. After hearing their ideas, I made some major changes to the new building.

The first priority was childcare. We added a fully staffed, state of the art facility that operated around the clock. Not all women worked nine to five. We also offered casual care for when the women needed a babysitter, wanted a night off, were sick, had things to attend to, appointments to keep.

I also included a medical centre. Women's health was a major issue. A group of female medical practitioners were happy to rent out the space.

It also became obvious we needed a commercial kitchen, not only as a canteen, but a place where women with food based businesses could rent the facilities. The Government required that kitchens be certified. It pissed me off that women could no longer cook from home to start small food enterprises. What woman could afford to build a commercial kitchen when she was just starting up? Most of the world's largest food brands had humble beginnings in the family kitchen. And this kitchen could make us some money as well. A group of chefs and bakers operated a catering business and increased their service by providing a range of take home meals. Many of the tenants told of the chore of cooking dinner every night. Hated the sheer grind of putting together a meal after a hard day at the office, trying to think of something interesting, nutritious, affordable and easy for their family.

Lastly I set up a financial advice centre. A place where women could meet with professionals, bankers, accountants, financial planners. A place where they wouldn't feel intimidated asking the most basic questions. Things such as how to get a loan, buy a house, invest, make sure they had enough superannuation to retire with financial security.

I tried to spend at least a few hours keeping in touch with the women, the tenants, chatting about their various projects, my eye out for any of the top performers. Always with a view to invest. After all, the next big thing might just be right under my roof.

To outsiders, I was unstoppable. Happily watching the business grow. Constantly delivering the feel good messages of the possibilities the world offered to those willing to take them.

Even the guys at the top end of town were beginning to take notice. The informal social networks of gallery openings, dinners and charity events were often peppered with the none too subtle inquiries about what price I would put on my business. I was flattered by the tens of millions being offered, but not prepared to let go just yet. I worried that the altruistic nature of the business would be forgotten if I sold it off to the highest bidder. I didn't want to see the sweatshop fire fuelled. And, more truthfully, what would I do if I didn't have my business? Work wasn't enough, but it was all consuming, because I chose it to be that way. Filling my days with projects was a good way to avoid thinking about my desolate personal life.

Every day that I returned home to my dingy little flat, I got more depressed. I needed to create a retreat, a place to escape to. That dream house might just be the catalyst I needed to start to get a life. I needed an architect. This would be my way in, my excuse for calling him. It had been well over six months since that messy Boxing Day lunch. Enough time had passed to lessen the sting.

First Approach

I dialled his number. Would he pick up or would he let it ring out when he saw the caller ID. It seemed to ring and ring...

'Darcy,' he answered coldly.

I was startled.

'Adam, Tina here, how are you?'

'Busy, what do you want?'

I knew immediately by the tone of his voice that this was a bad idea.

'I need an architect,' I replied and quickly explained that I knew this was only a small job, by his standards, but perhaps there was someone looking for a private project who he could recommend.

Adam was completely thrown by the call, by her voice. She was saying something about an architect, but he could barely concentrate on the conversation. He had spent the last six months throwing himself into work, after that disastrous time that started with his brother's violent outburst and finished with her betrayal. She had every right to be furious at him after he had treated her so badly. He should never have let Justin speak to her like that. He should have dealt with the overpowering relationship with his brother. He should never have left her there alone in the car park, with Sam to take her to the airport. He should have jumped on the next plane to LA.

When he'd seen her on Boxing Day, she had confronted him about the photos in the paper. He hated that she'd seen him with Justin and Fiona. He could just imagine how she felt, remembering those times in the uni bar twenty years ago, when they had made her feel so unwelcome, so alienated. Letting her know she wasn't one of them. If only he had behaved differently, she might still be his. He had tried so hard to get her out of his head, dated other women, worked longer hours, even tried taken down the painting of her, a reminder of what he had lost.

Tina didn't want to see him. She had moved on. She had taken another lover. He had seen them kissing on that fateful Sunday in LA. Today she wanted an architect, someone he could recommend. She didn't even want him for what he did best.

'I've got someone here. I'll get her to give you a call,' and with that he hung up. No 'how are you' or any polite chit chat to keep her on the phone longer. No, his social clumsiness had put paid to that and he'd stupidly terminated that small window of opportunity she had opened.

'Fuck, fuck, fuck!' he cried out, slamming his fist onto his desk.

He wanted her more than ever, but knew nothing had changed. He didn't know how to break the destructive bond he had with his brother. He didn't know how to stop feeling responsible for him. She was right, he didn't know how to not choose Justin.

I stared blankly at the phone. I understood perfectly. Adam had closed that door and moved on. What an idiot for thinking that my little ruse might bring him rushing back, that we might have a chance.

Building

The phone rang and I didn't recognise the number.

'Hi, this is Davina Newton. I believe you're looking for an architect?'

Shit, I'd forgotten that I'd actually asked for an architect, when all I'd really wanted was to reconnect with Adam. At least he'd followed up my request. We arranged a time to meet.

Davina wore no make-up and her fair hair was cut in a rather severe bob. She wore a straight grey skirt, black tights, orange and grey leather flats and a cropped, but beautifully tailored brown shirt. She looked 'architectural' and ever so slightly intimidating.

She said that she had just finished working on a multi storey housing development and was looking to take some leave, work on smaller, private projects.

I talked to her about my vague ideas, although I edited out the more salacious details of the big bathroom.

'I hear you and totally get it. I work full time and I completely understand your desire to have a simple, practical working house. But, Tina, can I suggest we make this not only functional, but beautiful, stylish and fun?' she said, cocking an eyebrow and grinning.

I had no idea what that would look like, but I liked her attitude and I knew we would get along. That austere outfit was just a facade. We ordered lunch and after a glass of wine, I loosened up enough to tell her about my childhood dream house. She told me she had also written a similar essay. Her bedroom, built in the attic, had a slide to the ground floor, all the rooms had purple carpet and there was a fountain in the lounge room where she kept her pet dolphin. I liked her even more.

She knew about me via the blog. She knew nothing about my relationship with Adam.

I asked her what we should do next, then realised how premature this meeting actually was. There was no land, no house to renovate or knock down. In reality I was years away from stepping across the threshold of my own domestic nirvana. I felt a bit foolish, a bit exposed.

'Maybe I should get online and see if there is anything available in Fitzroy?' I said sheepishly.

'Or maybe not?' she returned.

Davina then told me of a project she had been working on that had unexpectedly stalled. She had designed a house in George Street, not far from my flat. It was to be the dream home of a newly married couple, second marriage for both. Construction was halfway through when the couple split up. Apparently their incompatibility became increasingly evident as the house progressed and they couldn't stand each other any longer. The site was up for sale as part of the divorce proceedings.

'Now I know this isn't the way things usually go, but it does vaguely fit your needs and the interior could be tweaked to suit you. If we make no major changes that require council approval, you could be living there in a few months.'

'When can we see it?'

'Well, now if you like.'

Davina took me to the site. From the front, the house looked like a fairly typical Victorian two storey, double fronted terrace, with an ornate white facade. She opened the front door and we walked along the corridor, very traditional, with a room on either side and up a staircase to the same configuration on the floor above. I opened the door to one of these rooms and saw they were almost finished, obviously a bedroom with an ensuite and dressing room at one end.

'The front rooms will be the bedrooms, two up, two down, just like the one we are in now. Pretty traditional and best suited to the space. We had to keep this part of the house intact, heritage rules are pretty strict around Fitzroy,' said Davina.

At the end of the passageway the new construction began. Three storeys faced us, with a large central courtyard in between, effectively dividing the house in two. Davina explained that a moveable glass skylight could completely cover the space, depending on the weather. A deep rectangular pit had been dug centrally to contain a lap pool that would reflect the sky above. What an interesting idea. I loved the thought of being able to swim all year round, naked if I chose, without the prying eyes of neighbours. Across the courtyard we entered the ground floor of the new build.

'This is the lounge/dining area with bi fold doors that open up the entire ground floor to the courtyard, creating a massive space. The kitchen runs along the length of the back wall. I'm sure we could accommodate a butler's pantry at one end, this area is pretty flexible.'

It was as if she read my mind.

'And maybe somewhere to store wine?' I asked, getting into the swing of things.

'You're jumping the gun, follow me.'

She took me to a gap in the wall and I saw where a lift shaft was under construction.

'The previous owners were much older than you and wanted a lift so that they could use the house well into old age. It connects the basement car park with each floor, right up to the roof deck. The car park is accessed from the lane way behind the house. The back of the site is quite steep and the garage is entered at that lower street level. It holds three cars, but I'm sure one of those spaces could become a wine cellar,' she continued.

'Wow, I had no idea there was such a drop.'

'I'll take you around there in a minute. But let me show you the rest of the house first,' she said.

We climbed a ladder to the next floor, a large empty room, with a wall of glass overlooking the older part of the house and the courtyard below.

'This room could be whatever you want. It was originally designed to be a quiet gallery, library, lounge room. I had designed shelving to cover the entire back wall, with a ladder connected to a track, allowing easy access to the upper shelves. The previous owner was an avid collector of antiquarian books. All of that could be easily changed, have a think about what you might want.'

We climbed to the next floor where the room was identical to the one below.

'And what was this space intended for?' I asked.

'This was to be the master bedroom.'

'But there are four bedrooms already?' I said.

'They both had kids from previous relationships, with grandchildren on the way. I guess they wanted to make this into one big happy Brady Bunch house, with enough rooms for when their adult children came to visit. There's no reason why you couldn't convert some of the bedrooms into an office space or a media room or even a gym. The possibilities are endless. What do you think?'

'Well, it's a bit overwhelming. I lived in a great big house once and barely used half the space even though I had a family and we entertained. Now it's just me and I'm living in a flat that could fit into this one room.'

'Who's to say that it will always be just you? You never know things might change?'

'Yeah, the thought of grandchildren already seems abhorrent.'

'Not grandchildren, you're too young!' said Davina.

'Well, I'm hardly planning on having more kids, I don't even have a partner.'

'You never know. I met my husband when I was thirty eight. I had thought I'd never find Mr. Right. Two kids and four years later it still shocks me how my life has changed so much. I'd already started that housing development before all of this happened and I was determined to finish the job. I remember being on the phone to the engineer hours after giving birth to our first child, determined to prove all those people wrong. People who said I couldn't possibly work and have children at the same time.'

'So why take time off now? You seem to have everything under control?'

'Because the downside of having kids so late in life is that I'm completely exhausted and, quite frankly, I've got nothing to prove to anyone anymore! Plus after all those years of being single, I was able to accumulate enough money to be completely financially secure, independent of my husband's income.'

I really liked this woman.

She took me up the last ladder to the roof deck. We entered a large glass room taking up half the space. The view of the city was spectacular.

'The deck has been plumbed and I have designed the space to contain a fully functional kitchen. Like the courtyard, it can be used all year round, the glass walls can be opened or closed. And the outdoor deck has the capacity to take the weight of at least fifty people.'

'Again, wow! But it just seems too excessive,' I pleaded.

'I understand it's a lot to think about and that it's all been a bit sudden, but there's a little secret I'll let you in on,' she said conspiratorially.

'What's that?' I asked.

'Well, the owners are keen to sell, can't stand each other and are carrying a very large debt. I've read your book, and if nothing else, it would be a very good investment. They are desperate to get rid of it at any price and quite frankly with the slump in the property market, there just aren't that many buyers prepared to shell out at the top end.'

Now she was talking.

There was a lot I liked about this house. I looked over the drawings and started to play around with some ideas I had about making it my own. I knew Davina could make it work and I had already grown quite fond of her and the way she operated.

I rang the real estate agent and after doing some research found that the asking price was way below market rates. I'd be a fool to say no. I arranged for Ruth, my lawyer, to look into all the legal ramifications and, after a meeting with Davina and the builder, I was keen to get things started.

'There's just one thing that concerns me a bit,' I said.

'What might that be?' she asked.

'How will this affect your job?'

'It won't affect it at all. I have my boss's approval. In fact he said you were a very dear friend and that I should take as much time as I needed, that he would always be available to assist me in any way.'

'You know Tina, he's really a great boss and a really good man.'

And that was another member of the Adam fan club to add to the ever growing list.

A really Great Man

In August the Tim Nolan retrospective was staged, thank God I was in Cambodia for the opening night. I really didn't want to see that portrait hanging so publicly, perhaps with Adam gloating at his ability to rid himself of the last reminder of our brief affair. Luckily the painting had been abstract enough that it wasn't completely obvious who Christina Maxwell, the subject of the painting, was. There were probably many portraits of people much better known than me and that is why I presumed the press left me alone.

Buying that shitty tabloid on a Sunday morning had become a self whipping ritual. I was starting to believe that Adam's recurring picture on the back page was a signal, letting me know what a fuckwit I'd been to think there was any possibility of us ever being a couple. The roll call of bimbo's he dated, getting younger with every new photo, pissed me off immensely. He rubbed it in by turning up to many of Gabriella's openings with a more spectacular beauty at each new show.

I countered Adams moves by being seen more and more often with Raphael. That too was creating a quiet little drama of its own. Although Raphael had declared on Boxing Day that we would no longer sleep together, it was impossible to remain celibate in his company. Rarely would our 'dates' end in a goodbye kiss at the door. Almost always we ended up in bed, fucking emotionlessly, no tender caresses or words of affection, simply satiating a need and slowly killing a friendship. Sex with someone you don't love starts to become a very soul destroying act. The notion of a fuck buddy was great in theory, but the reality was different story. Discovering my sexual self, ironically thanks to Raphael, gave me a huge carnal appetite. Being with him was fulfilling nothing more than hollow animal lust. We both needed more, I just didn't know how to break the addiction.

The Finestra family wasn't buying it either. I sensed an impatience from Massimo. He would see us together and wondered why neither of us would to commit to something that resembled a traditional relationship. 'Would he never be a grandfather', was a tirade I quite often heard. Gabriella saw right through the charade, and Lola simply showed a sister's possessive jealousy. This game was becoming costly to both of us.

I had become used to Raphael being around. Someone to go out with, someone in my bed. I was trying to convince myself that perhaps it could be more. Many a couple grew to love each other, why not us? Though when this would actually happen, I had no idea. We were both so busy, he spending longer stretches in Italy and me being utterly consumed with business. Perhaps this type of loveless arrangement was the only form of relationship I understood, after all I'd had eighteen years of practice.

He was back in town, rang me, wanted to talk, said he had something he needed to tell me. Was he feeling the same way about me? Was he after all the special someone Aura had talked about? Had he been there all along? Perhaps we'd both been too busy to see.

We met at our favorite restaurant in Gertrude Street. Easy for him, easy for me. We could drink and stumble home afterwards. Probably end up in bed. He looked sexier than ever. He always looked good after he'd been in Italy, but there was something different this time. He had a new self assuredness.

'Ciao Bella, come va?'

'I'm good, and you?'

'Good to be back. It's been a long time.'

He ordered our usual antipasto. I requested a bottle of Nero D'avola, it sounded like Black Devil, a perfect wine for dinner with Raphael Finestra. We talked about work, new projects, but I could sense Raphael was slightly distracted.

'You said you wanted to talk to me about something. It's driving me nuts, what was so urgent?'

'Well, you know I've been spending much more time in Italy,'

'Yeah, your new range is coming out, it's as I would expect.'

'It's not just that..., I've met someone, I think I'm in love.'

I paused to take in what he'd said and was surprised at how I felt. We weren't in love, but I had become quite possessive of our friendship and felt resentful that someone else might interrupt what we had, what I'd grown used to.

'You. The charming, no girlfriend, free to fuck whomever he chooses, Mr Finestra, is in love?' I responded, trying to make light of what he'd just said. Good sport and all that.

'Why does it seem so incredulous?'

'It's just that I never thought I'd hear you say those words. I thought fucking was more like a sport for you. That you liked sex, didn't like commitment.'

'What are you saying? Are you jealous, did you want commitment from me? I thought our little arrangement was mutual? We were good in bed, liked each other's company, but that was all.'

'No, no, I'm not jealous at all. I'm just surprised, it was a little unexpected.'

'It was for me, too,' he said, pouring us both another glass.

We drank the wine. I could feel this was affecting me much more than was comfortable and had to snap back to reality. A relationship with Raphael was not what I wanted, I didn't really love him. Was probably more enamoured with the idea of being in love. And in my heart, I knew I'd never really resolved my feelings for Adam.

'So who's the lucky girl, how did you meet?'

He paused before he answered, took my hand and looked me straight in the eye.

'It's not a girl. His name is Antonio.'

'Shit Raphael, I didn't see that one coming!'

It's funny, both men and women had always been attracted to him, but I was still blown away by what he'd said.

'Are you ok, you looked shocked.'

'No, no, it's cool, just a little unexpected. How did you meet? What does he do, where does he live?'

'He's a furniture designer. I met him in Milan, at the Salone Internazionale del Mobile. He's one of Italy's hottest new talents. We had a few drinks, talked, had so much in common. It was as if we'd known each other for years. We've been seeing each other for about six months.'

'And does anyone else know?'

'Yes, I've told Lola. We spend so much time in Italy together, I could no longer hide it from her.'

'What does she think, how did she react?'

'She was great. Told me she always thought I was gay, that the Casanova thing was always just an act.'

'And your parents? Have you told them?'

'Are you kidding! Papa would have a fit. Me falling in love with a man won't give him the grandchildren he so desires. Haven't you heard the way he goes on about it?'

'I know, I know, he's not been very subtle about it when we've gone out together.'

'And Lola's not the slightest bit interested in kids.'

This I had always known. She had told me of her many lovers, men that fall in love with her, treat her like a goddess, can't understand why she doesn't want to make babies with them. Men wanting to be fathers was always her sign to leave.

'Jesus Raphael, you can't always live a lie. Surely your parents would come round eventually?'

'Not in a million years. You must remember my father comes from a peasant culture that treated gay men very badly. There are many stories of men found executed with their balls cut off and stuffed in their mouths.'

'Fuck, I had no idea those old superstitions ran so deep.'

'Not superstitions, just fear, hate and bigotry.'

'But the world has changed since the sixties when your parents left Italy.'

'Yeah right, how many openly gay men do you see in the South? Didn't you see that episode of the Sopranos?'

'Well, I haven't actually been there, but I did see that on TV and I get your point.'

'It's still taboo, the north, Milan, is a little better.'

Our pasta arrived, we had a few mouthfuls and I continued the conversation.

'So how come you have sex with me? I don't get it? If you've always been this way, how could you possibly be able to make love to a woman?'

'Not all men are the same. I love women's bodies as much as men's. Yours in particular. It's just that I've never felt like this before towards anyone. The person who I've fallen in love with just happens to be a man.'

'Now I'm really curious. Did you know I've always had this thing about gay men? Had this fantasy that I could convert them? Find my perfect man. A kind of man-wife.'

'Now that sounds really interesting. You know I'd be quite happy to take you back to my place and explore this idea a little further.'

'Raphael, you are incorrigible! I thought you just told me you were in love.'

'Christina, don't confuse lust with love.'

'Fuck Raphael, you can't have it both ways.'

'Why not, I find you beautiful. I'm getting hard just thinking about what I'd like to do to you right now. Here feel.'

He grabbed my hand and placed it on the base of his torso.

'Raphael!' I yelped, as my hand felt his stiffening cock.

'We have to stop. It's not fair on Antonio, I really don't want to be the 'other woman'.'

'What? You don't lust after me too? I can't think of a time when we've been out and the evening hasn't seen us fucking madly at the end of the night.'

'You're right, that's exactly what it's been. Fucking. And you telling me you've found love makes me really sad. Not because I'm mad at you, but because what you've found is exactly what I want for myself.'

'There, there my beautiful Christina. Don't cry, it will come. I think we both know who the right one has always been. You are both just too pigheaded to do anything about it.'

'But he sees other women?'

'And you sleep with me, but this doesn't mean I'm 'the one'. I think this is how it is for him too. Surely if he'd found someone to replace you, he wouldn't be dating all those different women. Don't think I haven't noticed. Him bringing those bimbos to Mama's Gallery is just a pissing contest between him, me and you.'

'I guess what you're saying has some truth. I hadn't really thought about it that way before. The thing is, we've been playing this game of petty jealousy for so long, I don't really know how to break the cycle.'

'You should be the one to act first. Give him a call.'

'I did and he could barely put down the phone quickly enough.'

I told Raphael about my call to Adam, to ask if he knew of an architect.

'And you wonder why he was so mad?'

'I don't understand. I thought the call would break the ice, open a line of communication.'

'Jesus, Christina, are you that stupid! You rang and asked him to find you someone to do the thing he does the best. He should've been your architect, that was the call that would've broken the ice, but instead you slapped him in the face with your request. To a man like him, it must have been the ultimate rejection.'

I'd never thought about it like that before. I couldn't use that line again. My beautiful new house was almost complete. What other excuse could I find to call? Raphael had no answer to that specific question, but said something that hit a nerve.

'I don't think you really know what you want. You've thrown yourself into your business. It's become your whole life and it threatens to eat you up. You work ridiculously long hours, commit yourself to all these other projects, so you don't have to face up to what it is you actually need.'

'And the point you are making?'

'I think you need some time out, you need to get away, clear your head. You know Cindy is quite capable of running the business. In fact, I bet you're working around the clock, micromanaging everything and driving her nuts.'

'Yeah right, I've got a new book coming out, a house that is nearly finished and a multimillion dollar fashion business that I can't just walk away from.'

'I'm not saying you should walk away from anything. I'm just saying you need some time out to gather your thoughts.'

I took a big exasperated sigh, knowing he was perfectly right.

That night he walked me home and for the first time in many months he didn't stay.

Farewell Beautiful Lovers

Tim had rung to say that he was having another show, new works. He was fine about me not making the opening night of the retrospective, knew I was in Cambodia. Told him I would call in to the National Gallery when I returned. He didn't need to know that I had absolutely no intention of seeing that picture, Adams painting of me, ever again. Tim and I had kept a pleasant casual friendship, bumping into each other occasionally on the streets of our shared turf.

Raphael was still in town and had asked if he could escort me to the opening. I needed a night off. Naturally I said yes. I was looking forward to seeing him again and he knew I would be happier turning up to the opening with a partner.

He called past to pick me up. He looked his usual raffish, charming self, but tonight he was not alone.

'Tina, bella, I want to introduce you to a friend of mine, Antonio.'

'Ciao, Antonio. Pleased to meet you.'

'The pleasure is all mine,' he responded, kissing me twice, with an accent to charm and dark Latin good looks. I could see why Raphael had fallen so hard. Burnished bronze skin, brutish three day growth accentuating a strong jaw reminiscent of someone Michelangelo might sculpt. Definitely sexy enough to bed. We walked together along Gertrude Street and like that time over a year ago, I was aware of the stares of passing strangers. We made a very handsome threesome.

The opening was no different from many of the others, except that it was Tim's work and I felt a strong personal connection to the paintings and the man.

Antonio was visiting Australia for the first time. I took him under my wing, Raphael was busy working the room. Antonio was as charming and flirtatious as any red blooded Italian could be. He made me feel desirable, which was a good thing to feel as Adam walked through the door with another of his women. Sissy seemed to be no longer on the scene. I was unnerved that tonight's bimbo had appeared more than once and a surge of jealousy coursed through my veins. This was a very toxic game. Adam ignored me and I pretended to ignore him. How on earth would I ever break this cycle?

The champagne flowed and the red stickers appeared quickly. The retrospective had made his painting much more valuable. A very good night for Tim. I made sure Adam noticed I didn't leave alone.

Raphael suggested we continue the night back at his place and I was curious about what this might mean. I had heard of threesomes. Always assumed it was the fantasies of men wanting to have two women. Not one woman with two men. The thought of being made love to by these exquisite men was a very tantalising prospect. The flirting, the teasing all evening with the sexy Italians had made me very aroused and a little more open to push the boundaries.

Raphael poured us all a glass of Prosecco.

'Cin, cin,' said Raphael.'

'And so, Raphael, tell me about this beautiful woman,' said Antonio, looking at me admiringly.

'Christina is a woman of many talents. She runs a very successful business and is wealthy enough to fill her house with your expensive furniture. She owns property and makes money on it in a way that would even make the Germans envious. But she has another talent I am sure you, Antonio, would be very interested in.'

I was a bit taken aback by his praise. No one had ever put it that directly. I was curious about what he would say next.

'And what would that be my dear friend?'

'She is a gifted lover with an insatiable desire.'

'And do you think she would desire me?' quizzed Antonio.

'I would think she desires both of us.'

My body shivered at this indecent, but utterly tantalising prospect and I was intrigued at the way this conversation made me feel like a voyeur in my own fantasy.

'Let us look at what is hidden under this clothing,' said Raphael, walking around me and unzipping my dress.

I felt a rush, a thrill, a shot of electricity straight to my sex. It seemed that Antonio shared Raphael's ambiguity, that sex with a woman was something that he too enjoyed.

'Are you sure she is ready?' said Antonio.

'Why don't you see,' said Raphael.

Antonio moved towards me and lifted my dress at the knee, then ran his hand up my leg, slipping his fingers beneath my panties.

'She is ready.'

Raphael looked at me invitingly. I held out my hand and let him take it. Antonio took the other hand and together they led me to the bed.

My dress slipped easily from my shoulders, Antonio unhooked my bra, Raphael slid my panties down my legs. I stepped out of them and stood before these two gorgeous men ready to be completely and utterly possessed. Raphael and Antonio undressed, and then kissed each other hungrily, their cocks rising in response. Rather than feeling jealous, I felt wickedly turned on. My gay man fantasy was going to be played out.

Raphael pulled back the sheets, I understood his signal and lay down on the bed, parting my legs ever so slightly. He followed and lay beside me, reaching for my nipples, twisting them until they were erect. I opened my legs further, inviting Antonio to play. He joined us.

I pulled both men towards me, running my fingers through their hair, as I savoured the intense sensation of having them suck, one on each breast. Their legs were wrapped around mine and I felt the nudging of their rigid penises.

Antonio released my nipple, licked the surrounding areola, then playfully moved down my stomach, kissing as he went. His hands parted my thighs and his mouth continued its exploration. Raphael kissed me then followed his friend. They both knelt either side of my hips and each took a thigh and stroked the sensitive interior as they eased my legs apart, exposing my sex, exposing me.

Raphael took Antonio's hand, leaned in close, linking their fingers then passionately kissed him. As they kissed, their intertwined fingers found my engorged cunt and together they fondled me, their fingers exploring every fold, entering me and opening me up, a shared intimacy, highly erotic, taking me to a sexual place I never imagined. I begged for more.

Raphael got up and found the condoms in the drawer beside the bed. He took out two and, in an act of loving intimacy, rolled one down

Antonio's cock, then Antonio did the same to Raphael. Antonio looked me in the eyes and held me close, as I felt his thick cock enter me. I groaned at the sheer pleasure, this feeling of fullness gave me.

He toyed with my anus and gently eased in his finger. I guessed what he was preparing me for, but didn't know if I was ready. What surprised me was what happened next. As Antonio lay between my open thighs, deep inside me, I saw Raphael walk to the edge of the bed. He knelt behind the two of us. I felt his hand between my legs, briefly disengaging Antonio's penis, then pushing his fingers into me, gathering my juices and coating his rigid cock. Antonio reached under and pulled my body closer and re-entered me. Then, to my surprise, Raphael deftly pushed down on Antonio's back and, using the slick wetness on his hand, stroked Antonio's anus. Raphael then took his own cock and gently nuzzled it against Antonio's tight hole. Slowly he eased it open and I felt the pressure of both men's bodies on my own. Raphael's movements became stronger and with each thrust into Antonio, I thrilled at the sensation of the force directed deep toward my throbbing core.

The pounding action of both men quickened, the pressure on my clitoris excruciating, until finally my body erupted uncontrollably into an electrifying, mind blowing orgasm. My lovers soon followed. We lay together in a hot crumpled heap, reluctant to move, to break the chain of physical connection we had just shared. I felt Antonio's penis soften and slowly withdraw. Raphael dismounted and lay on one side of me. Antonio rolled off to the other. They both kissed me and stroked my body as we quietly recovered from the ferocity of our intense fucking. Antonio reached for Raphael and together they held me close, till we fell asleep in each other's warm embrace.

I woke very early the next morning and extricated myself from their arms. I returned from the bathroom to find the two men spooning each other. Antonio's arm was draped over Raphael's hip, holding his cock, gently stroking it back to life, speaking softly in Italian, words of affection to his rousing lover. It was time for me to go and let them be together, alone.

'Thank you my darlings,' I whispered, then kissed them goodbye.

The faint glimmer of light was just beginning to show. I knew that this was now most definitely the end of the game we had been playing. I wanted Raphael to find love.

Temporarily Homeless

As with all building projects, some things didn't go to plan. Davina's estimate of a completion date was not to be. The lease on my apartment was due to expire at the end of October, my beautiful new home would not be ready until late November and my landlord had already signed up the new tenants. Technically, I was homeless and, truthfully I couldn't stand another minute in the flat. I really had moved on.

It had been a ridiculously busy time. I had written the second edition of Escape Money and it was now in the hands of the printers. Once again advance sales of the book were through the roof, and this time a long book tour was not needed. The dress business had continued to expand under Lana's watchful eye and I now employed an army of designers and IT people who knew exactly what was needed. The business functioned like a well oiled machine, the orders continued to flow and the company continued to grow. And I made sure that absolutely everything was approved by me before we signed off on any project or facet of our business.

'Why don't you take a break?' said the ever wise Cindy late one night, as we were finishing up a teleconference with the team in New York. Had she been talking to Raphael?

It was obvious I needed some time out. I had become obsessed with spending every waking minute immersed in work. Sometimes I found myself sleeping on the couch in my office, ordering in food from the staff canteen, showering at the gym, changing into one of the spare outfits I kept at work. I doubted I could fool Cindy, I'm sure she suspected many nights I didn't make it home. I gave Cindy every reason why I couldn't possibly take time off and she responded with one of her usual blunt reality checks.

'Jesus boss, sometimes I wonder if you have any faith in us at all. I remember a time when you could go away, let me take charge and return pleased that I had let nothing slip. Your approval of the way I did things gave me more impetus to succeed.'

'But Cindy, you are in my second in command, without you this would all fall over. I don't understand where you're coming from?' I responded, slightly exasperated by her statement.

'It's something to do with the shit that went down after Adam, after the trip to America, after Christmas. You've changed. You've become almost manic in your need for control. Nothing can go ahead unless it gets your approval. You're here seven days a week, you arrive before us and leave long after even the cleaners have finished. Don't think I haven't noticed the rumpled blanket on the couch when you've slept at the office. You are setting impossible standards that none of us can, or want to, live up to. Some of us have a life!'

'But I have to be in control, because it's me who's ultimately responsible for anything that goes wrong. I'd like to think that by being thorough, we can be on top of any situation before a problem arises.'

'I get that, but you need to see what all this micro managing is doing to staff morale. I heard you asking the office manager if she could give you an inventory of the amount and type of paper we were using in the printers.'

'I wanted to make sure we were getting the best deals on stationery,' I snapped back.

'And don't you think she isn't already doing that?'

'Well, when I checked, yes I did find that she had sourced the best deal.'

'And what do you think this does for her self confidence when you question her ability to make even the most trivial decisions?'

'She needs to know that every aspect of this business counts.'

'No, you've got it wrong. She needs to know that you trust her. Buying paper is not one of the big decisions that will make or break this company. Questioning every little thing we do undermines the confidence of everyone. It's building a resentment towards you that's getting dangerous.'

'You're pissing everyone off. You have no idea of the bitching that's going on behind your back. You've got to let your management team have the authority to do their jobs well. One meeting a week to look at the big picture should be enough. We would come to you if there was a major problem. This new mania of yours is driving me nuts! The ship won't sink without you, but if you don't give us all some breathing space, I can't guarantee who will stay around to keep things afloat!'

Ouch, that hurt, but she was right. I had become impossible to work with, micromanaging more maniacally than Kevin Rudd and driving everyone mad. I wanted to have a nice little dummy spitting tantrum. Vaguely thought I might make a speech about how this organisation would collapse without me, when I realised I had, in fact, created a business that very cleverly almost ran itself. It would be quite feasible to leave it for a short time for some well earned rest. The real problem was that I had let my business fill the gaps left by my less than perfect private life. I had not had a break since Christmas and apart from the odd few days Cindy had organised, I had not had a real holiday for many years.

'I'm sorry Cindy, I didn't know you and the team felt this way. I guess I've become obsessed with work. I've got nothing else.'

Tears welled in my eyes. She gave me a hug and a knowing look.

'Think about it, where you might like to go and I'll clear the diary.'

I had a site meeting with Davina and when we'd finished I took her out for a drink. She had the night off, her husband was looking after the kids. I told her about my conversation with Cindy.

'I'm envious. It's the one thing I miss from my single days. I long to simply chuck a few things in a bag and head off. Now just getting in the car and nipping out to the supermarket is as well organised as any military operation.'

'And I'm some poor old cat lady with nowhere to go!'

We both laughed at this melodramatic exaggeration.

'Have you been to Tasmania?' she enquired.

'No, why do you ask?' I replied.

'I was reading about a photographic exhibition of sixties Australian houses at a gallery in Hobart, and thought of you, knew how much you loved this style of architecture. Apparently there were a large number of these houses built after the fires of 1967. And of course you'd have to check out MONA. Tasmania is only a small place, you could hire a car and drive yourself around the island in under two weeks.'

She had me interested. I went online and checked out the exhibition. I was intrigued and did a bit more research. Tasmania was full of interesting wineries, boutique food producers, great restaurants, old Georgian architecture and pristine national parks. I booked my tickets, car and hotel that night.

They were all telling me, their message was quite clear, I had to take a break. I had become impossible to be around. I had done none of those things Aura and Henry had suggested, far from it. They had said to find someone special, someone to share the journey with and I had done almost the complete opposite. Kate and I had become estranged. Raphael, my pretend boyfriend had found true love. Cindy could barely stand working with me and I'd pushed Adam so far away, I knew there was no prospect of even achieving friendship, let alone anything more.

The house was almost complete. I tried to convince myself that this would be my retreat, my place to escape to. But who was I kidding? It was only a short walk away from the office, meaning that I could be on call twenty four seven.

And a life away from work? Work was my life, I had no other interests.

Fun, they had told me, 'don't forget to have fun'! I was not even fun to be around! What hope did I have?

The Four Commandments of the wise people had been completely ignored.

Anna Buckley

Part 3

Tasmania

Tasmania, the island state to the south of mainland Australia, was only a short flight from Melbourne. But it felt like I was heading on some great adventure to a very remote place, worlds away from home. I couldn't understand why it seemed like this? Perhaps I really did need a holiday and by crossing Bass Strait I could truly feel disengaged. Put some space between me and my work, my hectic life in Melbourne.

Flying low, as we began our descent into Hobart, I got my first close view of the island that would be my holiday escape for the next few weeks. Myriad waterways, secret coves, white sandy beaches, dark bushland, towering mountains. A place of wilderness. A friendly cab driver welcomed me, chatting as we drove through a landscape of dry eucalypt forest, not as lush and green as I expected, on our way to the city. He told me fire was a continuous threat in this part of the world and the blackened trunks and bright green regrowth on the trees bore testament to this. Slowly the bush gave way to the suburbs, residents pushing the boundaries, tentatively encroaching on the edge of nature's territory.

I was amazed at the architecture. It was as if time had stopped. Hundreds of sixties and seventies houses sitting proudly amongst neatly tended gardens, built on the sloping sides of the Derwent river valley, with spectacular views of the water below. It was obvious I wouldn't need to go to a gallery to see this iconic Australian architecture, it was everywhere I looked.

'Last big fire was '67, wiped out hundreds of houses. Suburbs had to be rebuilt. Funny how people forget,' he said. And how easily it could happen again, I thought.

We crossed over a bridge into the older part of the city. Mount Wellington loomed on my right.

'Usually see snow up there for most of the year.'

Snow in Australia was rare, snow in a city even rarer. He told me that even in summer the temperature rarely rose above thirty. How the icy southerly blasts from Antarctica usually put paid to any heat wave lingering around Australia's southernmost city.

The heart of the city was like a big old country town. Thriving retail streets, not too many tall buildings and a decent show of its famed Georgian architecture. All very well ordered along steep streets running down the valley towards a bustling harbour. I remembered the ugly Neo-Georgian house I had lived in as a young bride. It had been a horrible reproduction that bore no resemblance to the beautifully proportioned, two hundred year old buildings I saw in the much older part of the city on the drive down to the port.

I had booked an apartment on the waterfront in a converted warehouse built on a pier. The rooms were standard hotel style, neutral colours, nothing special. What was special was the view from the balcony, a sweeping panorama of the harbour, ships, and the land across the bay. Ice breakers loading up with supplies for the next Antarctic expedition gave a surreal confirmation that this place really was somewhere distant, remote.

I wondered what the first settlers and convicts thought of this same view when they arrived in 1803 on this remote British penal colony, an island tens of thousands of miles away from London, from home. No buildings, strange landscape, bizarre animals, nothing familiar, just a wild place needing to be tamed.

A quick survey of the map showed I wouldn't need a car just yet as everything in Hobart was only a short walk away. The fridge was bare so I headed across the street and loaded up with supplies. A great little grocery store that, unlike generic supermarkets, sold a range of locally produced goods. Smoked wallaby, sheep's milk cheese, crusty sour dough, heirloom apples and Tasmanian Pinot to name a few of the things filling my basket. I returned home and put together a simple platter of the food I'd gathered. Sitting on the balcony I felt a pleasant sense of contentment on this the first night of what I hoped would be my quiet little Tasmanian adventure.

This was the first holiday I'd had in many years. When I was married, we rarely went away. Paul was a fairly parochial man and couldn't understand why people bothered to travel great distances to unfamiliar places in the name of fun. Our vacations usually consisted of heading to his mother's beach house in Portsea, the place where we had spent our short honeymoon. Somewhere predictable and familiar. Fortunately Margot would move to her city town house during this time. I couldn't bear the thought of spending summer under her roof, pretending to get along. Luckily she thought the same.

Portsea was where Melbourne's wealthy families decamped for the summer, it had a kind of Hamptons feel and was only just over an hour's drive from the city. Kate spent much of her time hanging around with her little pack of close girlfriends. They swam, had sleepovers, ate ice creams and giggled at the boys who cheekily tried to intrude on their blissful childhood turf. I liked having the girls over. We cooked, did little craft projects. Was more than happy to be the mum with the car, ferrying them to surf lessons and shopping expeditions. The other mothers, happy to be relieved of the burden of their children, preferred instead to meet for coffee, for long lunches, to gossip, swapping bitchy stories, re-establishing the pecking order.

Paul seemed to always find a reason to head back to the office. Often not bothering to make the long nightly commute home to us, his family. Sometimes we would not see him for days, work, or so I thought, always took precedence. What a naive fool I'd been. How different my life was now. It was as if that other woman, Chris Brown, submissive little wife and mother, barely existed.

This was the first time I'd holidayed alone. I'd travelled such a lot in the last eighteen months, always for work, never for pleasure. It was strange to have no busy schedule, deadlines or meetings. Even stranger to have absolutely no plans at all.

That night I curled up in bed and watched a movie, 'The Hunter'. It was about a man sent to the island to look for the supposedly extinct Tasmanian Tiger. His mission was hampered by a group of disenfranchised people living in an ex logging town near the forests, where his search was to take place. I hoped the film would give me some insight into Tasmania and its people. I fell asleep before it finished. I don't think I'd realised just how exhausted I really was.

The following day I took a ferry ride up the Derwent river to MONA, Museum of Old and New Art. There was a buzz on the boat, foreign languages spoken, an air of excitement in anticipation of what lay ahead. The gallery looked like a giant rusty steel bunker built into the river side cliff. It housed an eclectic mix of extreme new and ancient art. It was the collection of an eccentric millionaire, a maths genius who had made his fortune by calculating the odds and beating the casinos. He had built the gallery only a few years ago to house his collection.

The exhibits were confronting and at the same time exhilarating, many installations questioning what art could be. A series of wheelie bins spewing out a continuous foam of detergent bubbles. A gut machine that tried to replicate the human digestive tract complete with the smell of decay. Or the dark sarcophagus with the electronic scan of the contents of a coffin's Egyptian mummy. I loved the sheer mind fuck of a place like this existing in such a staid old town. That such an obscure gallery could revitalise a whole city. Tourists flocked to Hobart from all over the world to witness this most extraordinary display, a kind of conundrum, modern art in a town where time stood still. Tasmania now famous for more than just its pristine wilderness.

When I returned to my apartment, I downloaded more books, one by the Tasmanian author Richard Flanagan, and as I'd not stayed awake to finish the movie, The Hunter, by Julia Leigh. Maybe they could give me some insight into this enigmatic place? I had plenty of time to read.

That night I walked across to the tree lined row of Georgian terraces that made up Salamanca Place and through a lane way into a quadrangle housing a mix of old and new buildings. It was remarkable that any of the Georgian structures survived at all, considering how happy Australian developers were to demolish our history in the fifties and sixties. I found a restaurant called Veldt. It was housed in a very ugly new office building, behind the row of gorgeous old shops. But again the contradictions delighted as I walked into a very well designed, uber groovy space that was, metaphorically, sticking it right up its ugly exterior.

The food was a spectacular display of skilled cooking, showing a reverential respect for very fine local ingredients. Being a lone diner was made easy by the friendly sommelier who was happy for me to taste a range of his favorite Tasmanian wines. A particularly good aged Riesling finished this superb meal and I walked home quietly loving this esoteric little city. The level of sophistication of the art I'd seen and the food I'd eaten, at odds with my perceptions of the 'nothing more than a large country town' tag once used to describe Hobart.

I was woken by the percussive sounds of a ship's rigging clinking against its mast. The clock said 9am. I'd slept in. I had gotten into the rhythm of this slower paced town and felt truly relaxed. It had been three days of playing tourist, walking, eating out, galleries, no newspapers, no television. I checked in with Cindy just to see that the world hadn't ended and she happily informed me that everything was good back in Melbourne. Davina had emailed with an update on the house, telling me all the finishing touches were going to plan, but that the completion date was still three weeks away. No one needed me and I was at last at ease to let go and truly begin my adventure.

I had decided I wanted to see more of Tasmania and organised to pick up a car tomorrow. But before I left Hobart I would check out the exhibition Davina had suggested. The official opening was last night. I had an invitation, but didn't feel like hobnobbing it with strangers and decided a more leisurely visit the following day would be better.

Picture after picture of sunny, hope filled modern houses adorned the walls, classic mid century domestic architecture. It was as if Tasmania was saying 'enough of the old' after the destruction of the '67 fires, 'the future is a modernist one'. And then it stopped, transfixed in time, Tasmania's dabbling with modernity had been nothing more than a brief aberration. Then a few years ago, all that changed, cheap land and houses led to a property boom. During this time many new houses were built and the small island became a bit of a mecca for the works of some the big name mainland architects. This was the subject of the exhibition in the next room.

'Darcy Shack, Lands End Lagoon' said the typed descriptor below the photo. I was stopped in my tracks. It was obvious whose house this was. I just wasn't prepared for its, or his, intrusion. The photo showed two shipping containers rusting away, almost camouflaged under trees in a secluded estuarine cove. A deck connected the two vessels. To view the interiors I needed to point my phone at the QR code to link to the website showing a more detailed set of photos. The battery had been flat this morning and the phone was still charging back at my hotel room. How clever but how stupid, not everyone would have the technology to do this, but then again maybe they did? Regardless, I would not to get to see inside his shack today.

As I walked home, I couldn't get my mind off the man who had converted the rusted shipping containers. So much for getting away from it all. He was here as well. He got under my skin. I had been tossing and turning all night. On one hand I hated that he had invaded my space, on the other I was drawn to him like a moth to a flame.

The map said that Lands End was about 100 km south of Hobart, just over an hour's drive. I had not driven much since moving into Fitzroy. No need, most things were a short walk away. A simple day trip, not too far, would be a good way to get back behind the wheel. I was curious. I had all the time in the world and decided to hit the road, take in a bit of the scenery and see just what these shipping container houses actually looked like.

Lands End Lagoon

The drive was easy. I had forgotten how much fun it was just getting in a car, free to go wherever I chose. Kate had wondered why I hadn't purchased a vehicle, she loathed the whole chauffeur driven thing. My new house had parking space in the basement, I would buy something when I got back to Melbourne.

It was a perfect day. The sun was shining, the sky a magnificent bright blue and surprisingly hot for spring. The countryside south of Hobart was beautiful, more what I expected Tasmania to look like. Cherry and apple orchards, lush green fields, rolling hills, tall pine forests set against the backdrop of the fertile Huon River valley and its hidden estuarine waterways. It was what I imagined the English countryside to look like, what the settlers and succeeding generations had tamed it to be.

By one in the afternoon I was starving. I had taken my time stopping off at many of the small towns, picking up some of the local produce, easily bought at roadside stalls and general stores. But this was not the food I craved. I had noticed, rather peculiarly, many little shops and cafes advertising 'scallop pies'. They seemed to be a speciality of the area. This was what I wanted to taste.

When I finally reached Lands End I stopped at a small service station. The landscape had changed dramatically. I was at the gateway to the vast southern Tasmanian wilderness and surrounded by rough mountainous terrain and dark tall timbered forests. The sparsely populated town was scattered with abandoned buildings, suggesting more prosperous times when logging once brought hundreds of people to the area. It had an air of despondency, of a fading ghost town, a place with no sense of future.

'Best Scallop Pies in Tassie. Fresh Wallaby Meat. Last Petrol in the South', the sign said in front of the only occupied building in sight.

I ordered a pie from the man behind the counter. He told me it wouldn't be long, another batch was just coming out of the oven, so I looked around the shop while I waited. This was a very peculiar little store. Not only did it sell basic supplies, but I also noticed an eclectic mix of food. Not the boutique regional fare I had picked up along the way, but obscure things like truffle oil, tinned foie gras and other very expensive imported foodstuffs.

When I thought about it, it was no stranger than a modern art gallery selling soap in the shape of a woman's vagina. I had learnt to expect the unexpected in this baffling place.

'That'll be $4.70 luv. You new around here?' said the old man.

'I'm just visiting. From Melbourne,' I replied, biting into the pie.

'Bet you've never had a scallop pie before. Mine are the best in these parts,' he said proudly.

I took a bite and yes, it was delicious. Crispy pastry stuffed full of succulent scallops in a curried bechamel sauce. The last thing I expected to find deep in the southern Tasmanian wilderness.

'Yum, these are very good. I'd better take a few more. Save cooking dinner tonight.'

'Where you off to next?' he asked, as he placed two more pies in a cardboard tray.

'Well, I'm actually looking for a place at Lands End Lagoon.'

'Jesus, there's not bloody much down there. Some bastard, architect bloke, dumped down a couple a containers there a few years ago. Thinks he can live in 'em. Why would you wanna do that?' he replied, in a slow drawl.

'I wondered about that myself. Saw some photographs in an exhibition in Hobart, thought I'd go and have a look at the real thing. Is it very far away?'

'Come out here, I'll show you.'

He took me behind his shop to the back porch and pointed to a headland across the water.

'There it is, just a few kilometres away over the inlet.'

I saw the green tip of land over the water.

'It looks quite close. Can you get there by boat?'

'Don't be fooled, one of the most dangerous bits of water down south. That rip has claimed many an experienced fisherman.'

'So, how do I get there?'

'Come back inside. You'll need a map, no GPS or phone coverage down there.'

He grabbed the map and spread it out across the counter.

'You've got to do a big loop around the lagoon. The turn off's about 30 kilometres down the road, just after Moon Bay. It's a bit of a bush track after that, but you'll be fine in that rig.'

I filled up with petrol and he playfully slapped the roof of my car, yelling 'see ya' and waving as I pulled out of the driveway.

For the first time I felt slightly wary about my decision to come down this far south. The map showed vast areas of national park, with tangles of tracks through the remaining land not owned by the state. The verdant forests now looked dark and menacing. No towns, just the odd ramshackle hut, yards strewn with abandoned car bodies. It looked more like 'Deliverance' country. I could almost hear the banjos playing.

He was right, 30 kilometres south, along a well maintained dirt road, I saw the turnoff. Moon Bay was nothing more than an intersection and a perfect description of the lunar landscape that lay in the direction of the sign to Lands End Lagoon.

It was a rough, gruelling, one hour drive over a track that barely passed for a road. This too, seemed abandoned and was nothing like the easy drive of the last half an hour. Luckily I had opted for the upgraded four wheel drive, and although at the time I thought it a bit excessive, was glad I'd accepted this sturdy truck. The treeless landscape was completely denuded, logging had taken a heavy toll. Deep eroded gullies had formed where the topsoil had been washed away. Why on earth had Adam chosen this ugly, barren part of Tasmania, when there was so much stunning natural beauty nearby?

I reached a ravine with a fast flowing river below. The only way to access the long spit of land further ahead was to cross a narrow bridge. The sign said 'Private Keep Out', but there was no locked gate. 'Piss off,' I thought, with a devil may care attitude. I'd come this far, I wasn't turning back now. I got out and walked down the steep drive to the bridge. It was solid and I saw that it would easily take my car.

For a brief moment I wondered what the hell I was doing miles away from civilisation, but then I remembered, Hobart was just over two and a half hours away. It was three in the afternoon, and as long as I left by four, I would be on the main road by five. The trip back to Hobart would be easy from then on. That was the weird thing about Tasmania, a sense of remoteness, when in actual fact, nothing was that far away. This small island could be quite deceptive.

The road on the other side of the bridge was much better, this was obviously private land that someone cared about and looked after. As I drove further into the property, I began to see the attraction. It was a completely different world. It was an extraordinarily place. On my left were a number of small sandstone coves with sheltered pristine white beaches. The water was the most intense blue I had ever seen. The tall forest grew almost to the lagoon's edge. Bright green tree ferns looked like nature's umbrellas. A little further away, on my right was the open ocean, a wilder coastline of craggy cliffs. The spit was probably little more than a kilometre wide.

At the end of the road I could see what I had come looking for. Tucked into the rocks and almost completely shrouded by trees, were the shipping containers. I pulled off the track and got out. The containers were sealed up, I couldn't see inside. I could understand the attraction of being in this beautiful paradise. It was such a contrast to the barren area I had just traversed. A sanctuary. I walked the short distance to the beach and saw that the spit formed a broad arc, creating a massive lagoon, broken only by a narrow waterway, where the headland on the other side seemed close. I could see no sign of the petrol station on the other side. Perhaps it was much further than I perceived.

The sheltered lagoon beach faced west and I could imagine sitting there watching the sun go down. Maybe with Adam at my side, away from Melbourne, away from his brother, a true escape. I sat for awhile in quiet meditation, contemplating what might have been. Dreaming like this was foolish, as was this little expedition. The clouds were getting heavier and it looked like a cool change was on its way. I should get out before the weather turned. It was already 4 o'clock, I had seen enough, it was time to go.

'Fuck, fuck, fuck!' I yelled as my tyres spun uselessly.

I had absolutely no traction and the more I tried, the deeper the tyres tore into the sand. The car had become hopelessly bogged. Stop and get a grip, I thought. This was not an impossible situation. I had driven the farm truck since I was a kid and Dad had taught me how to get out of loose sand. Dig away the sand from the tyres and lay the area with sticks and leaves, I could imagine him saying. As I was digging, I felt the first heavy drops on the back of my neck. I would have to work quickly. Within seconds the rain was beating down. The more I dug, the more the water caved in the sand, burying the tyres even deeper. This was becoming a futile exercise and I realised I would have to wait until the downpour subsided.

Sitting in the car I was aware of how foolhardy this trip had been. I was ridiculously under prepared. My phone had no service, I was cold and wet, and had nobody waiting at home, wondering why I hadn't returned. I contemplated walking out, but knew it would be hours before I got to the main road in the dark, and even once there I couldn't assume anyone would be driving by. It would be best to wait it out. The rain turned into a storm and I resigned myself to the fact that tonight I was going nowhere.

I scampered over to the containers to see if I could break in, find somewhere dry to shelter from the storm. Another exercise in futility. They were tightly sealed. I was dripping wet and exposed. My food purchases along the way meant that at least I wouldn't starve, but were little consolation for the stupid situation I'd gotten myself into. I ran the motor, turned on the heaters and stripped off so that my clothes would dry. A linen dress and sandals was hardly appropriate attire for such an intrepid adventure. I had lots of fuel, so at least that wasn't going to be a problem. When the clothes were dry, I turned off the engine. I wasn't so stupid as to suffer the added humiliation of a flat battery.

Sleep was all but impossible. The wind howled and the rain pounded down all night. I felt spooked. My mind began to conjure up images of some kind of Wolf Creek nightmare happening. Every time the car shook, I expected to see a crazed gunman staring back at me. Perhaps one of the inhabitants of those run down shacks I had passed on the main road?

By morning the wind had stopped but the rain had settled in and it was freezing cold. I got out only to find that the water had washed away all the sand from under the wheels and that the car was balanced precariously on its axles. This car was going nowhere. My options were narrowing, and in realising the hopelessness of the situation I bawled my eyes out. What an idiot I'd been. I would just have to wait until the weather cleared, then take my chances and try to walk out. The weather got worse, the rain had turned to sleet, reminding me that Antarctica was the nearest landmass south. I remembered seeing the icebreaker ships taking on supplies at the wharf across from my apartment in Hobart.

The time passed slowly. I rifled around in my bag, found a pen and began to write a piece about the idiotic situation I now found myself in. Sure that my readers would find this predicament absolutely hilarious. Hopefully I would find it funny one day, too.

By late afternoon I knew I was in for another long night stranded in my car. The rain had gotten much heavier. Laughingly I looked at the hipsters picnic of gourmet food supplies. I'm sure Amundsen had not thought to pack sheep's milk cheese and aged Riesling as part of his supplies when he made the first expedition to the South Pole. The wine helped to calm me and, at long last, in a drunken stupor, I nodded off to sleep.

Rescue

I was falling, the door had opened and I had nothing to hold onto, someone grabbed me, disorientated, I screamed.

'It's ok, I've got you, you're safe.'

I could barely comprehend what was going on. It was still dark, the storm was raging, thunder and lightning exploded around me. I thought I was hallucinating. Only vaguely conscious, I felt myself being wrapped in a blanket and carried in the rain to a warm place. I remember being put into a bed. My alcoholic haze let me fall into a deep, intoxicated sleep.

I woke with a shocking hangover. Someone had left paracetamol and a glass of water on the bedside table, thoughtful, and most desperately needed. My brain throbbed against my hard skull, it felt like irreparable damage had been done. Why did I do this to myself? Kicking off the covers I could see I was still wearing all my stinky old clothes. Light was coming in from a narrow glass door on my left. I got up and had a look around. Where was I? The bed was jammed into a small, dark, claustrophobic room. Outside, across a deck I could see another building.

'Hello?' I called out sheepishly.

No one replied. I took a few tentative steps and saw I had slept in one of the two shipping containers. Across the deck I could see a kitchen. Only part of the structure was open, the rest of the long container remained tightly sealed. There was no one in sight.

I walked out, my car had been moved and it appeared that I was free to go. The keys were still in the ignition, so I got in and drove down the track to see if I could find out who had rescued me. In the distance I saw a battered old, army Jeep. Maybe the guy at the petrol station had come down after all? He probably knew every passing car and would have been alert to the fact that I hadn't driven past, back to Hobart. Back to where idiotic tourists like me really belonged.

There were trees across the road, blocking my path. I could hear the sound of a chainsaw. In my drunken stupor I'd been only vaguely cognisant of the ferocity of last night's storm. The damage was extensive. The noise stopped, a person emerged from the behind the tangle of fallen trees.

Shirtless, wild, sexy... Adam! Fuck! Of course it was him! Didn't he always turn up when I needed rescuing? He walked towards me. He looked pissed off. No knight in shining armour.

'What are you doing here?' I asked foolishly.

'It's my place and what the fuck were YOU doing here, is more the question?' he said angrily.

'Do you know how stupid it was coming down here alone!' he spat.

'I know, I'm sorry. It was idiotic. I've no right to be here. I'll get going as soon as the road's clear. Can I give you a hand?' I said, like a kid who'd been caught doing something wrong.

'You can give me a hand, but you're going nowhere,' he replied.

'I think that's up to me to decide,' I said indignantly.

'I think not. Follow me.'

He walked silently ahead, me just a few steps behind, not quite able to keep up. In front of us, the ravine had become filled with water. The entire area flooded. The bridge was nowhere to be seen. We had been cut off and the spit of land was now an inaccessible island. I didn't understand why the water just didn't flow out to sea.

'The ravine has been jammed up with old logs. We're stuck here until the water seeps through. I won't know what condition the bridge is in until the water level drops. Hope you had nothing urgent you needed to do,' he said, with mocking concern.

His coldness towards me was more than evident. I had intruded on his space and was obviously not welcome. Nothing had changed.

Although I had one of those dry retching hangovers, I was too proud to let it stop me from helping. I needed to show him I was not completely useless. We worked until the road was clear and stacked the Jeep with the cut firewood. Surely he would be impressed with my effort? He didn't thank me, didn't seem to notice.

Back at the house we unloaded the wood. I became aware I needed to eat. My hangover was turning into a terminal disease.

'Would you like me to get you some breakfast?' I asked, hoping the offer of food might lift the mood.

'I've been up since dawn and already eaten. You can eat if you like, but I've got work to do.'

And with that he drove off, leaving me standing there humiliated, like an errant child. It looked like I would have to endure my punishment for a while yet. What kind of juvenile romantic fantasy had I harboured? Coming down here, hoping to reconnect, missing what never was. The sooner I got out of here the better.

I walked back to the kitchen to see what I could find. It was a utilitarian space with a stainless steel bench and a sink, the kind of stuff I'd seen in commercial kitchens. All my supplies had been put into the cooler, a kind of upright refrigerator with a huge block of ice in the top compartment. I had purchased a lot of food and knew we could survive out here for a few days at least. The only other food I could see were a few cans of baked beans sitting on a shelf above the sink. A terracotta urn sat on the bench, at least there was clean drinking water. I filled a tin mug and guzzled thirstily. An Aga wood oven meant that cooking was not going to be too onerous. The only thing difficult was the thought of waiting out this flood with someone who didn't want me around. I rifled through the cooler and opened up a packet of smoked salmon, spreading it on rye bread and wolfing it down. There seemed to be something quite miserable about my lonely little breakfast, inappropriate food, inappropriate place and inappropriate company.

Eventually my body started to rehydrate, I could slowly feel my hangover abating. I reeked of someone who had slept in their clothes for two days. My dress smelled of the wine I had spilt on it last night. I desperately needed to take a shower and wash these stinking clothes. I looked around for a bathroom but could find only a pit toilet. The lagoon looked tempting. The sun was out and warmed my skin. I would take a swim. As I undressed, I was saddened by the thought of a much gentler morning almost a year ago when Adam had rescued me from the riots. What a pathetic reunion this was. A less than happy anniversary.

I remember waking, that morning last November, naked. He had carried me off to bed after I had fallen asleep in his arms. He'd told me he had removed the robe, so I would have a more comfortable night. He'd said he had wanted to make love to me, but knew it was not the right time.

He had rescued me again, but this time I had awoken fully clothed. No tender ministrations after my latest ordeal, just an angry man pissed off by an unwelcome intruder.

I found a grubby old towel hanging on a hook above a bucket of water near the toilet. It would have to do. I walked the few metres to the small sheltered beach in front of the bedroom and stripped off. The coldness took my breath away. This was not tropical northern Australia, the turquoise waters were deceiving. I washed quickly, watching my body turn blue, then scrubbed my dress and underwear clean and spread the clothes out on rocks to dry. The towel would have to do for now and I sat back in the sun hoping the rays would warm my shivering body.

I heard his footsteps behind me.

'Take these,' he said, tossing clothes into my lap, looking at my nakedness, making me feel ashamed.

'Thanks,' I replied forlornly.

He had given me a pair of worn faded jeans, softened through years of wear, and an equally old grey tee shirt. 'Beggars can't be choosers', I thought. The jeans were way too big, I wondered how I would keep them up.

'Here,' he said, cutting a piece of coarse twine and throwing it in my direction.

The silence was unbearable. I watched as he quietly went about his day, doing odd jobs. After a few hours I tried to make polite conversation.

'How long have you had this place?' I asked.

He told me he'd discovered the place many years ago, when he had tried to stop the logging. I was surprised to find this out. Green Adam? The thought of the billionaire business man hanging out with the greenies seemed incongruous.

'The only real estate available was this narrow peninsula. So I bought it. The land you drove through was owned by a timber company that went broke. They intended to replant, but timber prices crashed and they could no longer afford to do it. It's been left like this for a very long time. This flooding is a direct result of the land's mismanagement.'

'Surely there's something you can do?'

Hooray, an actual conversation!

'Follow me.'

He took me into a cleared section of forest and I saw hundreds of seedlings, protected under wire cages.

'These are ready for planting, they're all original native species. I'm hoping to eventually generate enough seed stock, so the whole area can be replanted. It's not much, but at least it's a start. It's why I'm here.'

'Wow, you've done all this? When do you get the time?'

'Sadly, I don't. Joe, the old guy at the petrol station, keeps his eye out and makes sure the plants are watered and the property is kept in order. I pay him to look after the place.'

'That old guy, the pie maker?' I asked.

'Yeah, he knew I was coming down yesterday and when I rang him he said that someone had been nosing around, hadn't come back. I told him not to worry and that I was already on my way. What the hell made you come here?' asked Adam, brow wrinkled, annoyed.

'I saw the photos of this place in an exhibition. I had plenty of time and was curious. I thought it might tell me something about you.'

He was silent as he went back to work, pinching off dead leaves, pulling weeds, his back to me, ignored. His anger still palpable.

'Can I help?' I asked, prepared to pull my weight.

'Just go back to the shack and don't touch anything. As soon as the river drops you can leave.'

It looked like a truce was still a long way off.

He continued to work around the property and by sunset was hungry enough to eat the meal I had prepared from some of my food. It was a peace offering that he quietly accepted.

By nightfall I was ready for bed. I saw the swag he'd set up on the deck, and that is where he retreated to after dinner. I went, alone, to my bed inside.

A cacophony of birdsong woke me. It made me think it was quite early, the sky was still a dawn grey and the air chilly. I had no idea of time, no computers, no clocks, a completely useless phone. My bladder was ready to burst. I hated the pit toilet, convinced there were spiders hidden in its dark depths. Adam was not around, the Jeep was gone. I walked, naked, out to the trees and squatted down, relieved to piss.

How long would it be before we were able to get back home? Cindy wouldn't be worried just yet as I told her I would be on the road for the next week or two, with limited phone coverage. She said she'd leave me alone and wouldn't ring unless it was a life or death situation. I knew she wanted me to keep my distance. To prove that I could take time out, that the business would not fail and the world, as we knew it, wouldn't end. I'd kept my reservation at the apartment in Hobart, to use as my base, not knowing if my travels would require overnight stays. Told them not to service the room. Nobody would notice my absence.

Again breakfast was a lonely affair.

'Been busy this morning?' I asked, when he eventually came inside to grab a drink.

'Yeah, I want to plant the first of the seedlings today. I've been sorting out the most mature plants, the ones I think will have the best chance.'

'Please let me help. I might as well be doing something.'

'It's pretty hard going.'

'I think you forget, I grew up on a farm,' I responded defensively.

Perhaps if we could be civil towards each other, we would get through the day.

He tossed me a pair of heavy duty gloves and for a brief moment I sensed his guard lowering.

The day was warming, Adam's shirt was off. He caught me looking at his body and turned away. We worked hard, digging holes in the ground and gently placing the seedlings into the freshly turned soil. The landscape was a mixture of older forest regrowth and bald patches that had failed to regenerate. These were the areas he was hoping would heal. When we finished we looked, proudly, at the day's achievements.

Before we went back, Adam checked on the flood waters. There was still no sign of the bridge. We would be here for at least another day.

I hated the way he was treating me, this petulance, this sulky tantrum was becoming exhausting. Couldn't he just let it go? What more did I have to do to show him that I was sorry I'd intruded on his 'boy's own adventure'? I was trying to be of help and was just as keen to leave, as he was to see the back of me. How could I ever have imagined a future with this sullen, solitary man?

The day's work was both mentally and physically exhausting. We were almost too tired to eat. Beans were all we could be bothered preparing. After a wordless dinner, we both retreated early to our respective beds.

I heard him get up. I was awake, ready to help with another day's planting. We ate quickly, loaded up the Jeep with the next lot of seedlings and drove to the site.

I couldn't believe what I saw. It was heartbreaking, all that effort, gone. Rabbits, trapped by the flood, had eaten the little trees. All that was left were a few bare twigs sticking, pathetically, out of the ground. Neither of us could speak. The disappointment left me feeling so empty, I could have wept. Head lowered, shoulders drooped, Adam's body language said it all.

We had placed sturdy guards around the plants, but they had just dug under them. Planting more would be a complete waste of time. We drove back to the plot and returned the remaining plants to their rabbit proof nursery. What an exercise in futility. I started to hate this island. It felt cursed.

Adam went back to the camp site, grabbed his shotgun and threw it in the back. I jumped in. He drove to the edge of the swollen creek where we had seen some of the shitty little devils. BOOM, reload, BOOM. The rabbits scattered, only to pop up a few metres away with contemptuous disregard. He was a hopeless shot, but I sensed that this aggressive act helped calm his frustration and anger.

We had nothing to say to each other. I had nothing to do. I didn't know how long I could keep this up, his tantrum had gone on for long enough, it was exhausting. I would keep my distance. He disappeared for the rest of the day.

Inside I found Richard Flanagan's book 'The Sound of One Hand Clapping'. This depressing tale of struggle and survival set in fifties Tasmania was probably not the best thing to read right now, but it was the only book I could find and I really didn't have anything else to do.

He returned late in the afternoon.

I'd finished the book and guessed it was about finding salvation. Was this what Adam was looking for?

He didn't need me to nag him about his disappearance. I understood his need for solitude. The silence was uncomfortable. I sat outside, the sun setting behind the distant mountains. Another melancholic evening.

And then it occurred to me. I had a plan. I grabbed the keys and climbed into the driver's seat.

'What the hell are you doing?'

I didn't answer, so he jumped in beside me and I drove to the place that had caused us such grief this morning. I turned off the engine and could see many rabbits. I knew they would all be out at sunset. I went to the back of the car, grabbed the ammo, the gun, loaded it and aimed. BOOM, hit, reload. BOOM, hit, reload. I felt a surge of power as I took my revenge, adrenaline coursing through my veins. The anger and frustration of the past few days finally finding release. My father had taught me well, one shot, a good clean kill.

Adam was only just comprehending what he was seeing. He couldn't control her, she seemed possessed. She was firing at the rabbits and every creature she set her sights on fell. She was a crack shooter, an Amazon. It was the sexiest thing he had ever seen. Any that were not yet dead she quickly dispatched with a deft pull and twist to the hapless creature's neck, stashing them in a hessian bag. He was speechless and could only shake his head.

'Something I picked up on the farm,' I said back at him, as we loaded the Jeep.

Was that a hint of a smile, had this finally broken the ice? I would need to skin and bleed the rabbits quickly, if they were going to be of any use to eat. A welcome change from tinned beans. Cooking would give me something to do. The kill had left me feeling exhilarated, the blood pumping through my body, igniting a kind of bloodlust that was strangely sexually charged. My heart was pounding, I was on heat.

When they got back to the camp site they unloaded the dead rabbits. She got him to hold the animals' back legs firmly and, after a few exacting cuts, pulled at the pelts and skinned the rabbits, as if removing a slightly difficult glove. She then slit open the belly, spilling the guts out over the ground. The cleaned, headless creatures were mounted on a long stick, bound at the feet and left to bleed dry.

She was extraordinary. Her action made him want to fuck her senseless. He hated that he had no control over his feelings for her, his cock begged release. He needed her and he needed her now. He walked straight up to her, took the knife from her hand and tossed it to the ground. He grabbed her body and held her head, kissing her with an animalistic ferocity. The killing had ignited something primitive. He needed to fuck her, to own her body, to reclaim what had been his.

He ripped open the tee shirt she wore, her breasts tumbled out, he pinched the nipples hard until they stood erect, she groaned, her chest rose, she begged for more. Her mouth, their tongues met hungrily, beginning to satisfy a demanding need.

She stopped, then with an equal savagery tore at his belt, ripping down his fly, freeing his constrained throbbing dick, kicking off her own loose jeans then climbing his body like a preying cat. He lifted her up, felt her hot wet cunt, and slammed his hard cock into her. She arched her back and screamed a carnal cry as he mercilessly pounded her.

His orgasm came quickly, his cock pumped its fluid deep into her. His mouth, his tongue, hungry for her taste, devoured her with his kisses, never wanting to let her go. Carrying her, still mounted on him, he walked back to the kitchen. He placed her on the wooden table. She lay back and languorously stretched her arms above her head, her legs casually falling open, exposing her deliciously newly fucked sex. She looked at him hungrily, he kissed her passionately, roughly, in response.

My heart was pounding. Adam was kissing me and my cunt throbbed with the tingling of post orgasmic euphoria. What had just happened? His response had been visceral, all that pent up anger and rage had been taken out in the most brutal fucking I had experienced. But my desire had not been quenched.

'Fuck me again, please. I need to feel you inside me,' I begged, breathlessly.

He hurriedly removed his clothes, then rolled me onto my stomach and dragged my body to the edge of the table. My legs dropped to the ground, he wrenched my thighs apart and placed his penis to my cunt. I was dripping with his cum, enough to lubricate himself, rubbing against my labia, until he began to stiffen again. I raised myself up on my elbows, arching my back and presented myself eagerly to him. He groaned and grabbed my belly, pulling me hard against him, fucking me from behind, penetrating me deeply, agonisingly, inside. I moaned, my arousal was off the scale. I lunged back at him, wanting him to thrust harder. He moved his hand down my stomach, his fingers searching, till he found my swollen clitoris. In this position he held me, able to grip my hips, giving me pleasure as he slowly and deliberately rammed my womb. Each thrust was a considered blow, building my need for more. This was not a loving act, but an expression of brute force, telling me he was in charge and would control when I came. It was astonishingly erotic. I wanted this game to continue. After each drilling, I responded by squeezing my cunt tightly around him, a guttural groan escaped, he couldn't hold back much longer. He reached for my breasts and savagely pinched each nipple, holding me firmly against him as he quickened his actions. Within seconds my whole body exploded and I screamed as waves of pleasure rolled over me. He bit into the back of my neck as his orgasm engulfed him, possessively holding me until his trembling body quieted. Exhausted, we both collapsed onto the table, his weight encasing me, my body, my mind completely captured.

I made the first gestures of movement and he responded by nuzzling his lips against my neck, biting, sending shivers down my spine.

'You undo me,' he groaned hoarsely.

'You make me feel alive.'

He reached out, stroking the length of my arm, stopping when his fingers intertwined with mine. It was over, we both succumbed to the animal passion that had simmered just below the surface, the impasse had been broken. His hands were black. Dirt, blood, sweat and sex, a filthy, heady mix of aromas and sensations, covering our bodies, filling the room. He rolled me over, wiping a streak of blood from my face, sniffing the air, kissing me again. He stood, then effortlessly picked me up and carried me outside. He walked across the deck to the back of the kitchen and placed me tenderly on a wooden chair. I watched as he bent and released the catches that had been holding down the steel casing of the back of the shipping container. Lifting them high, a large tub and shower were revealed, fully exposed to the outside. He turned on the shower and began to fill the tub. I saw steam rising.

'This has been here all the time?' I asked, with a look of shocked indignation.

He smiled.

'I've been bathing in that freezing cold lagoon!'

'I know, I liked to watch you naked and I've enjoyed watching you piss by the trees,' he replied with a wicked grin.

I got up and walked to the shower, holding out my hand to feel the blissfully hot water.

'And this, hot running water, where does it come from?' I asked.

'The stove in the kitchen heats up as much as I want. The rainwater tanks are on the roof.'

I stepped in and almost cried with the luxury of something so utterly needed. The toiletries were from his hotel. I lathered my hair and started to feel civilised again. He soaped my back. When he had finished I climbed into the tub. Naked, his body glistening hard and wet, he walked into the kitchen, returning with a bottle of wine and two glasses.

'Welcome to my place, Tina. I'm glad you're here,' he said with a wicked grin.

I held the glasses while he got in behind me. I handed him his wine and leaned against his chest.

'You merciless bastard, Adam Darcy! Don't think I've forgiven you that easily!'

The alcohol did its work, my body began to calm, my heart stopped racing and slowly my anger dissipated. We both lay back, watching the setting sun, serenaded by birdsong, exhausted, but at long last at peace.

Let's Eat

We were both wrinkly when we emerged from the tub. He handed me a clean towel from the cupboard next to the bath and I wrapped myself up in its soft luxuriant warmth.

I watched as he lit the kerosene lamps.

'Are you hungry?' he asked.

'Starving, what have you got on the menu, Sir?'

'Rabbit au Adam. Stay there, tonight I'll cook for you,' and with that he walked, still naked, into the kitchen. Gorgeous ass, hard body.

A cleaver hitting a board and pots clanging on the metal stove top were the sounds coming from the kitchen. After about five minutes he came back outside to the deck with another bottle of wine.

'How long before dinner, chef?' I asked.

'Looking at the size of those rabbits, I'm guessing a good couple of hours.'

'What do you propose we do to kill time?'

'How about I shag you senseless?' he replied.

'What a brilliant idea,' I said, looking at his stunning, strong body standing before me.

'But first I need to do something,' I said, getting up and letting the towel fall as I walked toward him.

'What?' he responded, looking slightly puzzled.

'This,' I whispered, kneeling down before him and putting his soft penis in my mouth.

Before long he was hard again and we spent the time, waiting for the meal to cook, fucking ourselves senseless, just like he'd said.

We had fallen asleep on his swag, waking to the smell of burning food.

'Shit!' he yelled and we both raced into the kitchen to find our dinner turning into a barbeque. The stove had been too hot, the stew too dry, he had only added a tin of beans. Picking at the charred, inedible remains, I realised we should have paid more attention, been less distracted. But my body hummed with the tingle of post coital satisfaction. I didn't care how much food got burnt, if this was the reason why. Shooting and cooking were not his strong points, fucking me most definitely was.

Neither of us were really that hungry, it was late and we were both tired.

'Your bed or mine?' I asked.

'Ours,' he replied and gently took my hand and led me to the bed where I had slept alone for the past few nights. It was cold, he pulled the covers over and wrapped his body around me.

'Stay with me,' he whispered.

'I will.'

Settled

Another morning awoken by birdsong. Something had changed. Adam was not in the bed. Gone was the poky dark room, instead I was surrounded by glass walls, light flooding in around me, the lagoon was in clear view at the far end of this now large elongated room. A worn leather armchair sat in front of the fireplace, positioned to capture the panoramic views. I knew this style, a mid century Danish hunting chair. I'd seen one in a store on Smith Street. It seemed so appropriate. The trees on my right were just an arm's length away from the bed. The strong perfume of eucalyptus wafted into the room. The glass walls slid right back to let the fresh air in, a mosquito net billowed in the morning breeze. It was as if I had been transported into a magnificent light airy pavilion within an enchanted forest.

I looked over to the kitchen and saw a similar transformation as well. The whole space had been opened up. The deck now a huge outdoor room created by lifting up the side panels, forming a roof along the entire length of the two shipping containers. The two rusty boxes now a series of three interconnected, breezy, open rooms. I had gone to bed in a dark metal box and woke in a modern architectural dream, all glass, timber and sleek, minimalist furniture. The space had a Zen like quality.

On the deck, a long trestle table was set for breakfast. White canvas butterfly chairs were waiting to be occupied. I could smell coffee and got up to investigate. Adam was in the kitchen cooking bacon and eggs. A newly exposed wall of shelves showed an abundantly stocked pantry. And at the end of this equally bright sunny space was a lounge room with a long rawhide sofa positioned to capture the view of the lagoon and woods outside. Coarsely woven rugs broke the hardness of the polished timber floors.

'What happened?' I said, wide eyed, like Alice in Wonderland.

'I wanted to show you how beautiful this place could be.'

'Why didn't you do this a few days ago?'

'Because I didn't want to get attached to being here with you. I was determined to get you away as soon as possible and now I don't want us to leave.'

'God, it's so beautiful here. What you have created is magical, I don't want to leave either.'

He pulled me into his arms, kissing me roughly, his unshaven face and tousled hair giving him a very sexy 'beast of the wild' look. He ran his hands down the length of my bare back and playfully squeezed my backside. He picked me up and sat me on the bench next to him and teasingly sucked hard on both my nipples.

'Here, you're cold, I can tell,' he said taking off his sloppy old sweatshirt and pulling it over my naked body. I could still feel his heat, smell his scent.

When the food was cooked, he lifted me off the bench and we both saw where my wetness had left a slick snail trail on the cool steel. He ran his finger through it and put it to his nose, inhaling deeply.

'This is the scent of you,' he said, breathing heavily.

'And that is what you do to me,' I replied, smiling seductively, licking the same finger.

We hadn't eaten last night and I was starving. I could easily have taken him back to bed, but the smell of bacon won, for now.

After we finished breakfast, Adam said he should check the flooded ravine. If the water had receded, uncovering the bridge, we could get back. Being on our island, marooned, gave us no choice, making it easier to forget about the world that had become impossible for us to share. We had only just reconnected, I wasn't ready to return. It was with some trepidation, that I went along for the ride. But I didn't have the guts to get out of the Jeep, dreading what I might see. He walked to the ravine, still wearing only his jeans. He looked strong, his muscular body well formed and powerful. He aroused me so much. I was made weak with lust and could easily spend every waking minute being fucked, over and over by my exquisite lover.

Eventually he turned around and headed back. He gave no clues. I got out and walked toward him. He held my face in both hands and looked me straight in the eye, not speaking, for what seemed like ages.

'It's not good,' he said grimly.

I stared back looking for answers, not sure what he was about to say next, when his mouth broke into a large grin.

'It's completely fucked. Most of the timbers have been washed away, the bridge is impassable, we ain't goin' nowhere just yet.'

He grabbed me by the hand and ran to show me the skeletal metal frame that was all that remained of the bridge. The water had subsided, but the river was still raging and swollen. I noticed the flood waters on the other side of the ravine had subsided also. I could barely make out the track I had driven along just a few days before. I shuddered to think of what could have happened if Adam had not turned up. Would this reconciliation have ever occurred? How long before anyone would know I was missing? Who knew where to look? Who would care? We danced around, two mad things, giggling and hollering like drunken teenagers. This isolated island paradise was ours, alone, for a little bit longer. I loved that fate had played this trick.

Joe

I was keen to get back to our beautiful sanctuary. I wanted to see what was in that kitchen, to explore the house he had created, to cook for him, feed him, nurture him, make love to him. Play at being his woman. This desire was almost primordial. There was so much food. A perfect pantry that would sustain us for quite some time.

'Did you stock this pantry?'

'Why do you ask?'

'I can't work it out. It's got all the basics. But it has other stuff, extras, it looks like it's been put together by a chef. By someone who really knows their way around a kitchen.'

'What are you implying?' asked Adam, looking slightly crestfallen.

I grabbed a jar from the shelf and hid the label.

'Well Mr Smarty Pants, what are these?'

He peered at the contents of the jar.

'Easy, grapes.'

'Yep, grapes in a jar. Try caper berries.'

'And these?'

'Ah, sardines?'

'Absolutely not. They are the most exquisite anchovies in the world, Ortiz. They cost a fortune.'

'Ok, ok, you've caught me out. I get Joe to stock the pantry. I let him buy anything he wants. I tell him he can keep anything left over. He knows I usually eat whatever is easiest, which is pretty much always baked beans, bacon and eggs. Occasionally I surprise him. It's a game we've played for as long as I've been coming down here.'

'Yes, but it still doesn't explain why some old guy who runs a service station in the middle of nowhere knows about Ortiz anchovies?'

'It's a long story... '

Adam told me Joe had once been his father's personal chef. On his yacht, his polo property, in his numerous homes all over the world. Graham Darcy liked the status symbol of having Joe around him wherever he went.

'Joe went wherever Dad lived. He was more Dad's mate and confidante than just someone on the payroll. They drank together, even partied together and when my dad needed a new kidney, Joe donated his. In fact their relationship lasted longer than any of my father's marriages.'

'As a kid, I always liked Joe, he was the only constant in my dad's ever changing life. No matter how many new girlfriends my father had, Joe was always there. He made sure there was always something for us to eat, knew when to bake a cake on our birthday, knew what our favorite foods were, even introduced us to new stuff that most kids had never heard of.'

'About ten years ago, Joe was in a bad car accident and his passenger was killed. The courts heard Joe and this woman had been drinking heavily that night and neither one of them were capable of driving. However, in a mistaken act of gallantry, Joe opted to drive the woman home. My father made a big song and dance about not supporting drink driving and completely disowned his former mate. Joe went to jail for three years. I always knew there was more to the story.'

'It turns out the passenger was one of dad's ex girlfriends and her diaries showed she'd been having an affair with Joe for many years. Dad was affronted that they had shared the same woman, after all Joe was just an employee, not his equal. Dad cut off all ties and left him without a cent. Dad's ego was bigger than their friendship.'

'I found Joe in a boarding house in Saint Kilda, after he got out of jail. At about the same time, I bought this land from the owner of the petrol station. A condition of the sale was that I had to take the petrol station as well. I didn't want it, but had no choice. I kept it open because I knew it would be perfect for Joe.'

'I can't understand why he would want anything to do with your family?' I questioned.

'We were the only family he had and the dispute wasn't with me. Anyway, we have a legally binding contract that says if he stays with me for more than ten years, he will own the petrol station outright. In summer the national parks around here fill up with tourists and campers and the store makes a killing. He cooks incredible food and the tourists pay a premium to eat it in what must be one of the world's most bizarre fine food restaurants. During winter, the off season, he experiments, hence all the weird stuff here.'

'And the weird stuff on the shelves of the petrol station,' I said finishing his sentence.

'Yeah, and when he's not playing around in his kitchen, I pay him really well to look after this. It works for both of us.'

The kitchen was now starting to make sense, as were the scallop pies.

'So how come he hasn't come down here to rescue you?'

'Because these types of storms are not unusual at this time of year. He'd have no idea the bridge has been destroyed. But what really keeps him away is that he knows I want to be left alone, that I come here to escape. He knows not to come back to the property until after I call in on my way out.'

'My plan was to stay for a month.'

'So we really have got the place to ourselves.'

'You bet, now take your clothes off. I need to finish what we started before breakfast!'

I jumped back on the bench ripped my top off and spread my legs.

'Hurry up, I'm still hungry,' I begged.

Domestic Goddess

I showered quickly. Adam had gone to tend the plants. I was keen to explore the kitchen on my own. Joe had put together a good basic pantry. Along with the rabbit meat, there would be enough fresh supplies to last us for a quite few more days. After that we could survive on the pantry staples. I knew I could do better than tinned beans.

Large blocks of ice packed in layers of straw, were stored in a big insulated chest dug into the ground behind the bathroom. I remembered reading Elizabeth David's account of the ice trade in ancient Rome and how the compacted snow, if stored correctly, could last for months in purpose built ice houses. The straw, the ice blocks, in this slick modern house, seemed like such an archaic touch. Every few days I would need to replenish the refrigerator in the kitchen with a new block.

Tonight I would cook a rabbit ragout, red wine, tinned tomatoes, olive oil and garlic would make this a hearty meal for us to share.

A pantry stocked by a pie maker explained the sack of flour. I suppose that was the only way Joe bought it. Pasta, bread, I could make it all. I remembered how much Paul had loved it when I made bread and how much those loaves contributed to the money I had hoarded during my marriage, during that bleak time not so long ago. Although Joe had done a good job stocking the pantry, I'd noticed no rising agents. Beer, I remembered, and made a slurry of flour and ale and put the paste in a warm spot near the stove. After about ten minutes the brew was bubbling away and I knew I had created a yeasty culture that could be used to make bread.

Keeping the oven stoked with firewood was another task I would have to remember, if I wanted to cook or take a hot shower. I busied myself with domestic chores, reminded of just how much time these simple tasks took when there was no electricity or a supermarket down the road.

Before the end of the day I drove back to the ravine and shot a few more rabbits, determined to rid the place of the destructive vermin. Adam returned just as I was burying the latest batch of carcasses.

'You been shooting again, Annie Oakley?'

'Huntin', shootin' and cooking,' I replied in my best cowgirl accent.

'Mmmm, smells good, I'm starving,' he said coming up behind and pulling me roughly into his arms. He smelled masculine, sweaty. It was intoxicating.

'It's dinner, but first you need to wash. I've run you a bath.'

He smiled and kissed me, then stripped off outside and walked naked along the deck to the bathroom. I noticed the deep tan of a man who had worked shirtless and thrilled at what holding that perfect virginal white ass would feel like, gripped in my hands, as we fucked. Just the thought of him, while I cooked, while I cleaned, while I ran his bath, had kept me in a state of arousal all day.

I felt such a deep sense of satisfaction as I surveyed the kitchen. Two golden loaves of bread and a pot of simmering ragout. The rabbit was almost done, so I moved it to a cooler part of the stove. I didn't want a repeat of last night.

Excited by the thought of his body, and tempted by what I had just seen, I stripped off and followed him. He was lying back in the bath, with his eyes closed. I quietly picked up the soap. He sighed with contentment as I massaged his broad, strong shoulders. I watched as his penis

191

stiffened and rose above the water. I walked to the front of the bath, then lifted my leg to the edge of the tub exposing my pink sex to his view. Seductively I rubbed the bubbles over my parted legs, then delicately used the soap to unfold my labia and teasingly insert the hard bar just a small way in. His chest rose as he breathed heavily, then, to my surprise he took his cock in his hand and firmly began to rub the length of his shaft until it reached full rigid thickness.

I climbed into the tub and slid my cunt easily down on him. He took the soap from my hand and lathered my back, moving along my spine until he reached my ass and soaped the cheeks that sat pertly above the water. Then with one slippery hand he slid the tip of his finger into my anus, my back arched in response to the slightly painful intrusion, then gradually as the tight muscle relaxed he eased the finger in further until I groaned in response to this new found pleasure. Then he rubbed his other hand down the cleft of my buttocks and assertively entered me with a second finger. The pain was more intense this time, but again, as the muscle began to accommodate the stretching, my pleasure senses took over. With his fingers now deeply anchored inside me, he began to deliberately push me forcefully onto his cock, his hips rearing to greet the action of his hands and I relished this exquisite new sensation. He thrust faster, his pounding more brutal as he worked our bodies together in perfect synchronicity, and spectacularly brought me to a shattering, climax, rolling over my body in wave after wave of indescribable ecstasy.

'I need you... I love you,' I whispered breathlessly, barely audible.

'I have always loved you,' he panted, holding me tightly in his strong embrace.

A Cold Day In

Pulling the covers a little higher, I woke to a dull, wet, day. I looked over at my handsome lover and watched him peacefully sleeping. Walking to the kitchen, I was taken aback by the intensity of the cold Arctic blasts of wind shooting along the deck. Sleet peppered the rain, hitting my skin like icy needles as I scurried to the kitchen. Adam had loaded the Aga with firewood before we went to sleep, and I could see the fading glow of the dying embers as I re stoked the fire. All my clothes were getting very dirty. Walking around naked on this freezing cold day was almost as insane as driving through the Tasmanian wilderness alone. I scooted back to our bedroom and put on one of Adam's shirts. It covered me enough to take the edge off the chill as I waited for the kettle to boil.

Last night was very special. For the first time, I told Adam I loved him. I had never said this to any man before. I thought I would feel vulnerable, exposed, but was surprised at how contented I felt when, finally, I let Adam know of my true feelings toward him. I wanted to shower him with affection and nurture him with love and food. We had hungrily wolfed down the meal last night and he marvelled at my ability to create such a splendid feast.

'I love you for your body. I love you for your mind and I love you even more for your food!' he had declared last night as we ate.

The kettle whistled, I made a pot of tea, boiled some eggs and found butter and strawberry jam for the toast, adding it to the breakfast tray, before taking it back to feed the man waiting in my bed.

He had woken and I found him piling logs into the fireplace at the end of the room. He was also naked and I noticed his early morning erection had not yet subsided. So sexy. I hadn't thought about warming the space until now, as the weather had been glorious. I understood why he had designed the room to be a series of smaller cells as heating the whole space in a freezing Tasmanian winter would be difficult. Today was just a temperamental spring cold snap. I looked forward to spending the day inside this well lit, big room, in front of the fire, watching the panoramic views of the wild weather outside. Protected in this big glass case, with the man I loved.

I put the tray on the bedside table and crawled back under the covers, waiting for the fire to take hold. I removed the dirty shirt and thought tomorrow I would take the clothes down to the river to be washed. Within minutes the fire was blazing and Adam came back to bed. We sat together and ate, occasionally playfully feeding each other. Adam took the jar of jam, dipped his finger in and smeared some of the bright red fruit on my nipples and hungrily licked them clean. He gave me a sweet jammy kiss and I put the tray down on the floor.

'You got up before me. I woke needing to fuck you. I was dreaming about you!' he said lustfully.

'I wanted to cook for you, feed you,' I responded.

The room was warming up now and I kicked off the covers, exposing his body spread languorously across the white cotton sheets. His cock was sleepily nestled amongst dark curls of pubic hair. He watched curiously as I took the glass jar from his hands, spooned the merest drop of jam on the tip of his penis, then delicately used my finger to smear it all over the now protruding head. The jam oozed into the slit and folds of skin and deftly I used my tongue to penetrate every contour licking it all off. Then I scooped out a small handful and used the sticky sweet nectar as a lubricant, wrapping my fingers firmly around his now fully aroused cock, stroking harder and faster till he closed his eyes and groaned with pleasure. He was close to coming, so I leaned down and licked the glistening head with my mouth and sucked, taking him deep into my throat. I felt a slight pulsation in the thick vein along the shaft and within seconds he spurted into my mouth. He ran his fingers through my hair and stroked my face as I lay there, against his belly, with him in my mouth until he softened. He took my hand and licked all the fingers clean, then took me into his arms, holding me close, kissing away the last traces of sweetness.

Eventually we got up and showered together in the completely open bath room, the scorchingly hot water tempered by the icy blasts of the rain and the wind raging around us on this wild stormy morning. We raced back to the shelter of the bedroom and dried each other in front of the fire. He found some clean sheets and remade the bed. It must have been quite early, as we both soon drifted back to sleep.

Awoken by his kisses, enfolded in the warmth of his arms, I gazed into the face of this man whose love had completely and utterly claimed me. How long, I wondered, would we be able to live like this? This isolated utopia, could not last forever. My eyes welled with tears as the truth of the future invaded my mind.

'What's wrong?' he whispered, wiping the tears and the loose strands of hair from my face.

'How do we do this when we get back home? Your brother, those women, our lives.'

'I know,' was all he said, his eyes pleading for answers, as we lay silently together.

Adam was the first to speak.

'Those women, I'm afraid to say, I used them. None of them meant anything to me. I wanted you to see them, the photographs, I wanted to hurt you. You are the only woman I have ever loved.'

'My treatment of you that morning, my brother's behavior, was unforgivable. It's a pattern I don't know how to break. I hate that it took me those few days to realise I had to apologise in person, and I hated that I took so long to get to LA, only to find you had moved on. Seeing you in that man's arms almost killed me. After that day, I retreated back into the cold, disengaged behavior that had protected me for most of my life.'

'The last ten months have been torture. Seeing you with Raphael, getting small bits of information from Davina, not knowing how to fix up this mess. I knew you were in Hobart, Davina had mentioned it. I came to the opening of that photographic show hoping you'd be there, that I could pretend to bump into you, away from Melbourne, away from the people who got in our way.'

The sadness and vulnerability of this man was raw and painful for me to witness.

'I came here, to Lands End, looking to connect with you. I imagined what it would be like being here with you, but didn't know how I could make this fantasy happen,' I sobbed.

He held me close.

'How can we have a life together? I can't make you choose,' I pleaded.

'I have already chosen. A life without you would be impossible for me.'

We kissed and the tears of relief flowed, no more words were said, we just lay there holding each other and made gentle love. I needed him to be inside me, as physically close as possible, his cock filling me, his tongue in my mouth, our bodies intertwined, embracing and fucking till the desperation ceased.

Muse

The wind was still howling. We ate lunch and then retreated back to the long bedroom. Adam put more logs on the fire, keeping us warm enough to remain unclothed. I lay back on the bed and decided to spend the remainder of the day reading. For a long time I watched as he just sat at the window and stared at the wild coastline outside.

The warm room, wine at lunch, I nodded off.

I woke to a room strewn with sheets of paper. His empty armchair facing the bed. I didn't quite understand what I saw. There were drawings depicting me in various states of repose. The pictures were very good, dark charcoal sketches, subtle shadows where the sheets draped over my slumbering body. There was something highly erotic about being drawn whilst asleep, oblivious of the artist at work.

His footsteps could be heard, he was coming back to the room. I wanted this to continue and pretended to still be asleep. I heard him pick up the sketch pad and he sat back down in the chair. I moved slightly, just enough to let the sheet slip from my breast. Scratching sounds of charcoal scuffling across the paper told me Adam liked the new pose.

After some time I rolled over onto my stomach, my backside completely uncovered, the sounds of his sketching continued. My heart was racing as, next, I slightly opened my legs, tempting him with a glimpse of what had been hidden. He continued to draw and, as I heard the sound of another sheet of paper being ripped from the pad, I slid my knee along the sheets to expose the folds between my legs. I heard him groan and wondered whether he could see the subtle changes in the skin as my sex engorged. Footsteps across the room and the sensation of someone sitting on the bed. He opened my legs wider and continued to draw. Another sheet ripped then I felt his fingers take my inner lips, tugging them until they stood out, distended and swollen.

He then rolled me onto my back and I stretched out languidly, arms above my head, knees bent and my legs sprawled open, another groan and a rush of air as he breathed deeply. The scratching of the charcoal even more frenetic. When the next sheet of paper was ripped away, I put my hands between my legs. I stroked my cunt, spreading my lips to expose fully the delicate pink skin, my eyes still closed to keep the mystery of this game alive. The charcoal tore across the page until he could take no more, tossing the pad across the room, grabbing my slippery wet hand and placing it around his stiff dripping cock. Quickly I guided him into me, wrapping my legs tightly around his back, drawing him in close, pulling him down onto my aching clitoris and fucking as frantically as he had sketched. Sex with this man was extraordinary and my appetite for it was insatiable. I wanted to stay in his bed forever.

That night the sky cleared and we watched through the windows as the stars twinkled brightly. The storm had passed.

Anniversary

The sun was up and a faint northerly breeze heralded an unusually hot spring day. I had enjoyed padding around naked yesterday and liked the idea of doing the same today. All the clothes and sheets needed washing. Doing the laundry naked seemed quite practical, if I was going to go down into the river to scrub. But I also had another idea. I prepared him omelettes and we ate the last of the bread.

'What are your plans for today?' I asked, noticing the tool pouch he had left on the bench.

'The wind did quite a bit of damage. There are trees down, the wire around the nursery has come loose, some of the awnings need tightening. Just general maintenance around the place. How about you?'

'Well, I thought I should do some washing, drive down to the river. I saw a place where the ravine wasn't too steep. The muddiness has cleared and I want to use fresh water, my dress is still as stiff as a board after washing it in the salty lagoon.'

'I'll come with you. I want to see if I can salvage any of the timbers from the bridge.'

'There's one more thing,' I said smiling.

'What?' he asked, a little puzzled.

'I've been thinking about dates. I've got no idea what day it is today, but I think it's about the first week in November, and it's my birthday,' I said

'Oh fuck, Tina, I had no idea, I'm sorry.'

'No, no, please don't apologise, I hate birthdays. What I do remember is that the day after my birthday I went to that book launch in King Street and...,' before I could finish, with the realisation of what I was about to say, he picked me up in his arms and kissed me passionately.

'Happy anniversary, Adam,' I said smiling, feeling such love and joy that we were here, together.

'My God, it was a year ago. Best book launch pick up I've ever had,' he said with a cheeky grin.

'We should celebrate,' he said enthusiastically.

'Yes, we should, but I've already got you a gift. Put your tool belt on.'

Again he looked puzzled and ridiculously sexy, shirtless, wearing only jeans, the leather kit hanging from his lean hips. I put the small bottle I'd found in the bathroom into the pouch.

'What's this for?' he said, reaching for the unfamiliar object in the pouch.

'It's coconut massage oil.'

'Why?'

'You'll need it if you're going to use your present today.'

'And what present might that be?' he asked, still completely confounded by my cryptic game.

'The present is me!' I said letting the towel I'd been wearing drop to the floor, effectively unwrapping his gift.

'Today I will not wear a scrap of clothing. I will be available to you all day, to fuck whenever and wherever you choose. Your gift to me is that I want to be taken by surprise, no warning, no foreplay. The coconut oil is for you to rub onto your hard cock so you are ready to take me, to pour over my cunt, so that I can receive you.'

I looked at the shocked expression on his face and saw his erection pushing at his jeans. He obviously liked the idea.

'Ahh... can we start now?' he begged.

'No, because it wouldn't be a surprise and that is what I lust after.'

Adam took the Jeep to the bridge. I would follow once I had collected the dirty laundry. As I was loading the car, I remembered I needed to make bread. If I prepared the dough now, it would have the chance to rise while I was at the river. I peeled back the cloth covering the starter culture and was pleased it was still alive, bubbling away nicely. I halved some for today's bread, the remainder to be fed with some more beer, flour and sugar for the next batch. There was something so satisfying about making bread. The kneading, the rising, the forming of the dough, the smell of it baking. Trance like I stood over the floured bench and vigorously worked the dough with my hands, kneading until it had just the right elastic texture.

I gasped as his hard oiled cock rammed into me. He took me from behind holding my belly as he began to pound. I bent forward to take him deeper, my cunt coming alive with the thrill of his first surprise encounter. His voice hoarse as he spoke of how much he loved me and that he could do this all day. We climaxed quickly and sunk onto the bench desperately panting for breath, my breasts landing in the soft pillow of dough. He turned me around, kissed me, and fled across the deck.

'See you soon, wench!' he called out as he departed.

Breathless, I retrieved the dough and put it into the bowl, doubting whether I would need the coconut oil, his cum, the juices of my arousal and the excitement of expectation would be enough.

I found him at the bridge crawling precariously along the frame, inspecting the structure. I felt fearful for his safety as he slowly crossed to the other side, relieved when he eventually got there. Where he stood, on the opposite side of the river, was a twenty kilometre walk away from the main road. He looked around, checking the flooded land, surveying the distant horizon, the outside world. What was he thinking about? Was he trying to come to terms with our imminent return? He turned and made the slow, dangerous crawl back. I breathed a sigh of relief as he finally stepped back onto our side of the river, safely into my arms, back to our sanctuary.

'What do you think? Can it be fixed? Could we ever get the cars across?'

'The bridge is nothing more than a steel frame, the structure seems sound, but it will take a lot of time and work to attach enough planks for us to drive over it safely,' he answered.

I was happy to stay longer, he could take all the time in the world.

After gallantly helping me carry the washing to a natural rock pool formed at the water's edge, I watched him drive off, leaving me alone with just the sound of the water gurgling across the rocks. The sun felt good on my back as I scrubbed. This was a lengthy task, the sheets were awkward to wash. I thought about how much time our great grandmothers would have spent doing what is now usually such an easy job.

I remember asking my mother why some of the old bushmen that came past the farm always smelt so strange and she said that they didn't wash very often and got used to the smell of their own sweat. Had people lost their scent? Have we washed away the pheromones humans used to instinctively choose a mate? Is this why the sex with Adam had been so intense? Were we simply responding to an innate desire previously hidden, washed away, one that gave us no choice about the deep attraction we had for one another? My body was responding as if I had no control. My sex seemed to be in a constant state of arousal whenever I was near him. I had to stop thinking about him, stop daydreaming about what I wanted him to do to me or I would never complete even this most simple task.

I focused on the sheets. Doing these repetitive tasks gave me time for contemplation. I knew I needed to think about how we could make this, us, work. We had spent so little time together in Melbourne and now, even though it had only been a few days, it felt like we had been a couple forever. We had slotted into a matrimonial nirvana as if it was the most natural thing in the world. Maybe my new house could replace what we had found here? Could it be a sanctuary for both of us? By now Davina would be close to completion. The house could be ours to share, the island wasn't the only place to escape to, to feel safe. I needed to make this work.

Momentarily distracted, I looked up. Was that a vehicle I could hear? Not the Jeep, a different sound coming from the other side of the river. I listened more intently, but the noise had become indistinct. It was possible that vehicles would use the track, just highly unlikely in this sparsely populated part of the world. Nobody knew of our plight, so a search party was just as implausible. Perhaps it was it coming from Lands End? The sound seemed very close, as it was carried by the north wind. Perhaps my hearing was just a little bit more acute, without the white noise of a bustling city to deaden the senses.

The strawberry stains on the sheets needed a more brisk scrub. I found a smooth rock and spread them out, lathered up the brush and scrubbed until the red turned to pink and the stains started to fade.

First the sweet smell, then the luscious sensation of the warm coconut oil running down my buttocks, a firm hand sliding forcefully between my legs, pushing them apart, his hand quickly replaced by the brute strength of his thickened cock keenly opening me up. I arched my back and he lifted me from behind, his strong muscular arms tucked under my knees, holding my back against his firm belly. Fucking me in this new position, I felt his cock rubbing hard against my anus as he punished my cunt, deeper than any penetration before, pounding my womb, reaching my very core. He grunted with each thrust and I held on tightly, submitting to his control, until our bodies shook with the sheer physicality of the orgasm that ensued, sweat dripping from his body, his cock pumping me full of his cum.

He let my legs down slowly and I stood up, on tip toes, still impaled by his engorged penis. As he softened he naturally withdrew, and a stream of his fluid ran down my leg. He took my hand and led me to the rock pool where he gently washed me, the cool water soothing against my burning swollen sex.

And that would be the pattern of the afternoon. Woken from my afternoon nap, being spooned, cocooned against his warm chest, and filled with his hard dick. Taken on the forest floor, after he watched me piss. Fucked missionary style, late that afternoon, as I lay on the beach.

The sun was beginning to set. Too cool to be lying naked on the sand, time to finish this wonderful day. A white poster could be seen on the tree at the forest's edge. It was one of the sketches, *The Bath is Waiting*, he had written.

The bath was full, scattered with acacia and gum flowers. Another note placed on the towel told me to take my time.

When You Have Finished, Follow the Path into the Forest.

And after a long soak, I did as he asked. The dusk light showed a new path, strewn with more acacia flowers, and as I ventured further into the forest, candles illuminated the way.

At a small clearing I stopped and before me I saw the shrine he had created. A bed, canopied by the fine white mosquito net, the freshly laundered sheets on a soft pile of fern fronds, blankets and pillows, scattered, harem like, across the expanse of white cotton. I sat down on the bed inside the gauzy tent and waited, not knowing what to expect. The silence was interrupted by the occasional sounds of birds, and the faint rustling of the night creatures. I sat alone for what seemed a long time and was starting to wonder if I should stay, when I heard the crunch of twigs underfoot. My heart raced with expectation. His hand parted the curtain and he stood, naked, before me, his finger to his lips, gesturing for me to remain silent. He drizzled the last of the coconut oil down his belly, into his curly black pubic hair, slowly trickling down his soft penis. A surge of blood heated my cunt as I began to understand what he was about to do. He picked up his cock and very slowly began to rub. Longer strokes signalled him stiffening, preparing himself, as he had done during the day. The oil glistened in the candlelight and I watched as his cock rose proud, thick and ready. My body was reacting spontaneously to this deliberate slow ritual and I opened my legs, letting my fingers part my lips, toying with my swollen sex, coating my hand with the warm wetness. I saw his chest rise as he breathed heavily with expectation. He knelt down in front of my parted thighs, then gradually moved his slick chest up my belly and against my breasts, stopping when his hungry mouth met mine. His hard cock slipped easily into me, my muscles clenched around him. He held my ass pulling me closer, pushing deeper and thrusting, slowly, deliberately till my body came alive in rapturous ecstasy. Soon after I felt the uncontrolled pulsation of his own powerful orgasm.

'Happy anniversary,' he whispered, holding me close.

That night we slept the sleep of the deeply sated, under the canopy of the trees, beneath the big southern sky.

The Bridge

Another sunny day greeted us, the earthy smell of the forest filling my lungs, birdsong welcoming us awake.

We walked back to the shack hand in hand, like wood nymphs emerging from the forest.

It was a clear, crisp morning, too cool to continue my bare bodied adventure and anyway I needed to wear work clothes, as today I would help Adam gather the timber so we could make rudimentary repairs to the bridge.

After a hearty breakfast we drove to the ravine. Adam showed me the scant pile of timber he had collected. We would have to try and salvage more logs that had fallen deeper into the ravine if we were to have the slightest chance of making the bridge passable.

All day we worked, Adam tying planks to ropes attached to the Jeep. Me driving, hauling them up the steep sides then unhitching and tossing the ropes back down to Adam.

The work was back breaking. We barely had the energy to cook, but if we were going to complete the task we needed to eat. The pantry was looking bare. I hadn't had time to make bread or cook more rabbit, tiredness left me uninspired.

Tonight the tinned beans were all I could muster. With sore muscles and spent bodies, we collapsed, exhausted into bed and slept, without sex. I felt a touch of sadness.

The next day we started early, the odd dark cloud made us aware of the unpredictable nature of the weather. We would have to work quickly or risk losing it all again with the next big downpour.

More of the hard slog of retrieving the planks deep in the ravine. This was dangerous work that became more precarious as we tried to extricate the most deeply embedded planks. As a snake slithered past, more frightened of us, I realised how vulnerable we were. We could eat, had water, but were miles away from any help if either of us were injured or got sick. Slowly the flaws in our escapist fantasy started to appear.

We barely spoke, just continued to repeat this arduous process, too tired for conversation. Our nerves were frayed by sheer exhaustion.

By sunset we had almost gathered enough timber and, as had been the routine of that long day, I drove cautiously dragging last piece of wood up the steep cliff. I sensed a slight resistance and thought I needed to apply a bit more power, when I heard the chilling sound of the rope whipping through the air, the echoing of the thuds as the plank crashed against the rocks, splashing into the river below.

'Jesus fuckin' Christ, didn't you feel the strain!' roared Adam, his voice filled with rage.

I looked down and saw him holding his arm, wincing in pain. I scuttled down the steep path, scared of what injury I might find, fearful that I had no plan. The rope had lashed its way across his skin, opening up the flesh, leaving a raw bleeding gash. The sleeve of his shirt, torn open at the site of the cut, ripped away easily, exposing only a shallow wound. I said a silent prayer of thanks, as I bound the cloth around the cut to staunch the flow of blood. I felt guilty for not being more observant, for screwing up and started apologising like some kowtowing serf. He stormed back up the path and got into the truck, tyres spinning in the dust as he tore off. I followed, ashamed at my idiocy, but aware I needed to put my feelings aside. I had to clean and dress the wound, make sure this situation didn't get any worse.

'Here, let me do that, it needs to be cleaned,' I said, as I found him attempting to rip the edge of the sheet, one corner in his mouth, pulling at the cloth trying to make a bandage.

The rudimentary first aid kit had the basics. I washed the wound in antiseptic and bound the arm with the improvised dressing.

'Fuck, Christina, you've got to be more careful! Any little slip could cost one of us our lives. Didn't you hear me yelling out for you to stop? All you had to do was drive. I'm the one doing all the hard work. This isn't some kind of game we're playing at, I'm trying to get us out of here...ALIVE!'

The anger had returned.

Another sexless night, his back facing me, telling me, 'don't touch'.

Beans for dinner and breakfast, another day, racing against the weather to fix the bridge.

His behaviour reminded me of the Adam I had witnessed the day after he'd dragged me out of the car, surly, barely being able to tolerate my presence. He had a vile temper. I remembered his road rage, his outburst when the restaurant was closed, when his brother kept ringing and when he called me a bitch on Boxing Day. He needed to be in control. Didn't know how to cope when things didn't go to plan.

And instead of confronting him I retreated into my old submissive self. Behaving drone like as he barked new commands, fearful that he might erupt again if I didn't obey him or do the job right. I hated what this did to us, hated what it made me become. I didn't know how to make it better.

There was so much work to do. For the first time, I wanted the bridge to be finished, I wanted out. We had to lift each of the weighty timbers onto the rail like track spanning the frame. Adam could then secure them with fencing wire he found tangled up with the debris at the bottom of the ravine. Each plank would take ages. There was only one set of pliers. Adam knelt down and I watched as he carefully twisted the wire, binding the wood to the steel frame with an engineer's precision. First plank fixed and he kicked it with his boot to see how firmly it sat. The wood didn't budge, the crossing would be possible. This was not a quick process and I could see we wouldn't be leaving soon. I felt useless, standing there watching, not knowing what to do.

'Does this look like enough fucking wire to tie up these planks?' he yelled, pointing to the meagre lengths he'd cut.

'Don't just stand there, I'll need a shit load more than this.'

Chastised, I climbed back down into the ravine, to the tangled mess, and began scavenging for more wire. Luckily it didn't take long to find a whole coil. It was rusty, but not so badly corroded that it couldn't be used. I took my find up to Adam hoping for praise. He chucked a pair of cutting snips at me and went back to his job.

When that was done he told me to help him lift the remaining planks into place. He would stay and wire them up himself. When all the wood was finally down, we saw that the timber barely covered half the bridge. Even with gaps in between, it was painfully obvious we had nowhere near enough. We would have to go back down and search even harder. This project was going to take way longer than we thought.

When my usefulness had expired, I returned to the shack, leaving him alone with his temper, upset by his imperious attitude, furious at my response. Why had I retreated into this behavior? It troubled me that I didn't stand up to him. It wasn't my fault the rope had snapped. I couldn't hear him, didn't know how to read his mind.

Sitting in the clearing where, just a few nights ago, we had made passionate love, I began to think about the reality of being with this man. I hated the sting of his anger, the rejection of the last two nights. I didn't know how to deal with it. Anger was an emotion Adam resorted to when he had no control. It was an emotion I had almost no experience of. My parents adored me. My marriage was a relationship of indifference, very little emotion was shown, let alone anger. My mind started to race. Could I think about building a life with someone like this? Could I live with my own reactions and all the insecurities it brought out? Over the last two days, my self confidence had all but evaporated. I longed to get back to Melbourne, to the people and the job I loved. I missed my daughter and wished to pick up a phone just to hear her voice. The bridge needed to be finished. I had to return home and stop pretending this utopia was real.

I buried my head in my hands and wept. I had hated being alone in my marriage and couldn't contemplate another relationship where I was being continually shut out.

Adam would be back at dusk and I needed to get things sorted before he returned. I ate a solitary meal then emptied a tin of beans into the saucepan. He would be hungry, but I didn't want to cook for him and sit with him, face his hostile silence. He could sleep in his swag and I dragged it onto the deck, not wanting another night of being shunned in our bed. I showered away the filth of the day and took myself on a long walk, the bright moon shimmering across the water, lighting the way.

He had understood my signals and was fast asleep on the deck when I returned. The bedroom would be mine, alone. I pulled back the covers and saw where the blood from his arm had seeped onto the sheets. The big bed seemed so empty.

He was gone by the time I got up.

Today I would clean, do the household chores, bake some bread to distract myself from the sadness and pain this needless fight had caused. I stripped the sheets. This time I washed them in the bath. No more idiotic scrubbing in the creek like some third world romantic. The blood stains were difficult to remove, I felt like a virgin cleaning away the necessary evidence of a torrid wedding night, perhaps sharing doubts, like a young bride, about what the future might hold.

And like yesterday, I disappeared before he returned. I couldn't face him. It seemed we had created an emotional impasse that neither of us was prepared to break. This was becoming a pattern.

The moon was waning, the sky less bright. I entered the bedroom from the opened glass door, on the forest side, keen not to pass him on the deck. I could just make out the outline of his rumpled bedding near the kitchen. The lamps were off. He must already be asleep. His oversized clothes slid easily off my body and I crawled into bed. The sorrow of loneliness swept me up and I sobbed into the pillow.

Calmer, but wide awake, I listened to the soothing night chorus, cicadas, crickets, distant birds calling across the water. I lay awake, wondering if sleep would ever come.

'I'm sorry,' were the words I heard hoarsely spoken from the hunters chair at the front of the room.

Startled, I looked toward the direction of the voice and saw him sitting there, faintly illuminated by the moonlight. He had heard my pitiful sobs, I felt exposed. This is what I feared. Adam got up and walked across the room, sat on the bed, and paused, head in hands.

'I resent having to build that fucking bridge to get out. I don't want to leave. I don't know how we do this when we get back. Deal with my brother, my anger. I've never been this close to someone. I'm used to being alone, it's always been easier that way,' he said quietly, then continued.

'I'm sorry I spoke to you like that. It wasn't your fault. I was mad at myself for letting such a stupid thing happen, I'm sorry I took my frustration out on you.'

He paused.

'Please forgive me'

I was still upset, didn't know how to surrender the hurt and despondency that had been building since the accident. I lay still, numb, broken. He moved closer, his hand reached out tentatively, brushing my hair away from my face. I opened my eyes and saw the sadness, pain and remorse in his eyes. I cried at how vulnerable love had made me become. He swept me up in his arms, onto his broad chest, holding me close, quietly touching my body, caressing as if he were discovering me for the first time.

'I need you, you make me whole. Please don't push me away. What I did was stupid and unforgivable. Please Tina, let me back into your heart. I couldn't bear to lose you again.'

He gently kissed away the tears and I began to let go of the resentment of the last two days. I needed to feel his warmth, his strength, his physical presence. I looked into his eyes and knew I needed him back too. He held me close, enfolding me, not letting me go. His rhythmic breathing soon told me he was asleep. I hoped we could work this out, perhaps we just needed time.

I was awoken in the night by his kisses, still in his arms. We didn't need words, his body told the true story. His erection pressed against my belly and I reached out, easing him into me. Sensuously his tongue entered my mouth, filling me, making me whole. There was no heated fucking, just the reconnecting both of us so desperately missed. All night I felt the need for us to remain connected, being in his arms was not enough. When I felt the softening of his cock, I gently rocked against him squeezing my cunt, keeping him hard, inside me, close, his arms wrapped around, holding me tight.

This is how we spent the night.

The dappled light of dawn gently woke me. I lifted my head from his chest and looked at his sleeping face, peaceful, no sign of the anger that had so tormented him. I relaxed back down onto his body and happily felt the rousing of his early morning erection. As he woke, I let his cock slip back inside. Gently we made love until I gasped with the surprise of the orgasm which crept up and slowly engulfed my entire body.

'I need you more than you can possibly imagine,' he whispered.

'I need you too.'

Hunter Gatherer

We shared a happier breakfast and spoke about what we might do when we got back to Melbourne. This was the first time both of us had the courage to talk about our return, finally facing the reality that we could not hide away on our 'island' forever. We both had lives, people to come home to. We had barely spent more than a few days together last year before Justin had broken the magic of that new encounter. We needed to do normal things, go out, sleep in, learn to be together as a couple. Talk to each other about the past, discover things about each other. Much of the behavior of the last few days had arisen out of fear. A fear that had created much of the anger that so nearly drove us apart.

It was with a new enthusiasm that we both returned to the bridge that morning, talking about the things we would do when we got back home. We stopped for a break. I'd packed a lunch and we sat under a tree and talked.

'Penny for your thoughts?' asked Adam.

'The house, I'm thinking about what it will look like. Davina said it would be finished when I get back. I really want you to see it, I think you'd love it. I can't wait to show you.'

Adam confessed that he had been following the progress of the house and had been hoping I would eventually invite him in. He even said he had gone on a couple of site visits with Davina in the hope I might show up.

He asked about Raphael. I told him part of the story, that we were just good friends. His unease about the level of intimacy in my relationship with Raphael was obvious and it was all I could do to put his mind at rest.

'The last time I saw Raphael he was with a man, a man he'd fallen deeply in love with.'

I didn't need to elaborate on what had happened on our last encounter.

'God, I had no idea. Do his parents know?'

'Hardly, they are a family with its own problems. Both Lola and Raphael have created new lives for themselves in Italy, a place where they can be themselves, away from the scrutiny of others. Lola hates the pressure put on her to find a man who could live up to Massimo's unattainable high ideals, and I don't think Raphael could ever come out to his father. Massimo's possessiveness has pushed them both away. Even the most perfect families aren't always what they seem.'

'God, it's nice to know that it's not just me who has a fucked up family! I'd always envied what I thought the Finestras had.'

'I guess Massimo's roots are not that easily forgotten. I'm sure he thought he would be a proud grandfather by now. It's sad that this will probably never happen and ironic that his kids have only found happiness in the country he left behind.'

'It's hard to know when you stop being someone's son, daughter, brother, sister and become your own person. An adult who's broken the bonds and constraints of the family you grew up with,' he said contemplatively.

'I don't know what that's like, it's a burden I've never had.'

'I'm sorry, I forget about your parents, about you losing them.'

'I've often thought about how different my life would have been if they'd lived. I know marrying Paul was an attempt at trying to create a new family, to fill the massive void left after they died. I married him for all the wrong reasons.'

'Did you ever love him?'

'I hoped I would grow to love him. He was a good man, he did the right thing. But ultimately I couldn't fall in love with a man I didn't desire, had nothing in common with. I never felt accepted by his family or friends.'

'So why did you stay?'

'I didn't want Kate to grow up without her father being around. I wanted her to have a stable family life and economic security.'

'I understand,' he said, squeezing my hand. I lay my head in his lap, looked up at him and wondered what he was thinking. It would be so easy to stop, make love, not return to the bridge. But we both knew it was something that needed to be finished.

'We should get back to work, there's still so much to be done.'

I think we realised how stupid this game had been, both of us too stubborn to make the first move. This pig headed obstinance had already wasted a year of a possible life together.

Adam had made quite a bit of progress with the bridge, but the timber we had collected had finally run out and we needed to find more logs.

'There are some saplings I planted a few years ago,' he said, pointing to a grove of small trees.

We walked over to the young trees and realised they were just the right size and could be easily felled with the chainsaw.

'What a shame,' I said, rubbing my hands along the smooth bark of the juvenile trees.

'We can always plant more when we come back next spring,' said Adam and I smiled at the prospect of his elucidation of our future together.

Compared to retrieving the planks from the ravine, cutting this timber was relatively easy and after a long day's work we looked satisfyingly at the pile of logs that would easily finish the bridge.

Cooking was my way of showing Adam that I cared for him and loved him. I hadn't realised just how hollow denying this made me feel. I needed to nurture him, show him that my body was not the only manifestation of our love.

Even though we had worked hard all day, I approached the evening meal with a renewed vigour. I left Adam in the shower and headed to the kitchen to round up some food. We would sit and eat on the beach, watching the sunset, just like I'd fantasised about that first afternoon.

This was a special occasion and I took extra care, combing my hair, sweeping it up into an elegant knot and putting on the linen dress. I had not worn it since waking up in a dishevelled heap after the storm. I caught a glimpse in the mirror and was pleased with the result, glad to be out of the masculine clothes I'd been wearing, remembering how much I loved to dress up. My skin was tanned, my body lean, toned and healthy. I wanted to look special on our 'date night'.

There was still some Riesling left and I had put two bottles in the fridge that morning. A whole loaf of bread and some of Joe's pantry treats would make up the bulk of the picnic. Adam met me on the beach and was surprised at the repast I had created from our dwindling supplies.

'You look beautiful,' he said and I felt a deep tenderness that he had noticed.

'You are amazing. This food tastes delicious, I can't believe you had the energy to put this together after such a hard day,' he said lovingly to me.

'Close your eyes, I have a surprise. Open your mouth,' and with that I fed him an oyster.

'Yum, where did you find these?'

'They were growing on the rocks in the cove, not far from here. I discovered them on one of my walks. There are hundreds of them. We could live off them for weeks.'

They were fat and fresh with that delicious ozone, umami flavour that only the very freshest of oyster have.

'Mmm, they are the best oysters I have ever eaten. They taste so fresh, they smell of the sea, they smell of you. Of your beautiful just fucked cunt,' he said running his hand up my leg, discovering my concealed nakedness.

I looked at his handsome face and felt flushed with desire at his wicked observation.

'You are incorrigible, Mr. Darcy,' I said, removing his hand and feeding him another oyster.

'It's you, Ms Maxwell. How can I think about anything else when you sit there, feeding me oysters, wearing no underwear?'

We continued our picnic and lay on the rug. The sun was setting and I was here, watching it go down with Adam, contented and replete. As the air began to chill he wrapped the blanket around my shoulders.

Despite our conversations about going home it was still very clear to me that we hadn't talked about the real elephant in the room, about Justin and how we would deal with the complex relationship the brothers had. Emboldened by the alcohol I spoke.

'I've been thinking about your brother and I don't want you to exclude him from your life.'

Adam sat upright, obviously surprised by the conversation I had initiated. He looked perplexed.

'He's your brother and I think we could come up with a compromise that wouldn't inflame the situation.'

Adam listened closely as I told him how he could start to break the stranglehold by not being available when we were at my house. That it could be our sanctuary, a Justin free zone.

'You could be honest with him. I don't want you to lie to him and keep our relationship a secret, but you could ask for what you want, to be left alone when you're at my house.'

'But I want to be with you all the time.'

'I just don't think it's fair to cut him off. It could backfire and make the situation worse for all of us. Don't get me wrong, I don't want to be his friend. What he did to my family was unforgivable, but I do want you to still have a relationship with him. Margot told me about the incident at the station, when you were little kids. After the way your father behaved, I understand your need to look out for him.'

Adam sat there shaking his head.

'My fucking family, I should point you in the opposite direction and tell you to run.'

Adam started to open up.

'Justin was a bully, because my father was a bully. As a child, he'd never been good enough for my father. Justin couldn't read, he was dyslexic. He was teased mercilessly at school and would cop a vicious serve from my father when reports came home. I tried to protect him by helping with his school work and it was then that I discovered he had an almost genius ability with numbers, something that had been kept hidden. We would work together, me helping him with words and he astounding me with his ability to read numbers like stories.

Unfortunately the brutalisation had an impact and when puberty kicked in, he became an aggressive teenager. The school boys, who once teased him, now feared him. My father seemed to hold a sick pride in the weakling son who now ruled with his fists and verbal abuse. Justin had become just like our father.'

'My father was an arrogant asshole. He had many affairs while he was married to Mum. I'd hear him bragging to his mates. We were all pleased when he finally left. Mum, although humiliated and ashamed, seemed lost when it was over. I think the thought of being alone had scared her. Sometimes people stay in dysfunctional relationships because they know no other way. They had married when she was young, her father didn't really approve. Dad wasn't one of them, but she was determined to prove her parents wrong. I think she thought she was in love, but maybe she was just quietly rebelling, charmed by this smooth talking man who could give her the escape from the straight jacketed life she was living. She would staunchly defend him, she was loyal even though everyone knew what was going on. It was quite pathetic to watch.'

'So what happened after your father left?' I asked.

'She got worse, leaned on me more heavily. I became like a surrogate husband, and the burden of my family grew.'

'But you obviously became independent eventually. We hardly saw you after uni.'

'Once Justin got his degree and found work, I knew I didn't have to be around to keep an eye on him so much. Fiona stepped in, she filled the gap and they seemed to be doing well enough. Like I said, he was good with numbers and accounting gave him his entry into the world of finance. He worked for a firm of stockbrokers before he went into business with Paul.'

'And your mother, how did she take your absence? You lived overseas for most of the time Paul and Justin were in business together.'

'Not real good, she drank pretty heavily. I sent her money, paid for her to go to some expensive clinics when she got really bad.'

'So what made you come home?'

'Felt like I was being drawn back. I'd just finished 'The Imperial', had built the penthouse and had somewhere to live. I realised I'd spent most of my adult life away, had nowhere to call home. Melbourne seemed like the right place to be. Mum was stable, Justin seemed to be doing good things with the business and Dad had moved to Greece. I felt for the first time I could live here without being quite so burdened by my family.'

He paused and I wondered what he was thinking about.

'And there was you.'

'But you did nothing.'

'I didn't know where to start. You were a grieving widow. I didn't how much time should pass before I could approach you and then that shit storm with your husband's company hit. Justin tried to tell me there weren't any real problems, just a cash flow situation. He inferred that you were making things difficult and I didn't want to get involved. It wasn't until after that gallery opening that I thought I should have a closer look and realised what a mess my brother had created. Gambled everything on that one Cambodian deal. Was paying ridiculous sums of money to bribe corrupt officials who supposedly gave him inside information on big infrastructure projects. He'd invested everything in the company that was going to be given the rights to build roads and railways in Cambodia. No one expected the company to withdraw, but when it did, it was too late for my brother. He'd gambled everything he had.'

'So why did you step in?'

'At first I was reluctant, but the more Justin spoke about the asset that was your house, and how it's sale could rescue him and the company, the closer I knew I needed to look. And then there was you. You suddenly kept turning up and I realised if my brother kept up his attack, I would never have even the slightest chance of being with you. It was after that night at Gabriella's gallery that I decided to act.'

'Yeah, I remember that night very well.'

We had been fighting a long protracted legal battle with Justin over the validity of the will. My lawyer, Ruth, was prepared to attack, but it looked like we were fighting a losing battle. All my money was being poured into the case, and I was beginning to wonder if it was ever going to end. Suddenly Ruth had called to say it was all over. I would keep the house, an undisclosed buyer for the company had been found. Finally I would be free of that scheming bastard and his intrusion into my life. We were both very surprised.

And then it dawned on me.

'Was it you? Did you buy out Paul's company?'

'I did. If the company had gone bankrupt, Justin might never have been able to work again. Numbers were all he knew.'

'But I have to be honest with you and tell you that my reasons weren't just to rescue him. I'd hated the way they were treating you. I wanted them to give up the fight for the house and leave you and your daughter alone.'

'I thought it would free you to grieve in private and move on with your life.'

I took his hand, intertwining my fingers with his, pulling him closer, tears running down my cheeks, as I realised the intense compassion of this man. He had put an end to the continual intrusion of court cases and legal battles that had been draining me emotionally and financially.

'I also hoped that one day we might be able to be together. That eventually enough time would pass, that you might consider me a friend.'

We held each other close.

'I love you so much,' I whispered.

My heart raced as I woke to screeching, hissing sounds and pots clanging in the kitchen. We both sat up in bed with a start and as our eyes adjusted, we could see a large brushtail possum, scavenging for food, defending its territory. Adam got up and tried to shoo the noisy creature away, but after continual interruption to our sleep, he finally took the drastic action of grabbing the gun, shooting some rounds into the air to scare the creature off. He kept the loaded gun next to the bed just in case the annoying animal returned.

We worked together the following morning to haul the next load of logs onto the bridge. This was a much more cumbersome task as the round logs, unlike the flat planks, did not sit easily. They tended to roll along on the metal frame. Eventually he worked out how to secure the logs with wooden wedges and once again we were back on track to finish the bridge.

Adam worked with a new found sense of determination. Last night's conversation had revealed so much more about him and seemed to have lifted an emotional weight off his shoulders. Getting home would be good. For the first time I could envision a life with Adam and felt encouraged that I could begin to cope with the ominous presence of the delinquent brother.

After lunch there was very little I could do. I left Adam to continue securing the logs and headed off on my own mission. Along with the oysters, there were mussels, sea spinach and in some of the more swampy parts of the cove and abundance of samphire, a salty almost asparagus like plant. I had read of the latest foraging craze amongst the food hardliners of Melbourne and was surprised at what I had so easily found. Amused at the situation I had found myself in, really needing to hunt and gather.

Back in the kitchen, I would make a seafood pasta, tossing the greens in at the end to provide us with a bit of vegetable matter that was severely lacking in our diet. The pantry yielded up the last of the olive oil, dried chilli and garlic. The supply of eggs had finished and the task at hand was to make the pasta with just flour and water. Making the dough was easy, the secret in getting it to taste like pasta was in the amount of salt needed for the boiling water. I remembered discovering that to produce perfect boiled shrimp, sea water was the best. This is what I used for the pasta and was pleased with the result.

All would be ready to cook for my man when he returned from the bridge.

The setting was perfect. The house had been cleaned, the table was ready. I had decided to treat Adam to a massage and had placed candles and the last of the coconut oil in the bedroom. My body responded lustily to the thought of what new heights our lovemaking might reach that night.

By sunset I decided to drive to the bridge to help him finish up. More selfishly, I was also excited to show him the feast I had prepared. I loved the way he responded to my primal domesticity and contemplated that a little pre dinner sex was worth bringing him home early for. From a distance I could see the awkward angle he had positioned himself in. His muscles must be aching, I thought of the massage I would give him.

'Hey, you coming home tonight or am I sleeping alone?' I yelled playfully walking down the approach to the bridge.

No answer.

As I got closer, I realised he wasn't moving. His leg was twisted at a strange angle, his body lay flat, his arm dangled over the edge. My heart raced and I felt sick at what I was witnessing. He groaned, he was alive, but his leg was badly broken. I could see bone protruding from a bloody gash on his shin. I could see that his leg had slipped between two of the logs. I had no idea how long he had been like this, but he was barely conscious and I knew I had to get him back to the shack.

'Adam, Adam, stay with me, you have to help me. You need to get up.'

He winced in agony as I released the log trapping his leg. He had enough strength to roll over and get into a sitting position and at a painstakingly slow pace he was eventually able to get up, leaning on me as he stood on his one good leg. I found a small limb to act as a crutch and we made the arduous walk back to the Jeep. He slowly climbed into the back and after what seemed like an interminable amount of time we finally arrived at the shack.

With the same amount of difficulty I got him onto our bed. The break was bad. I cleaned away the blood and bound the wound. He was shivering with shock and cold. I wrapped him warmly in blankets and lay next to him, awake all night in sheer terror at the thought of the impossible situation we were in and that he might not make it. I knew I would have to crawl over the bridge and make the long walk to the main road to try and get help. The painkillers seemed to make him more lucid and he understood that I had prepared as best as possible to attempt the walk ahead of me. Leaving Adam was my biggest concern. He was warm and I had put together food and water to last for several days, stockpiled by the side of his bed.

I calculated the walk would take at least ten hours across the rough terrain to the main road, maybe overnight. With as much food and water as my small day pack could carry, and wearing the ridiculously inadequate leather flats, I drove to the ravine.

The walk across the partially completed bridge was easy, the crawl on all fours along the metal frame, to the end was terrifying, but I knew it was the only way out. The mist of early morning fog made the rails slippery, the pack kept leaning to one side, distorting my sense of balance. I looked down and saw that the river, cleared of logs, had turned back into a fast moving torrent. If I slipped I would be quickly washed out to sea. My determination to get help made me want to race to the end. The continual sliding reminded me of that disconcerting feeling I remembered as a kid, when my bare feet would slip against the smooth bark of the tree I was climbing. Experiencing the prickling of pins and needles with the sudden rush of adrenalin from the soles of my feet to my tingling fingertips. Slowly, slowly I edged along. The mist turned to a greying drizzle. My hands became blue as I gripped the cold steel. Turning back was not an option.

Finally I crawled onto land. I had reached the other side. Now it would only be a matter of time before I got to the road. The sweater I was wearing was saturated. If I took it off and walked fast enough I would warm up. It drove me to go harder.

Time is such an abstract thing when you have no way of measuring it. As is distance and direction. The rain was now coming down hard. Heavy cloud blocked out the sun, the water and the flood damage obscured the road and I was only faintly convinced I was heading the right way. The wet loose denim of Adam's jeans was chaffing my thighs raw. The numbing cold at least stopped me feeling the sandy mud rubbing away the soles of my feet.

It must have been hours, but I would not let the fatigue or cold stop me. Completely driven, I was almost trance like in my effort to get out. Night fell and, after stumbling blindly into hidden potholes, I realised it was futile to continue. A rudimentary shelter under the tee tree bushes gave me some protection from the weather, but fear prevented me from sleeping. Sometime during the night the rain stopped and as soon as I could see the pink of dawn, I continued my journey.

It wasn't long before I realised that there was no road ahead. The track I thought I had been following, didn't actually exist. Luckily my survival instinct kicked in and I remembered that the sun would set in the west, the direction of the main road. With the morning sun behind me I now knew which way to head. The terrain was rougher and the sun was hot, all I had to do was keep drinking and walking, I told myself. Adam's life depended upon it.

Walking into the setting sun meant, that although I was heading in the right direction, I was running out of time. Before it became too dark to see I found a flat place to lie down and covered it with soft branches and weeds, knowing that I had to get some rest and sleep if I was going to make it through. Morning saw another clear day and with a new found vigour I pushed on.

When the sun was immediately above me I stopped to eat and drink. My clever rationing for what I thought would be a ten hour trip was now depleted. I still had the determination to go on, but had no water, no food, nothing to help me survive the trip. The denuded landscape around me provided not even a muddy pool.

Night three and the thoughts of despair were growing.

By day four, more scorching sun saw me fading into a stumbling delirium. My energy was spent, my body weak, my resolve gone. I had nothing left. I had given up hope.

Anna Buckley

Part 4

Captive

He'd watched as she shot the rabbits. He'd seen her as she'd been fucked on the river bank. Saw her haul the logs as they tried to repair the bridge.

But something had happened. Adam Darcy was not with her as she crossed the river. Where was he? Why was she alone?

Moses had tracked her for the last few days. Keeping his distance, following her progress through his binoculars. She had strayed from the road, but was clever and kept heading in the right direction.

He liked what he saw and he wanted her for himself. He'd watched her for long enough. She was weakening and vulnerable. He would rescue her, protect her, take her home. She would grow to love and understand him. She was perfect. She was Adam's. Now he would take her away and make her his.

Moses had his guns with him, he aimed and with a quick shot of tranquilizer, rendered her still. He would take her back to his hut without her being able to resist. She would have no idea of how she'd arrived or how she could leave. He drove his truck to the spot where she lay, surprisingly not far from the track, near the main road. She had almost succeeded and would never know just how close she had got. He lifted her into the back of the truck, placing her carefully onto a makeshift mattress of hessian sacks. The tranquilizer would last for a couple more hours, but he bound her ankles and wrists, just in case. He had seen her strong feisty spirit and didn't want to lose her now. His guns would need to be securely locked away, she knew how to use them against him.

The drive to his place was about an hour further west. Deep into the last tract of land not owned by the mill or the government, bordering the national park. It had been his grandfather's, then his father's land and now it was his. Not many people came this way. Most missed the track. The tourists were only interested in heading to the vast wilderness of southern Tasmania. Most of the visitors wouldn't start to arrive until after Christmas, six weeks away. They were isolated and would be left alone.

Moses hadn't planned on finding the woman. He'd been hunting wallaby in the wasteland that had once been the forest where he and his forebears had worked. He was surprised to see her travelling alone along the track a couple of weeks back. Joe had told him Adam was due to arrive the next day. Moses just assumed it was one of those city people, having their 'wilderness experience', although he couldn't understand why she had arrived early, before Darcy.

Normally he would have kept out of the way, but had become curious when distant gunshot had scared away the wallabies he'd been hunting. His gun sight gave him a telescopic view and he couldn't believe what he saw. It was that lone woman shooting, a crack shot, downing every critter in her aim. He was hooked and kept watch. He had enough supplies to last for weeks and became obsessed with observing the woman trapped on the other side of the river. He would dream about her. Waking up stiff, his cock hard for the Amazonian female who appeared on the edge of the river at the broken bridge. Some days he didn't see her at all and felt bereft. One day she had arrived completely naked and he looked on admiringly as she washed sheets in the river. He had pulled out his cock and eagerly stroked it as he observed her. She was better than porn. He felt she had known he was there watching, that her nudity was a gift to him. His wet dream turned into a nightmare when the asshole Darcy turned up and fucked her from behind. Moses raged at the thought of the brutal assault he was made to witness.

Slowly he saw the bridge being repaired and was coming to terms with the fact that Adam and the woman would soon leave. He dreaded the prospect of never seeing her again.

He almost wept with joy when he saw her edge her way across the metal span, alone and coming to him. Was she escaping? Had she been Darcy's captive? What had she done to stop Adam from following her?

He thanked God and knew it was a sign that she was coming to meet him.

He had stalked her, watching his prey weaken with every new day. And now she had surrendered to exhaustion and, in that broken state, he would rescue her, bring her home.

Lost and Found

Adam had spent the first night alone assuming that Tina hadn't quite made it out yet. He had been confident she would reach the main road and eventually get to Joe's. Find the help he needed. She was strong and resilient. By the fourth night he knew something must have gone terribly wrong.

Lands End Lagoon was his sanctuary. He loved the isolation of a place where no one could call. He'd intentionally not bought a satellite phone. Joe knew not to interfere. Adam remembered Joe commenting on how changed and relaxed he would appear after one of his monk like retreats. This was now Adam's new problem. If Tina had not gotten out, nobody would think to come.

His leg throbbed and he was rationing the last of the painkillers. Tina had ripped up enough of the sheet so that he could clean and dress his wounded leg. She had left ample supplies of food and water. He could possibly last for quite a bit longer. The biggest problem was that the antiseptic had almost run out. He was at high risk of developing an infection. The weather had been warm. He could smell the pungent odour of food rotting in the kitchen.

And if he was still alone, so was she. He had to find out what had happened to her. Getting out was no longer about him, but it now seemed it was about Tina's survival as well.

Why the fuck hadn't he got a phone? He wanted to scream at his idiocy. He was naive to think he could hide his head in the sand. That just by being here all the issues of his family, his business and his lonely screwed up life would disappear. He knew all too well they would be there when he returned to civilisation. And now, for the first time in his life, he had found someone he wanted to be with. Someone to return home to every night. He cried out in pain and wept at the agony of maybe never seeing her again. The tears helped. The release of adrenalin cleared his head.

He needed to contact Joe. He had no flares, but he did have a gun. He had an idea. Underneath him he felt around and was able to easily lift the weapon and the bag of ammo onto the bed. Adam hung the rifle on his shoulder and crawled to the door. The pain made every movement almost impossible. But he was driven, had to go on, had to get out. The gun acted as a crutch and slowly he hobbled to the back of the deck. It was a still, dark night. A faint southerly breeze might just carry the sound across the water to the headland. Aiming in the direction of Lands End he began to shoot. Three shots, evenly fired then a break, count to one hundred then fire again. He begged Joe to be at home, to hear his signal.

Joe and Bob

It had been an uneventful day. Pretty much normal for this time of year. A few customers, buying petrol and a pie. Joe didn't worry. The summer tourist season would be upon him soon. A busy time when he would give anything for a quiet night like tonight.

The weather had been warm for the last few days and the water was flat and calm. Bob, his mate, had just come ashore after a long haul at sea on his trawler. Bob was one of the last remaining residents of the town. He was a fisherman barely surviving on the dwindling resources of an overfished ocean. He was coming over with a bottle. The two of them would talk shit and drink themselves into oblivion. They sat on the back porch. Bob had brought some lobster and Joe was idly watching the fire, waiting for the pot to boil. He wouldn't start to drink until it was cooked, the timing had to be just right. He didn't want to fuck up the food. Even for the chef and the fisherman, this was a rare treat that needed to be respected.

They were men of few words and sat, content to stare into the embers.

'Can you hear that?' said Joe.

'What?'

'Gunshot. Some dickhead red-neck out there shooting in the dark.

Listen.'

They sat there, waited and heard the shots again.

'Sounds like its coming from your mate's place,' said Bob.

'Yeah, but it's not right. He hates guns and he's a useless shot. Somethin's not right.'

Three shots then nothing, and again, with repetitive monotony, the same volley.

'He's in trouble. I think we need to get to him.'

'Why wouldn't he call?'

'No fucking phone service down there.'

'Surely a rich fuckin' bastard like him would have a sat. phone. We all carry 'em these days.'

'Na. He likes to be left alone. But this isn't like him, somethin's wrong and we gotta get over there.'

'We'll take the boat. Water's as flat as a tack, real slack tide tonight. It'll only take twenty minutes. His place is right on the tip of that headland, isn't it?' said Bob.

'Yeah, let's get going!'

The Cellar

My head throbbed. My eyes were forcibly shut, a tight blindfold adding to the pressure in my skull. My mouth was jammed full of cloth, held chokingly in place with a suffocating gag. I couldn't scream. My arms and feet were bound and hog tied together. I could feel dense stifling heat and was aware of a vile odour. The smell of death, a bit like an abattoir truck on a hot day. I became aware my stiff and painfully constricted body was lying on a hard mattress. It made a crunching sound as I struggled against my bonds. A sound that reminded me of sleeping on an old horse hair mattress like the one I'd had on the farm.

I had no idea where I was or how long I'd been here. Was it night or day? Who had brought me here and why was I tied up? I couldn't even scream out to tell my captor I needed to piss, to drink.

Occasionally I heard a scraping sound above me, like a chair being dragged across a floor, footsteps and a door slamming. It seemed that I might have been beneath a room, the dank mustiness reminded me of the cellar under our shed in Greenhope.

For what seemed like hours I zoned in and out, bound and helpless.

I was terrified. I had no idea why I was here, tied up and captured. Who had done this to me? What did they want?

After another interminable stretch of time, I heard a new sound. Something familiar. A helicopter? Were they looking for me? Was it a search party? Was Adam still alive? Or was I somewhere near a city where the sound was simply the noise from a traffic monitoring helicopter?

I couldn't stay here. I had to get out.

There was enough give in the ropes that I could slowly edge myself across the mattress. If I could move around the room, I might find something sharp to rub against, cut the rope, free my hands. Falling hard onto a concrete floor added a new layer of pain. But now, off the bed, at least I had a better idea of the room. Big enough to hold a bed. Probably not the crawl space under a house.

I painstakingly wriggled to the nearest object and was sickened by the intense smell of decay. I rubbed my face across some type of pelts, rough hide and soft fur, animal skins. Not woollen sheep hide, no distinct smell of lanolin. They were probably wallaby, like the road kill I'd seen on the trip down here. Maybe I was still in the area?

Could I be in one of those ramshackle huts I'd seen on the road to Moon Bay?

Further movement allowed me to scope out a small room. It had a bed against one wall, a stack of pelts and a wooden stair on the far side.

I couldn't remain on the floor, if my captor knew I was able to move this far he might think I could escape. Again I continued to slowly writhe across the room and, using my shoulders and hips, finally managed to haul myself back up onto the bed. It hurt like hell and I was relieved to finally make it back to the place he'd left me. My body ached and exhaustion took over, I slept.

The loosening of the gag woke me. I was still tied and blindfolded. I could feel the presence of someone sitting next to me. I coughed as water was squirted into my mouth, unable to swallow while lying on my side. I felt his calloused hand hold my head up as he tried to help me drink, and this time I guzzled down the sweet, cool minerally water.

'Who are you?' I demanded when I had my fill.

No reply.

'You have to let me go. I won't cause any trouble. You could dump me by the road. Leave the blindfolds on, I'd never even know what you looked like, who you were. It's not too late,' I pleaded.

Again no response.

Silently he let my head down and his body weight shifted. A spoon clinking against my teeth alerted me to the food. I opened my mouth and tasted the cold, canned stew. Again he held my head so that I could eat. I was ravenous and gorged the disgusting mush. I felt him wipe my mouth with a cloth. Then the more disturbing taste of a pill and more water. When I opened again for another drink, he jammed the wad of cloth back in. I struggled against him. His knees held my head firmly as he tied the gag again. I heard the sound of steel capped boots walking across concrete, then up the stairs. The creak of a door being opened then shut, signalled he had left. The sound of a chain being looped through metal told me I was very securely trapped.

So that was it. My first contact. No brutal beating or rape, just the feeding.

It was obvious, escape was going to be almost impossible. Even if I cut the ropes, I couldn't break the door chains. I would have to think of another way, be clever about this. Perhaps I could gain his trust, become my kidnapper's friend?

After the food and water my need to pee was becoming more urgent. I decided that lying in my own piss would make my situation more uncomfortable. So I wriggled along my stomach, to the edge of the bed, and lowered myself to the floor, till my knees were firmly on the ground. The relief of pissing was overwhelmingly satisfying. I didn't care about the damp jeans and stayed in this position until the denim had dried. This must have taken quite some time, but at least it was a primitive way of occupying myself while I waited for his next move.

Searching for Tina

The two men were shocked to find Adam lying unconscious on the deck, the wounded leg bleeding profusely. They called the emergency services on Bob's phone. Joe reapplied a clean bandage and stopped the flow. Bob got off the phone, a helicopter had been dispatched. There was nowhere for the air ambulance to land. The men knew they had to get Adam back to town.

'Sorry mate, but we need you to wake up,' said Joe as he tossed a bucket of water over the comatose man.

Adam stirred and Joe slapped his face to keep him alert.

'Come on buddy, you've got to get up. We've got to get you back to town.'

'Tina. Gone. Need to look for her, over the bridge,' mumbled Adam.

Must've been that woman who'd driven down from Hobart. It seemed that Adam was reluctant to leave without her.

'Tell me where she is,' said Joe, knowing it would be easier to get off the headland if he could understand what Adam meant.

Joe managed to get Adam to tell him that the woman had tried to cross the broken bridge. Walking out to get help.

'It's ok. I'll ring Moses Smith, get him out with his spotlight. He knows this area like the back of his hand. He could get down there way before the cops,' said Joe, reassuring Adam that help was on the way.

Relieved that something was being done, Adam was more compliant and leant heavily on the two men as they took him to the boat.

Bob made the call.

'What'd he say?' asked Joe.

'Apparently the road's a mess. He was hunting in the area not long ago. Bridge got washed away. Said he'd go down and have a look. See what he could find.'

They sped across the water. They had to get to the playing field and light a signal fire before the helicopter could land. They docked at the old wharf. Bob drove his truck right onto the jetty. The two men laboured under the weight of Adam's unconscious body, eventually getting him into the truck and speeding off to the sports field. Joe grabbed the petrol can and emptied its contents onto a pile of logs, struck a match and watched the sky light up as the pyre burned. Within ten minutes the copter arrived and with expert proficiency the medics loaded their patient and were soon back in the sky. The trip to Hobart wouldn't take long, it was only an hour's drive away, even quicker by air. He knew he had to call Sam, the guy at the hotel where Adam lived in Melbourne. He would know what to do next.

Back in Hobart, Adam regained consciousness and was able to give all the details of Tina's disappearance to police. Within two hours the normally quiet town of Lands End was alive with police, sirens and flashing lights. Rescue teams had assembled and would be met by Moses at the Moon Bay turn off.

Wild Goose Chase

Moses kind of expected to be involved and was not surprised when Bob Hatcher made the call.

Luckily he had got the woman into his cellar hours ago, with enough drugs to keep her quiet for a long time. He tied her up well and knew she wasn't going anywhere soon.

He laughed quietly at the golden opportunity Bob had given him. He would be their guide, their hero.

He drove back to the bridge and tossed the woman's backpack into some bushes downstream at the river's edge. They would think she'd fallen and drowned. His tyre tracks would arouse no suspicion, they had asked him to take a look. Moses rang Bob and mournfully told him he couldn't find anything. No sign of the woman. Bob told him the emergency services were on their way and would assemble at the Moon Bay turn off. Bob asked him to meet them there, be their guide. He'd be the best man for the job. Moses loved the responsibility he'd been given. He took it as another sign and quietly thanked the Lord.

It took him forty minutes to get to the meeting point, he could already see flashing lights. He was met by Sergeant Barry Walters.

'You Moses?'

'Yeah.'

'Barry Walters, Search and Rescue. The locals tell me you know this place real well,' said the sergeant, shaking Moses' hand.

'Lived here all me life. Went straight to the bridge when Bob called. Couldn't see much. Been a lotta rain, road's bad. Bridge completely fucked, impossible to cross,' said Moses looking concerned.

'Do you think you could take us there? Is the track safe?'

'Sure, follow me.'

Moses guided the convoy along the potholed track, steering them clear of any hidden dangers. He wanted to show them how much he knew. Getting them there safely was part of his plan.

Finally they arrived. Armed with high powered torches, the team of men spread out along the edge of the ravine. They obviously saw how treacherous the crossing must have been and it seemed to Moses they were already resigned to looking for a body.

'Over here. I can see something,' yelled the young officer, his torch pointing directly at the bushes.

Moses felt a great deal of satisfaction as the sodden bag was retrieved from the bulrushes. The evidence he'd planted had been found. He watched as Barry pulled on rubber gloves and inspected the contents. He held up a wallet and read the name on the driver's licence.

'Jesus mate, this is hers, Christina Maxwell. It's not looking good. We'll get the chopper with the search light. Don't know how much it will help. She's probably been washed out to sea. Be well on her way to Antarctica by now,' said Barry with a look of despair.

'The current was pretty strong a few days back, full moon, big tides. You're probably right.'

Moses stayed up all night. Listened as they called her name, watched as their searchlights scanned the land in vain, hoping they might find her alive. He knew they would never find her. He'd made sure of that.

The helicopter was doing a massive search. At dawn he said he needed a break. He would be back in a few hours, ready to help again. He wished them good luck and they thanked him for his assistance. He drove off with a contented smile. What he really knew was that his beloved would be hungry and needed to be fed.

This would be the pattern for the next week. The longer they found no trace, the sooner he'd be left in peace. He hated leaving her.

Missing Presumed Dead

Adam woke from surgery to see Sam sitting by his bed. Where was he? What had happened? Then it hit him.

'Have they found her?' he whispered pleadingly.

'They're doing their best. I rang your mate Steve, the detective. He made sure a crack team, the best, was put together.'

'I can't stay here. I've got to get back. Be there when they find her. She needs me.'

'Listen Adam you nearly lost your leg. You're not going anywhere. Let me be your eyes and ears. Joe calls me every few hours. He said they've got that local tracker helping out. Moses, I think they call him. Joe reckons if anyone can find her, he can.'

Adam felt uneasy. He remembered the many altercations he'd had with Moses, when he first came to Lands End. But then he reconsidered. Moses was a man of integrity. And Joe was right, Moses knew the land very well. He was the best man for the job. Slightly relieved knowing they were doing all they could to find Tina, Adam allowed the painkillers to do their job and fell back into a drugged sleep.

Sam had been up all night, ringing the people most affected. He'd managed to contact Tina's business partner Cindy. She would let all the relevant people know, including Tina's daughter.

For now he just needed to be with his boss and sit by him. Ready to comfort him when the full force of the tragedy would strike. He cherished this time alone, looking after Adam, feeling needed.

Prisoner

The feeding continued. He only came once a day. I started to get a sense of time, birdsong at dawn and in the evening.

My captor had removed the suffocating cloth that filled my mouth. But the gag stayed, keeping me silent.

The smell of urine was starting to invade the space. Fortunately fear, dehydration and the scant amount of food, meant I hadn't needed to shit. My captor had cared enough to feed me and give me water. Hadn't he thought about the consequences of this? Didn't the odour give him the hint that he had to do something about my hygiene?

He did.

The familiar sound of his entry was almost a comfort. He hadn't hurt me and I hadn't upset him. A bond was forming. This time was different. The usual smell of canned food wasn't there. Again I felt him move towards me as the mattress shifted. He was behind me, tugging at the ropes, when suddenly I felt the blissful separation of my hands and feet. Though my wrists and ankles were still bound, I was no longer hog tied and, at long last, I could stretch out my near crippled back. I curled into a foetal position to counter the cramped, painful muscles of my spine.

He let me stay like this for some time.

I felt his rough hand stroke my cheek and I cringed defensively, scared by the thought of what this might lead to. But he was gentle and removed his hand when he saw my fearful reaction. Surprisingly, he then released my ankles and I stretched my legs like a cat waking from sleep. The movement of the piss crusted denim stung against my still chafed raw thighs, the smell an assault to my nose. I felt him undo the button of my jeans and tug them down. A grave sense of foreboding came over me. Surprisingly, he gathered me in his arms and lifted me onto a toilet of some kind. He rebound my ankles, then left me.

My hands were still tied behind me and my legs had no strength, but I was able to piss and shit and felt vaguely thankful at this small touch of humanity.

He returned, just in time to catch me as I nearly fainted from the shock of being upright for the first time in many days.

This time I sensed a new smell, soap. Before lifting me off I felt the pressure of his hand on my back, forcing me to bend over and, in an act of intimacy, he wiped my ass. When he placed me back down on the bed, I felt a rough towel beneath me. Then the strange sensation of being washed. I felt so vulnerable. He was so gentle. When he finished, I heard him scrubbing the floor. Cleaning the room until it no longer smelt like a filthy public lavatory.

He tethered my arms and feet to the bed then covered my naked body with a sheet. I felt clean. The room didn't stink so much. I could stretch out, and slept an almost comfortable sleep.

And this is how it continued for the next few days. All my most basic needs were being met. I had become totally dependent on this man who remained unseen and silent. I was thankful for the pills which meant that sleep filled most of the long boring days.

The changes were incremental. When he first took the gag off I learnt not to speak or it would be swiftly retied. Eventually I knew to remain silent. The interminable routine was altered slightly when once, after the same disgusting tinned food, he fed me a square of chocolate. I savoured this delicious rare treat and rewarded him with a smile. He touched my cheek, acknowledging my response. The bathing, the toileting also continued. This time he surprised me by dabbing a small amount of perfume at the base of my neck when he'd finished.

After he left, my mind started to race. How did he know how to care for me? Why did he have the perfume? Was he alone or was there someone else upstairs? A wife perhaps, oblivious to my presence. I had read of this, that some wives lived for years without knowing of their husband's hostage.

He had been clever in creating this dependency, because now I longed for his visits. I wanted to show him I earned the small rewards he gave me and became completely compliant.

My Eyes Opened

The bed was the first of the physical changes. Sheets, pillows, a silk edged blanket that felt exotic to touch, comfortable to sleep in, covering my exposed nakedness. The filthy clothes long gone.

The sponge baths were looked forward to and I felt no shame in being washed by the faceless stranger. My breasts, my face, the folds between my legs, delicately cleaned and attended to every day.

The routine remained unchanged.

My sense of hearing was heightened, new sounds amplified in my quieted prison, wood chopping, a dog barking, a motor running. I imagined we were somewhere remote, in the countryside, away from other humans. I heard no voices.

How many days, weeks, had I been held captive? The helicopters had long gone. Was anybody still looking? Or had they given up on me?

Mostly I tried to sleep, to kill time. The drugs seemed to be less effective and I now woke long before he came to perform the daily rituals.

The rattling of the locks signalled he was coming back. His footsteps on the stairs and lastly his weight shifting the mattress, told me he'd arrived. Most days he would sit for some time, barely moving, just being near, possibly staring. I didn't know. I couldn't see.

Our usual procedures continued, but this time, he took me by surprise and removed the blindfold. An assault of light, squinting, barely focusing, it had been so long since I had used my eyes. For a brief moment, I was almost too scared to look. I had built up an image of my silent captor and feared what I might really see. Was he some grotesque monster whose ugliness forced his solitude? Slowly I opened my eyes. His back was towards me as he went about the cleaning of my cell.

And then he turned.

An archangel, tall, well built, long curls, a beard. Not the ogre I'd imagined.

But he was my kidnapper.

I didn't speak. Knew not to look him in the eye. He picked me up and sat me on a stool in front of a bowl of hot water, then placed his hand on my back, signalling me to bend over. He had taken the blindfold off to wash my hair. The sound of an enamel cup clinking against the tin bowl, familiar. We used these things on the farm. He poured the warm water over my hair until it was saturated. Massaged in the sweet smelling shampoo. Then rinsed off the suds, careful to wipe away any water from my eyes. When finished I sat up. He towelled my hair dry, then delicately combed out the matted mess, careful not to hurt me. It felt so good, I almost wept.

Then he tilted my chin and I opened my mouth, communion like, as he put the sedative on my tongue. This time I did not swallow and pushed the pill into my cheek. He lifted me back onto the mattress, tied my hands and legs, spread eagled on the old iron bed. He fanned out my hair, combing it into a halo above my head. Free of the blindfold, I closed my eyes and pretended to go back to sleep.

He went about the usual cleaning rituals and after some time returned to the bed. I felt him lie down, pulling the sheets up to cover us, embracing me. It was his smell that dominated now. Pungent masculinity, stronger as he reached over, stoking my face and whispering,

'I'm here my darling. It's ok, Jessica, shh... '

Eventually his deep regular breathing told me he was asleep. I needed to remain focussed. I spat the pill, it dropped to the floor, hopefully hidden between the wall and the bed. I lay perfectly still, not quite sure what to make of his actions. Is this what he was doing every night, while I had been in my drugged, comatose state?

He was not in the bed when I woke.

This was the first time I was fully conscious and could think clearly about what was going on. My mind raced.

I had no idea how long I had been held prisoner. Did those helicopters find Adam? Was he still alive? Did Kate think I was dead? Would someone look after her? Who would love her as I did? But then I remembered, sadly, our last encounter, the hostility toward me. The boy who had stolen her heart. She no longer needed me and would not be alone.

I wept at the thought of never seeing the people I cherished. Of the mess I'd made of my personal life. Of being trapped here and the frustration of being unable to do anything about it. The tears reminded me that at least I was alive, and, after calming myself, I was more determined than ever to get out. My life had only just begun. I was a fighter, resilient and would do whatever it took to escape this prison.

The room was a concrete cellar. Small vents near the ceiling let the light and air in. The growing brightness and sound of birds told me it was early morning. A wooden staircase, my old iron bed, the pile of wallaby pelts, a sink and a stool were all that occupied the space. It was bleak and depressing. A trap door at the top of the stairs the only way out. The chained lock on the other side would be impossible to break. Without the drugs I was more alert and would spend the day awake, contemplating what to do next.

My strategy of offering no resistance seemed to be working. I had not been hurt and my fear of being raped had subsided. Especially after what I'd witnessed last night. He had called me Jessica. Who was this woman? Was she his weakness, the key to my escape? If he wanted me to be Jessica, then this is who I would become.

Seduction

After a tediously long day, my boredom was interrupted by the sound of the chains on the door. Tonight I would be able to see how he secured the lock once inside. If he trusted me enough, he might think to leave the door unlocked. My escape might be simpler than I thought.

My heart pounded as light filled the room. He entered, closed the door. Threaded the chain back through the handle, clicked the padlock shut, resetting the combination, locking us in. No key, just a set of numbers, safely stored in his head. I couldn't harm him. He was the only one who knew the code to get us out. If I killed him, we would both rot in this stinking hole.

I needed to pretend I was still in that twilight, drugged state. He didn't need to know of my heightened awareness and I hoped his hunter's instincts were not alert to any subtle changes.

Pretending to be just rousing, I blinked slowly and turned my head towards him as I felt his body weight move the mattress. I opened my eyes tentatively and looked at him, smiling faintly to show I welcomed his return. He looked away quickly, caught out by this intimate exchange. Strangely, I was quite touched by his sensitivity.

Tonight the ritual was slightly different. He undid all my bonds and held out his hand to help me walk to the toilet, a makeshift bucket with a wooden seat. This small independence gave me back some dignity, although I still needed him to hold my unsteady and weak body.

He removed the contents of a canvas bag. Soap, towels, sponges, tinned food, a spoon, all placed neatly on the stool. He carefully laid out a towel on the bed and carried me back. Gently he began to clean me. I offered no resistance. The soapy sponge gliding over my body, my nipples standing erect as the warm water cooled on my wet skin. My arms, my belly, my legs and lastly my sex.

The seduction would begin.

As the water trickled between my thighs and he delicately ran the sponge across the most intimate parts of my body, I let out a quiet moan and bent my knee to expose myself more openly to him. He hesitated slightly, taking in what he had just witnessed. I saw his chest rise as he sucked in air.

When the bathing was complete he fed me the usual tinned muck, a drink and lastly the pill. Again not swallowed.

He did not tie me up.

I pretended to drift off to sleep. He climbed into bed and pulled the covers over us both. This time I rolled towards him and placed my arm across his chest in a tentative embrace. I felt his heartbeat quicken. This would be all for tonight.

Again I awoke to an empty bed. I felt quite refreshed by the unshackled freedom that had allowed me a peaceful sleep.

He'd left all the things in the room. The granting of a small privilege, a sign of trust. I was eager to begin the day. After pissing in the bucket, I decided to explore the room in depth. Walking around made me realise I was in no physical condition to escape.

There was nothing to discover. I had seen all there was. No hidden doors, no possible way out.

The boredom drove me crazy. I needed something to do and so began a series of physical exercises to prepare my body, my mind. Sit ups, push ups, leg stretches, endless pacing, building strength. I was no longer prepared to wait and see what his next move was. I needed to be in control of the situation and of him.

Tonight I would up the ante to expedite my release.

At sunset he returned. There seemed to be no light switch in the room, no globe in the ceiling. That was why he carried a small kerosene lamp and again it reminded me of the farm, of the outbuildings where no power was connected. I was disturbed by the comfort these familiarities offered.

He knew I was able to clean myself. He had left me untied all night and day. But I wanted to show my dependency on him, that he had successfully tamed me.

As he sat on the bed watching me, I again opened my eyes and smiled. This time he did not look away. I got up and began to arrange the bathing equipment on the stool. I flicked open the towel, laid it on the mattress, then climbed back onto the bed, submissively. I wanted him to bathe me and he understood.

He picked up the sponge and again I responded to his touch. This time opening my legs further, inviting him to explore. I could see the tenting of his trousers and knew my actions were having the desired effect.

When he finished, he tried to give me the pill. This time I deliberately took it out of my mouth and placed it on the stool, then lay back passively on the bed. My heart raced as I waited for his response, fearful at how he might react to my new found assertiveness. He stood and picked up the lamp.

Don't go, I thought, as he moved toward the stairs. I needed him to stay if my plan was going to succeed.

He didn't leave. He placed the toiletries on a narrow shelf above the sink. Then put the lamp on the stool and blew it out. Pitch black. What next? I soon felt the rustle of the mattress, thank God he wasn't leaving. He pulled back the covers and climbed in beside me.

I was conflicted. I felt no desire, just an urgent need to get this job done. Is this what a prostitute feels like? Or was I returning to the all too familiar territory of my soulless marriage, where I was well acquainted with emotionless, unsatisfying sex? This would not be too difficult. The end goal drove me to succeed.

I moved towards him, nestling into his side, stroking his chest, feeling his body tense, as I began the foreplay that would lead to his submission.

My fingers explored his face, tracing around his lips, his jaw, along his neck and down his belly. His cock had already begun to stiffen. I dusted my hand over the cloth that separated me from skin, along his length, feeling the dampness at its tip. He lay back, not really knowing what to do, he was not an experienced lover. Without too much effort I continued to stroke him until his cock throbbed, ejaculating quickly like an adolescent school boy.

What happened next caught me unawares. I lay back down on his chest and became aware of muffled sobs shaking his body. He wrapped his arms around me, holding me close, and I responded by stroking his face till the crying stopped.

Who was this man, I'd begun to claim? What was his story?

Upstairs

Again I awoke alone, but this time it was different. The trap door was open. Light streamed in like God beckoning me heavenward.

A different sensation, a single metal ring around my ankle, attached to a long chain, shackling me to the top of the stair.

Pushing the bedding off, I got up and pissed in the bucket. What next? The open trapdoor was obviously an invitation to come upstairs. Why was I so reluctant to move? The place above intimidated me. I felt fearful of the unknown. I had become so accustomed to having my entire day controlled by this man, that I seemed to have lost my ability to think outside this room.

I could try and escape, but maybe it wasn't that simple. What if this place was miles from civilisation? How would I know which way to run? I had failed my first attempt at navigation. This was his territory. He would hunt me like prey and I feared what he might do if captured again. No immediate answers came. The solution to my problem definitely wasn't to be found in the cellar. I would have to venture upstairs. My curiosity was roused.

Tentatively, I began my ascent, the tinkling of the long chain dragging, reminding me of how limited my freedom was.

Adjusting my eyes to the brightness meant it took some time to clearly focus.

A large room, bigger than my cellar. To one side, a bathroom, door ajar. Corrugated iron walls and roof reminded me of the sheds on the farm. Small dots of light showing through the punctured metal, nail holes from a different use. Sheets of iron salvaged and re-purposed to build this hut. I was immediately aware of the heat. A hot December sun beating down on the uninsulated roof. Two windows illuminated the space. A patina of grime on the glass obscuring the outside view.

He was nowhere to be seen.

I was free to explore and stepped over the scrunched up rug that must have hidden the trap door. The chain around my ankle long enough for me to roam easily about the humble shack, too short for me to leave. Against one wall sat the kitchen. No more than a sink cupboard and a wood stove, a refrigerator meant there must be power. Next to this, a Formica table, piled high with papers, unwashed dishes, used empty cans. Three mismatched chairs stacked in the corner. A single ripped orange vinyl seat, pulled out from the table, as if it's occupant had just left, told me only one person dined here.

A double bed, similar to the one in the cellar, sat in the opposite corner. The grubby bed linen yellowing from much use, the pillows with visible circular spit stains, enticing no goldilocks to recline. A dilapidated brown couch and a junk piled coffee table completed this squalid interior.

The bathroom was as I expected. A rust dripped sink, a grime ringed bath, a stinking shit spattered toilet. The curled and cracked lino strewn with a pile of used toiletry containers. More rubbish, more junk, more chaos.

I was shocked that he lived like this. Especially knowing how meticulously he had bathed me and kept the cellar clean.

I walked to the door, the bolt was pulled back. I stupidly hoped my chance to escape would be as simple as pushing it open. The familiar rattle of chains told me it was locked from the outside. The barred windows were just as impassable. This place was sealed up so that nobody could get in or out.

The hut was far worse than the cellar. Claustrophobic, filled with the kind of junk and clutter that even kerbside fossickers would reject. It smelt of sweat, smoke, stale air, and the all too familiar stench of the canned food that had become my staple diet.

Disturbed by the primitive pigsty I'd discovered, I retreated to the relative safety and comfort of my cellar. There was no escape. This was an impenetrable jail. I had been locked in and wondered how long before my warder would be back.

I searched for the pill I spat out a few nights ago and on finding it, swallowed and took myself back to bed.

A day passed and still he didn't return. My stomach rumbled and needed to be filled. I would go back upstairs.

The fridge might provide some change from the monotonous diet. I longed for green things, salad, vegetables, real food. But it was turned off and bare. There was a supply of water and tinned food left on the sink, making me think he had planned on being away for some time. I needed to eat, but the smell was so overpowering that I retched between mouthfuls. Hot and sweaty, fighting waves of nausea, I reached the sink just in time, before vomiting up the contents of my stomach.

I longed to wash away the sour puke, rinse my body completely and cool off on this oppressively hot day. The vile bathroom was the obvious solution.

Re entering it I looked at the filth differently. It wasn't much worse than my first flat. Rummaging through the sink cupboard I found some detergent, a brittle curled up scourer, a couple of dried soap ends and a filthy tea towel. This would be enough.

I scrubbed the basin, ran the taps, washing away the suds to reveal a sparkling green sink.

It's funny how much joy I felt when cleaning, the sense of purpose it gave me. Boredom had become quite frightening and I was glad I finally had something to do.

The bath got the same treatment. The shower ran a little longer before the rusty water cleared. This was a job that would not be complete until the entire room had been scrubbed. Reluctantly, I would have to tackle the toilet. I longed to sit on a real toilet and flush away the shit and piss, rather than put up with the smell of that bucket. How bad could it be? Improvising, I pulled the head off a worn broom and used it as a scrubbing brush. Attacking the toilet until all the glued on shit was gone. Once that had been done I easily put my arm into the bowl and scoured away the last of the grunge.

I gathered up the rubbish, used shampoo bottles, tampon boxes, soap wrappers, all probably Jessica's, and stuffed them into one of the discarded plastic supermarket bags I'd found lying around the hut.

The tea towel had seen enough soap to render it cleaner than when I had started and it was with this that I lastly wiped over the floor and walls. My zealous effort must have taken hours but the end result was worth it. I looked at my handy work with pride and carefully placed my meagre toiletries on the side of the bath. It felt more like I had just entered a very exclusive spa, in this space I had now claimed as my own.

Nothing could compare to the feeling of the cold, refreshing water running over my head, my back, my entire body, rinsing away the heat, the vomit and the grime his sponge had failed to remove.

Sleep, that night, was the most relaxed I'd had since my capture.

The next morning I bounded up the stairs to sit on the toilet, happy not to use the bucket or be attended to by my captor.

'Don't touch my fuckin' stuff,' he yelled menacingly as I sat naked on the toilet. I screamed, startled by the shock of his unexpected presence. No gentle Jesus, just a very pissed off angry man.

Where did he come from? I hadn't heard the tell tale sounds of his return, hadn't seen him in my haste to get to the bathroom. Before he could do anything more I ran across the room, carrying the chains, down the stairs and back to the safety of my cell.

I huddled in a ball on the bed, scared at the punishment that might be meted out for my cleaning misdemeanour. He came and roughly retied my bonds. I screamed out after him, furious at the loss of this small freedom, no longer content to wait and watch.

'You filthy fucking animal, I only cleaned your stinking bathroom. I didn't touch your precious shit!' I yelled, as he slammed the trap door shut.

Hours passed. His boots scuffling on the floor told me he was still in the house, or the shit hole that passed for a house.

It was night time.

He eventually came down with food. When he tried to feed me I spat the slop back at him, twisting my head away, mouth firmly shut, refusing to eat this crap anymore. Pissing him off was entertaining.

Interestingly my outburst had not caused him to gag me again and it was with a sadistic delight that I shouted out to him as he headed back upstairs.

'Why do you live like this? Who was Jessica? Would she come back for this? This is not a life. That was not food. I'd rather die fighting, than be like you, you sad fuckin' loser. Piss off!'

He shut the door with a deliberate slam. I lay there tied up tightly, spread eagled on the bed, my punishment for speaking out.

After a few hours he returned and my mood lifted. He took off the ropes and replaced them with the shackle. This time on a much shorter chain, long enough to reach the piss pot, too short to do much else.

So what I thought was a small chastisement turned into day after day of the more excruciating punishment of isolation and abandonment.

He would come down once every few days with water and more of that disgusting food. He left no fork or knife and made me eat with my fingers straight from the tin. Not caring about the cuts from the jagged can, my grubby hand dived in greedily, scooping out the food and stuffing it into my mouth. A day without food had left me ravenous.

I longed for company, for his gentle ministrations and I longed for the drugs to numb the tediousness and boredom of my bleak existence. I feared I would go mad. Begging was useless and when the pleading got too much, he gagged me again.

This went on for days.

He didn't even empty the toilet and the smell became all pervasive. My hands, my body, my hair, filthy. I had no way to wash, to reach the sink so tantalisingly close, beyond the reach of my chains.

The cuts on my hand were turning red and starting to fester. Remembering a scene from one of those survival shows, I pissed on the wound, knowing that urine was quite sterile. Hoping it would stop the infection.

That night, without drugs, was made worse by waves of hot and cold engulfing my me, sweat pouring off my feverish body. Eventually I started to retch, throwing up that vile food. Too weak to move I just lay there. The acrid vomit caught in my matted hair, trapped on the stinking, soaked bed. My joints ached and I felt like death. I zoned in and out of consciousness, not knowing if the nightmares were real.

'Christina, wake up, open your eyes,' I could just hear his voice.

He knew my name, but I was too weak to respond. I was burning up. The coolness of a damp cloth on my forehead gave me brief respite. He lifted my head and tried to get me to drink. The familiar taste of dissolved aspirin filled my mouth. My mum had always given this to me when I was sick. I doubted whether it would be enough to alleviate the pain wracking every inch of my body. I could barely keep it down, but eventually was able to ingest enough to dull the ache and fall back into a restless sleep.

Was I dreaming of floating, being carried by warm water? My eyes opened. I did not recognise my surroundings straight away. Slowly I was able to focus on what was reality and what was just a dream.

The water was real. I was in a bath, green enamel, a familiar smell of soap. Startled by the change of surroundings I recoiled into a protective ball, holding my arms tightly around my knees, trying to sit up.

'It's ok, I've got you,' said the deep voice of the man who was my captor.

We were in the bathroom, the place that had made him so upset. But he wasn't violent or angry, just gently sluicing the clean warm water over my weakened body. Relaxing into his strong arms, I accepted his help, too frail to fight.

He picked me up, wrapped me in a towel, took me back to bed, and once again I retreated into sleep.

Unfamiliar surroundings greeted me when I woke, I was upstairs in the hut. The intense heat under the corrugated iron roof was gone, instead it was a cooler, dull grey day. He was leaning over the table, writing. He put the pen down and got up, walked to the stove, removed the boiling kettle to make a pot of tea. He then turned and looked straight at the bed, at me.

He came over and sat down, feeling my forehead with the back of his hand, checking for signs of fever. I turned my head away, not ready to face him. He got off the bed and went back to the kitchen. He returned with a fine bone china cup filled with real tea, a delicious scent, and placed it on the bedside table. Plumping up the pillows, he gently helped me sit up.

'You need to eat, to drink.'

Lifting the cup to my lips, I took a tentative sip. Not too hot, just right, he tilted the cup and I sipped again. He sat patiently until I finished, then stood and returned to the kitchen. Toast, that was the smell. He brought the narrow buttered soldier to my mouth and like a baby bird I gobbled the whole piece.

Opening my eyes fully, I looked into his sad, distant face. He quickly got off the bed, returned to the table and picked up his pen.

The first thing I noticed was the sheets, they were clean but had the musty smell of linen that had been stored for a long time. He had changed the bed. His bed?

The dim light through the windows and the sound of rain on the tin roof told me the weather had changed. It was cold. The glow from the wood stove made the room feel almost homely. Still weakened by the sickness, I drifted into a less fitful sleep.

The smell of bacon woke me. I was starving. He was at the stove again, back hunched, preparing food. This time the meal came on a tray, same intricate china, full teacup and a plateful of eggs and bacon. He helped me sit up and placed the food in front of me, then handed me a fork and an old bone handled knife. Salt and pepper came in two elaborate, but tarnished, silver shakers. He returned to the table and I was left to savour the taste of real food. I delighted at having something in my mouth that was familiar, comforting, delicious.

This nourishing food made me feel so much better, gave me the chance to think more clearly. I would stop the insolent behavior, not upset him, try to win back his trust.

'Thank you.'

He turned from the table.

'Would you like some more?'

'Yes,' I responded smiling faintly, indicating a truce.

I got up to take the tray back to the kitchen and he quickly stood, taking the things out of my hands and led me back to bed.

'Just rest.'

That night I stayed in his bed and woke to find him sleeping on the couch. He was fully clothed and I knew I would have to begin the seduction or more precisely, the courtship, all over again.

Feeding Moses Smith

My incarceration had gone on for what must have been weeks. The shackles remained. The days were boring.

My captor had a routine. Hunt when the weather was fine, usually at night. When he had enough, take the carcasses away, returning with supplies. Sometimes he would be gone for just a few hours and sometimes it would be days. These long absences meant I could explore the shack a little more. Always very careful to leave no evidence of my prying. Making sure all was exactly as he had left it. The punishment of those lonely, isolated days in the cellar were too much too bear. I didn't want to provoke a return to that dark place.

He allowed me the luxury of a box of books. Worn, dog eared novels, that looked like the rejects of a white elephant stall. A few thick best sellers and biographies of people nobody really cared about. Books that normally I would not have read, but now pored over as if they were the most exquisite prose.

When he was home, I was confined to the cellar. He didn't want my company. The chain was lengthened and I could pace the room, easily reaching the water and the wash basin, vague civility returning.

And when he drove away, he left the trap door open, giving me free range of the house once again.

The odd sticker on a window, a bundle of faded flyers calling the town to action, an assortment of newspaper clippings, told me he had been active in campaigning to save the jobs of the loggers of Lands End and Moon Bay. He probably hadn't always been a hunter, but had worked in the forests or mills like most of the men of the area. He would have known a more prosperous time, lived in a town full of people, been part of a community of hard working country folk.

I wondered why he no longer slept with me, like he had done in the first hazy weeks of my capture? Surely he craved the closeness and intimacy that those first surreptitious encounters had provided? He had become distant. I needed to get back his trust and offer him what I knew most men desired. Food and sex. Men were simple creatures with just these basic needs. I would assume he was no different.

Changing the power in this relationship was the only way I could begin to think about the prospect of freedom. Talking would be a good start. Scared of being gagged, I knew I had to start a conversation slowly, with just a few well chosen words. What did we have in common that he might let me speak about?

This time it was only a short trip and I scampered downstairs before he came inside. I heard the rustle of plastic bags being dumped on the bench. He must have gone out just for supplies. If the nearest store was in Lands End, he would have been to Joe's petrol station.

It occurred to me that maybe his avoidance of me might be quite simple. Apart from my bedding and a towel, I had no clothing. Perhaps my nakedness had now become intimidating?

A new smell wafted down to my prison, meat frying. He was cooking. Maybe he was sick of our monotonous diet also. After a short while he came down carrying a battered old enamel plate and left it on the stool. I sat still, didn't speak, waited for him to leave before I ate. Not wanting to break our unwritten code of conduct.

No knife or fork, but it didn't stop me from wolfing down the steak, ripping at the flesh like a starving cave woman. Even though the meat was tough and the potatoes had the distinct flavour of canning, the food was amazing. It was as if I was eating for the first time, savouring something special.

I was confident this gesture, the food, was a type of truce.

When he came to collect the empty plate I spoke.

'Thank you. That was good.'

No over exaggerated compliments, just a simple statement of truth. Nothing he had to respond to.

As he climbed the stairs, with his back to me and no serious threat of engagement, I spoke again.

'Could I please borrow some clothes?'

He hesitated briefly, then continued up.

Before shutting the trapdoor for the night he threw something down. I took my lamp and saw the crumpled checked flannel shirt on the floor. Thank God he responded positively, I thought, as I buttoned up the oversized garment. Now I might just be making progress.

The following evening I heard him up shuffling around in the kitchen. The sound of logs being loaded into the wood stove, the scraping of a steel poker loosening the ash. It was raining again and decidedly much colder. Even the cellar had dropped a few degrees.

'You can sit by the fire,' he called down, speaking from just above the entrance.

Grabbing a book, I slowly made my way up. Aware that he would not want this first outing to be too close, I sat on the couch, didn't speak, kept my head down and quietly read.

He couldn't hunt or get out. Drenching rain and raging winds prevented any outdoor activity, so he sat quietly reading what was probably yesterday's paper. No internet, no computer, meant a different kind of day spent inside.

My head was full of questions, but I knew I had to take it slowly.

'Those fuckin' politicians!' he mumbled, as he read.

'Don't give a fuck about people in the country unless they're in a marginal seat.'

I understood the gist of his grumblings, remembered state elections had been called when I was still in Hobart. He must have been referring to something in the paper. I thought about how to engage him, pausing before I spoke.

'I grew up in the bush, safest conservative seat on the mainland, never did anything for us either.'

A brief statement of understanding, nothing more. He might be interested and after what seemed like a lengthy pause he responded.

'That where you learned to shoot?'

He must have seen me. I wondered how long he'd been watching, what he'd observed? What did he know about Adam and me, and our time on the island?

'Had to, sometimes we didn't have enough money for food,' I replied.

Another long pause.

'Whereabouts?'

'Greenhope, western Victoria, Dad had a farm.'

We had found common ground. The ice was broken.

Not wanting to spoil this moment, hoping what I'd said was enough, I yawned, quietly took my book and returned downstairs.

'Goodnight.'

'Night,' I heard him mumble in response.

The weather got worse. He called me up to share the fire. I could see more food laid out on the sink and wondered how I could cook it for him, without seeming too pushy.

We read quietly. He was more relaxed, his body adopting a less aggressive demeanor.

'Tea?' he asked.

'Thanks.'

He was pouring the hot water from the kettle, when he was startled by the sudden frantic yelping of the dogs.

'Fuck!' he roared, as the boiling water spilled all over his hand.

Racing to the stove I could see immediately that the burn was quite severe, the hand becoming bright red.

An opportunity.

Acting quickly I forced his hand under the tap. He grimaced at first, but soon began to relax as the cold water did its job, soothed the pain. Eventually I inspected the damage. A massive blister had formed on his palm. The hand would be out of action and with his misfortune, I knew my luck had changed.

'Bloody possums spooking the dogs.'

I watched as he tried to start the meal preparation, attempting to peel potatoes with his one undamaged hand.

'Here, let me,' I volunteered and he stood aside.

I gently took the knife from him and quickly got to work.

Potatoes, onions and pumpkin sat on the sink, a big pot of boiling water on the stove, more steak sitting ready to be fried. Meat and boiled veg.

'Would you mind if I cooked?' I asked, knowing I could do so much more with the food.

'Got no choice,' he responded.

Taking this as tacit approval I began to work my magic. He was a man of simple tastes and limited supplies, but I knew I could make something extraordinary out of the things before me.

'Do you have any flour?' I asked, not wanting to seem too familiar with the kitchen, even though, due to my explorations, I already knew the answer.

'In the cupboard under the sink, there's a box of stuff. Might find some in there.'

Flour, salt and pepper was all I needed. Clearing some space on the filthy workbench, I began. Firstly I chopped the steak into cubes, tossed it in those three simple ingredients and fried off in butter till it was a rich golden brown. Next I added a couple of onions to ramp up the flavour. Like many Australian households a cask of wine sat on top of the fridge and it was with this rough red I deglazed the pot until a rich, dark gravy formed. The stew was left to simmer gently on top of the stove. In a battered old roasting pan, I placed the pumpkin, potatoes, onions, butter, salt and pepper and put this into the hot oven.

Delicious smells began to fill the room. Comforting, safe. I pushed the boundaries even further.

'Could I clean the sink? Do these dishes? Chuck out some of these cans?'

'S'pose so,' he replied.

And so I went about creating order in the small amount of space he'd given me permission to control.

Next I bandaged his wounds. The sink cupboard had given up a rudimentary first aid kit. When I was finished, he flexed his hand, smiled, pleased he would be able to use it again. Another small victory.

He responded by making space for one extra person on the cluttered table. I tried not to giggle as the towering pile of papers fell back down onto the newly cleared place. He shook his head and grabbed some cartons stacked up against the couch. I observed the careful placement of each item into different boxes. The clippings, tools, hunting gear, personal effects, being sorted, eventually removing all the junk, leaving the table completely cleared. I walked over and handed him a wet sponge to complete the process and when he'd finished, he stood back and contemplated what he had just done. His shoulders relaxing ever so slightly with the satisfaction of a difficult task begun. Avoided for so long.

From another box he retrieved the same delicate crockery and cutlery he'd used when I was sick and proceeded to set the table with surprising refinement.

What was the story behind this broken man?

When the meal was ready I took the food to the table and we sat. I watched, pleased, as he wolfed down my offering. The meat was meltingly tender and rich in flavour after its slow simmering. The roasted vegetables, salty, crisp and golden. He came back for more.

'You can bloody cook,' he said smiling, leaning back on his chair, fully sated.

'Thanks,' I replied and smiled back.

The power was shifting. Another win.

Again I cleaned up and took myself to bed.

He did not shut the trapdoor. Neither did he come down.

I heard him collect his gear, the sky had cleared, and he went out to hunt. The frequent sound of shots told me there was much game to be had that night.

The hunt had been productive and a full load would mean a trip to town.

'I'm heading off. Do you need any supplies?'

I carefully contemplated my answer.

'Anything you like to eat, whatever you can find. Maybe some more butter, flour, sugar, eggs, more veggies, meat? Actually some cleaning supplies would be good. Thanks.'

This would be enough for now. I didn't want to complicate things.

He returned many hours later, bringing in his purchases. Excitedly I unpacked the boxes like a kid on Christmas morning. Cooking would give me something to do to relieve the boredom. It was no chore. I loved food, and so did the hunter. He had bought most of the things I'd asked for, plus a whole chicken. Lots of ingredients for me to play with.

In a separate flat takeaway container I found the real treasure, scallop pies, still warm. I recognised the pastry, knew they were Joe's. His must have been the nearest store.

I had a plan.

A very stale loaf of bread sitting in the fridge would do. I cut off the mouldy bits and rubbed butter through the broken up crumbs along with a diced onion, some salt and pepper.

'What are you doing?' he asked.

'Making stuffing for the chicken.'

'Jesus, I didn't know you could do that? Thought it came out of a packet. Have you got what you need?'

'Well, I'd like some fresh herbs and lemon, but you don't have any. What I've got will have to do.'

He went to one of the boxes and got out some rope.

'Come here,' he demanded.

Not wanting to break our accord, I complied. He tied my hands behind my back and attached another metal ring to my ankle, securing my feet with a loose chain. Enough for me to walk, but not run, still his shackled prisoner.

'Follow me,' he commanded.

He walked to the door, holding it open, gesturing me to go outside. It had been weeks since I'd felt the sun and breathed fresh air. I shuffled to the door and took my first tentative steps outside.

I adjusted slowly to the near blinding light. When my eyes were finally able to focus, I was awestruck by the beauty of the spectacular landscape before me. We were in the mountains, surrounded by virgin forest, tall timbers, tree ferns. The hut sat in the middle of a clearing, a steep road the only way in or out. Miles into the distance, the sea was a faraway blue. The earthy smells, the eucalyptus, the fresh air, intoxicating. I inhaled deeply, every breath reaffirming life.

It was not what I had imagined and looked nothing like the hostile bush landscape that housed the shacks I'd seen on the road to Moon Bay. It was beautiful, nature at its pristine best.

Near the hut there was shed, covered in creepers. Through the open doors I could see it housed the usual assortment of farm equipment, along with a cool room and a generator. His truck was parked out front. The generator meant we were a long way from power poles, civilisation, or a main road. I had become quite used to the sound of the noisy machine which provided us with electricity. The exterior of the shack was just as I'd imagined. A simple square structure, pitched roof, rusty corrugated iron. A patchwork of metal sheets covering the most worn places. What made me curious was the partially constructed straw bale house sitting on a levelled site further up the hill. I guessed this crumbling, half built ruin had been the beginning of someone's dream house. Probably his and Jessica's. I did not pry.

'Over here,' he said and I followed him to the other side of the property.

An orchard, with an ancient bay and lemon tree, apples and stone fruit, was the manifestation of the self sufficiency dream. I could just imagine the hopes tied up in the overgrown and neglected garden.

A hedge of blackberries formed a border. A noxious weed at home, here, a treasure trove of dark purple berries waiting to be picked.

'Take what you need,' he said, as he removed the rope from around my wrists. I lifted the front of my large shirt, filling it with apricots, cherries, lemons and a handful of bay leaves.

The ripeness told me it must be mid to late December, the apples wouldn't be ready till autumn. I had been here for much longer than I thought, soon it would be Christmas. My mind started to wander, remembering who and what I'd left behind. I felt the prickle of tears. I took a deep breath and continued with the task at hand. I had to keep strong both mentally and physically if I was going to survive.

'Could you please hold these while I pick some blackberries?' I said, offloading the fruit into his folded arms. He looked away as I emptied the contents of my shirt, exposing my 'Eve in the Garden of Eden' nakedness. What had happened to the man who only weeks before had bathed me? Why had he become so embarrassed by my nudity, a state in which I'd lived for almost the entire time of my incarceration?

As I became more human and he treated me less like a captive animal, his attitude was changing. The anger, the madness was no longer there. He seemed calmer, almost normal.

What would he do with me now?

There were no longer helicopters in the sky, the search was obviously over. It had been such a long time since my disappearance. By now they must have thought I was dead. Lost in the bush, never to be found. No one would know I'd been kidnapped and was still very much alive.

Did he think he could hold me indefinitely? Releasing me would never work. Even if I said I wouldn't tell, the police would not stop questioning me, until they had the answers they needed. He'd backed himself into a corner with very few options. What was his plan?

I had to play this game very carefully and act quickly, if I was going to get out alive. I would have to pretend that I too loved this place as much as him and never wanted to leave. He needed to think I'd lost my desire to escape and trust me enough to unshackle me. Only then would I have even the remotest chance of leaving.

I grabbed a broken plastic flower pot and proceeded to pick the ripe blackberries, trying to remain calm, pretending this was the most important task at hand. In truth my mind raced, thinking of how I could escape, planning my next move.

Food and sex, food and sex, was the mantra I repeated over and over to myself. Keep focused, keep clear.

The lemon and bay leaves completed the stuffing and I put the chicken in to roast. I made a free form blackberry pie using the chipped enamel plate to contain the case. Then waited as the oven worked its magic. The rich shortcrust pastry and the sweet purple fruit smelt divine and the roasted chicken looked more tempting than Eve's apple. I looked proudly at the food and was sure it would be perfect to tempt my captor.

He set the table again, this time adding wine glasses. My job would be easy.

We ate and he praised my efforts, the wine loosened his tongue. And like the night before, I cleared up and then headed for bed.

'Don't go, it's too early, stay a bit longer. I've got more wine.'

He was mine. I sat back down.

'What's your name?' I asked.

'Moses,'

'Cheers, Moses,' I said, as I filled my glass.

'Do you ever eat the wallaby you catch?' I enquired, trying to keep the conversation going.

'Na, too dry. Rather sell it. What about you?'

'Yeah. It's really popular where I live. Kangaroo, wallaby, crocodile, young chefs are hungry for new ingredients. There's this restaurant near me that trains young indigenous kids. They serve bush tucker, tricked up city style. Their wallaby tartare is one of my favorites.'

'Raw? You're fuckin' joking!'

'No, really, it's great. You like my food, what I cook, bet I could change your mind.'

'Don't know about that,' he said, with a cynical curiosity.

The kettle was spluttering furiously on the stove and I got up to make a pot of tea. By the time it was ready I saw that my dinner companion had fallen asleep, head on his hands, snoring at the table. He had been hunting all night and up all day.

Tonight I would let him sleep.

Deep in the middle of the night I was awoken by the sound of gunshot. I guess he had to make the most of the good weather. With Christmas and the tourist season just around the corner, demand for wallaby meat would increase.

He came in late the following morning with another full load. Another trip to town.

'Anything you need? Like bread...' he said, staring at the last of the mouldy crusts I'd intentionally left out.

'Yeah... actually could you see if they've got any yeast? I can bake bread and then we'd never run out. I'll check the fridge.'

To my surprise, the first thing I saw was part of a freshly butchered wallaby carcass.

'Hey, what's this?'

'Thought I might let you change my mind,' he said, smiling. The proud hunter.

'Did you need anything special to make it edible?'

I thought about it for awhile.

'Some Worcestershire sauce, mustard and caper berries, if they've got them?'

'Write it down, I'll never remember half that shit.'

'Oh and Moses would you mind if I used the bathroom while you're gone?'

'Can't see why not,' he said taking the list and heading out the door.

With the chains and locks securely sealing me in and my shackles still attached, he left confident I would still be here when he returned.

He seemed unfazed by my requests and quite frankly I was kind of chuffed at his attempt to impress me with the wallaby.

The shower was blissful, hot, soapy and long. I wished I had something else to wear. The shirt was getting smelly, as was all the linen on my bed. The bath was big enough, so I stripped the bed and trod the grimy sheets like a peasant pressing grapes. A makeshift line of chairs would hopefully dry the laundry before bedtime. My only piece of clothing, the shirt, dried quickly in front of the wood stove.

He was gone for longer this time, the sun was already setting, perhaps he had to go further. Maybe he'd thought that Joe's shop wouldn't have all the things I needed. It was imperative that he got his supplies from the Lands End shop. Only Joe would spot the changes in Moses' grocery list.

'Jesus, can't you sit still?' he exclaimed, as he walked through the door, seeing the sheets draped all over the place.

'I looked at the sheets after I had my shower and didn't want to crawl back into a filthy bed. I just felt too squeaky clean and this shirt was foul, needed washing too. I don't like sitting around doing nothing, it's not in my nature,' I protested.

I took the bags of groceries out of his hands and started to unpack. Thank God, he got the caper berries, the same ones I'd found in Adam's pantry. Now I knew we were most definitely near Joe's. I prayed Joe had noticed Moses' unusual purchase.

'You managed to get all the things on the list?'

'Yeah, just about everything, had to go a bit further for the Worcestershire sauce, seems there's not much demand for it these days. And while I was in town, I got you these.'

He produced a cardboard tray filled with punnets of seedlings.

'I thought about what you said about the bread. Got me thinking that we could get the garden going again.'

He said 'we'. This was good. He was thinking about our future.

That night I served him the wallaby tartare and the last of the blackberry tart.

He ate everything and praised me for my efforts,

'Thanks, that was bloody good!'

But the night work was taking its toll and he politely excused himself and went to bed early.

I was surprised to see him still in bed when I got up that morning. Usually he would be up, loading his truck with the nights kill. Perhaps it was a weekend and he was taking a day off. I would need to pay more attention to his trips away, find out if there was any pattern to his movements.

I worked quietly as he slept. He woke to the smell of freshly baked bread.

I noticed his awkwardness at being served in bed. He was muscular, sinewy, strong. His nakedness made him look vulnerable. I let him eat alone, returning to the cellar, not wanting to upset his sensibilities.

By mid morning I could hear the sound of plastic ripping and went up to investigate. He had brought in a massive cardboard box from the shed and to my astonishment, was unpacking a brand new washing machine.

'Thought you might be able to use this, bought it for when the house was going to be finished. Not much use to anyone sittin' in the shed gathering dust.'

I clapped my hands with glee, pretending that it was the best thing ever.

'Tell me what you want washed and I'll try it out straight away.'

It was bizarre how something as mundane as a washing machine, a simple domestic appliance so taken for granted, now seemed so wonderful. I liked the sense of order and control it gave my strange little domestic world.

He handed me a bundle of clothes and helped me strip his bed.

Outside he took me to a clothesline and when it was hung, propped the line with a tall pole allowing the washing to flutter high in the summer breeze.

Back at the house, after the sheets had dried, we remade his bed.

'Why didn't you finish the house?' I asked.

He stopped abruptly, left the shack and locked the door. Had I just screwed up? Turned back the clock? Would I be marched back to the cellar and have to start this whole tedious process again? Fuck him. This time I would not retreat, I would continue doing what I knew pleased him and deal with his mood swing when he returned.

During the preparation of the meal he came back. Silently he placed the crockery on the table, setting for two. Thank God, he wasn't angry, just sad.

'Jessica was my wife. She died. The house was for her.'

He sat and I took his hand, looking him in the eye.

'I'm sorry, I didn't mean to upset you. These were her things, weren't they?' gesturing to the plates, the silver.

'The empty containers in the bathroom. I'm sorry for throwing them out.'

He didn't speak, but a tear rolling down his cheek told me enough. He coughed to clear his throat, take control before he spoke.

'No, it's me who's sorry. I've treated you badly and behaved like a fuckin' animal. I don't know who I've become.'

Discovering Moses

And so the cooking continued. I'd ask for things and he would do his best to bring them back. Never questioning even the most obscure of ingredients.

I had awakened his palate. He looked forward to trying what I cooked. Responding enthusiastically as if eating for the very first time.

Even with his few words, I knew he was astonished by my ability to work a kind of culinary magic. I lapped up his admiration and praise. He had only ever eaten for survival, not for pleasure. My food, cooking for him, was a way of connecting, slowly breaking down the protective emotional wall he'd built around himself.

Now I needed to know why he'd become so fucked up in the first place.

My shackles remained. I was still a prisoner, but eventually began to feel less trapped as Moses' mood lightened. Every day he would pack up more boxes and move them to the shed. A bonfire got rid of the rubbish. Eventually the hoard that had cluttered the room, and threatened to suffocate him, began to clear. He let me clean and slowly I was able to make the small house more habitable. One day he replaced the sealed windows with new ones, salvaged from the incomplete building. Windows that opened up, letting the fresh air in.

'You might like these,' he said, presenting me with a soft black garbage bag stuffed with clothing.

I peered inside and tentatively pulled out the first garment, a pretty dress with a fine floral print.

'Moses, are you sure?' I asked, holding the dress against my body.

'Yes,' he replied resolutely.

They were not what I was familiar with. They were pretty, ultra feminine, not my usual style. But at least they were dresses and made me feel like a woman, not a prisoner in a plaid shirt. I washed and dried the things I liked and hung them in a wardrobe he'd unearthed in the clean up.

Each day I put on something new, aware of the joy it gave Moses to see the garments his wife had once worn. Perhaps bringing a little bit of her back to life. It felt good to see him happy. Sometimes I felt like dancing around the room.

My plan to seduce him seemed pointless. The food was enough to gain his trust. I no longer felt threatened by him and knew I was not at risk of being harmed.

And I too was changing, beginning to enjoy this simple life. Even though I was still in chains, I no longer saw myself as a captive. I looked forward to Moses returning home, he eagerly anticipating the meals I prepared for him. I stopped giving him lists, as he now brought things home that he wanted to try. Keen to see what I would do to turn simple ingredients into delicious food. It was a new, uncomplicated game I loved to play.

We got on well and slowly I began to talk more freely to him. The more he drank, the more he talked. Backing away from his usual monosyllabism, replacing it with surprising erudition.

Satisfied after another meal and a glass of wine, I got the courage to ask him the question that had plagued me since my kidnapping. The more I got to know him, the less of a psychopathic killer he seemed to be.

He appeared to be a man in deep grieving. He was not violent, but quite gentle and did not fit the profile of some deranged criminal.

'Moses, why me?'

He paused, breathing deeply and looking into the distance, contemplating what he was about to say.

'I'd been out hunting in that waste land. That's when I saw you use a gun. Wondered why you were there on Darcy's land. Stayed around a few days to find out more. Saw you with him on the other side of the bridge, knew you had to be more than just friends.'

I remembered that day, washing the sheets, hearing what I thought was a vehicle. I was embarrassed to know that Moses had probably seen Adam fucking me on the banks of the river, near the bridge.

'I wanted to take somethin' from him, from Darcy. I wanted him to feel what it really meant to lose somethin', someone special. To lose the power he thought his money could buy. To feel the pain I'd felt.'

The mention of his name brought back floods of emotion. I wanted to know more. How did Moses know Adam. Did Adam get out alive? What was going on in the outside world? So many questions. Moses had begun to tell me he had some kind of score to settle with Adam, or 'Darcy' as he had called him.

'Was this about the anti logging stuff? I saw the pamphlets when you cleared the table, knew Adam had sided with the greenies all those years ago,' I asked.

'That and a fucking lot more.'

Moses told me that his family had lived in the area for many generations. The men worked as loggers, it was all they knew.

'Then the greenies arrived. I'd seen it in other places and knew their protests were inevitable. They were a rag tag bunch of lefties who thought that by saving this patch of land, they were doing their bit to save the planet. Their protests were pretty ineffectual against the trucks and bulldozers and we generally left each other alone. This wasn't pristine wilderness like the Tarkine or the Franklin River.'

'Things didn't get ugly till Adam Darcy showed up, flashing his money around. His lawyers got some expert in to say that the forest, that had been logged for almost 150 years, was the habitat of a rare species of wallaby. He was hailed by the mainlanders as a hero for trying to save the cute little creatures, putting his money to a worthy cause, defying the stereotype of the average billionaire.'

I remembered Adam telling me about trying to stop the logging but had never asked why he felt so strongly about it. It had just seemed obvious that it was worth saving beautiful forests like our island sanctuary. I had seen the desolation of the land across the bridge. Didn't ask why their protests had failed.

'They were able, through the courts, to put a stop to the logging, halting production, pretty much shutting down the local mill. He tried to talk to the townspeople, telling them that logging in this part of the world was barely profitable, that the yields of timber were too low. That the economic future was in tourism and with the opening up of more national parks there would be plenty of work. He even purchased the service station to show that he believed in the future.'

'No one bought the story and, while the court case dragged on, the jobs slowly disappeared. But in truth, this was a community too set in their ways for change. The people here just wanted things to go back to the way it was before the greenies turned up. Before the court case. The townspeople still held out hope that one day things would return to normal. The old men, my father, my grandfather still kept their axes sharpened. I got involved with the union to help fight for the men who would be disenfranchised by the job losses if we didn't win the court case. It took me to Hobart and I met a whole lot more people with a bigger view of the world,' he paused and took another sip of his wine.

'What did you find out?'

'I always thought the company that owned the plantation and the mill was one of those big businesses, owned by shareholders with a CEO keeping things running, keeping the investors happy. What I learnt was that Graham Darcy was the biggest shareholder and that Adam was his son. The union did some digging and found the two men had a bitter hatred for one another. I began to think that this dispute was about the enmity between father and son, not Adam Darcy's new found greenie leanings. Perhaps Darcy had sided with the greenies to piss his father off?'

I wondered how Moses came to this conclusion but let him continue so I could find out more.

'In the end we won. The courts found no case to answer, the population of wallabies was not under threat and the land was freed up to be logged like it always had. What we didn't see was Graham Darcy's response. Usually the logging was done selectively. We'd take out the mature trees, leaving the rest to grow. We'd plant new seedlings, continuing the life cycle of the forest, keeping everyone employed. It was early 2007, the Japanese were the biggest buyers of the timber, but there was talk of the market slowing. Graham Darcy ordered the whole lot to be clear felled, sell the lot for wood chipping, strip the land and leave nothing. He wanted to get out of the timber business. I wondered whether it was simply that Graham Darcy wanted to leave a reminder to his son of what happens when you 'fuck with the big players'.'

I was horrified to think this could be true.

'The land was eventually sold to a local timber company, but they were caught up in another long running dispute and didn't have the money to replant the forest. They eventually went broke and the land was tied up in legal limbo as the receivers tried to untangle the financial mess of the current owners. In the meantime the bottom dropped out of the timber market. It seemed like there may never be trees planted on that site again.'

'And your family, what happened to them?'

'My grandfather died. My father went to Western Australia. He thought he was young enough to be part of the mining boom, but he was too old and too unskilled. He lives in a caravan park, on welfare, a broken man.'

'And Jessica?' I asked quietly.

Moses shook his head and took a deep breath before continuing.

'Jessica had breast cancer many years ago. We both thought it had been successfully treated. The future looked good. We had just begun to build the house when the protests started. Jess didn't mind that we had to put everything on hold. She knew how important it was for me to continue the fight, to try and save the jobs and the town. So I returned to Hobart to continue the fight against Adam Darcy. The battles continued, on and off, for another two years'

Tears welled in his eyes and he paused to regain his composure.

'What she didn't tell me was that while I was away the cancer had returned. After one of her checkups the doctor rang me and said he was worried that Jessica didn't seem to understand the seriousness of her condition. I was shocked, it was the first I knew of the cancers return. It wasn't until I went with her to the doctor that he said I should prepare for the worst. Said there was nothing more they could do. He told me to make the most of our time together, as there was precious little left. I asked Jessica why she didn't tell me and she said she didn't want to upset me, thought the fight for the town and the jobs was so much more important. She died six weeks later. And I had spent the last few years of her life, wasting my time, caught up in a futile battle that ultimately saw no winners. I will never get that time back. I hated Adam Darcy for what he took away from me.'

He was silent. I didn't know what to think.

'I retreated into myself. Found that hunting gave me enough money to survive on. It was lonely and isolating, what I wanted, what I needed. Without trees the grass grew, was easy feed for the wallabies, and the population increased. Ironically, that land became a very good for the wallabies and a very good place for hunting.'

'A few weeks ago I was out hunting when I saw surveyors mapping out the site. They said, that after all these years, the land was to be sold. Naturally enough I was curious and rang my union mates to see if they could shed any light. They told me the area was going to be mined, that it's rich in rare earth minerals. The union was pleased, knowing it would bring jobs to the area and was working in co-operation with the company that was looking into buying the site. They told me that surprisingly Adam Darcy was the owner of the company and that his brother was manager of the new project. They said I'd better get in there soon and take out as much game as possible before the land gets locked up for good. They told me to keep it quiet until after the election, didn't want the greenies to interfere. That bastard had done it again, taken away my livelihood and this time I would have no support from the union. I understood what mining could mean for the area, of the jobs it would bring. I couldn't go to the papers because I didn't want to see another long drawn out dispute with the greenies who seemed to hate mining more than logging. This time I was on my own. I hated Darcy even more.'

I couldn't believe what I was hearing. Why didn't Adam say anything to me. I laughed at the thought of his feeble attempts at rehabilitating the land, planting those seedlings, hoping to save his little bit of paradise when all along his intentions were to mine the fuck out of the land across the river. My blood boiled even more knowing he'd put his asshole of a brother in charge.

'Anyway I knew I needed to act quickly, take as much as possible before being prohibited from hunting in that area. I planned to be away for a few days. The drop off point wasn't that far away. I could fill my truck, take the carcasses to the depot and be back to hunt in a much shorter time than if I went back home every night. I'd only been there for a day or two when I heard the shots. You shooting those rabbits spooked the wallabies, they disappeared. I had nothing to hunt, but became quite obsessed by the woman with the gun, stayed around to see what was going on. I watched as you attempted to walk out and, in a moment of madness, thought you could be mine, that I could take something that was his. As a hunter, I knew you would offer less resistance if you were weak. I didn't think you'd last as long as you did and was impressed by your tenacity. When I captured you, I fantasised about you being my wife. It was only when you screamed at me from the cellar that I realised what a fucked up fantasy it was and what an animal I'd become.'

Shocked by what he had just said, I didn't really know how to react. Moses sat there silently, looking at my face, waiting for a response after the enormity of what he'd just told me.

I got up and left the table, retreating to my bed, needing some place alone to contemplate the implications of what he had revealed.

I felt such a bitter sense of betrayal by Adam. I couldn't defend a man who had only told me part of the story. Adam had told me nothing of what Moses had just revealed. The full story was so much more than a timber company going broke. I couldn't believe I'd been caught up in this absurd circus.

I thought I loved Adam. But I had been kidding myself about who he really was? It was as if I didn't really know him at all.

Moses came down the stairs.

'Are you ok?'

'I just need some time alone. To think about what you've told me. I'm sorry for what they did to you.'

'It's not your fault. Can I get you anything?'

'Can you tell me if he's still alive?' I whispered coldly.

'Yeah, he survived alright, but no one knows where he's gone. Saw a story in the paper that he and his girlfriend have gone overseas. Press had been hounding them a bit. Rich men like that have always got some woman ready in the wings.'

Moses placed a ripped out page from a newspaper on the bed. It showed Adam climbing up the stairs of a jet with a woman. Not just any woman. Sissy Snelling. He was holding her hand. The caption said she was his girlfriend.

What an idiot I'd been. She must have been biding her time, waiting to step in when Adam really needed her. I'd thought it was over. She had obviously meant more to him than what Adam had chosen to tell. And when he was in trouble the clan had regrouped and, by the look of the photo, he had willingly come back into the fold.

The same old insecurities came flooding back. There I was stupidly fantasising about some blissful nirvana we could create for ourselves. This was never going to happen. He and I could never exist together in the real world. Adam was even more fucked up than I thought. It was as if he lived in two worlds. The real world of his family and the make believe one he thought he could escape to with me. I'd been the biggest fool in this charade.

Sleep eluded me that night. I tossed and turned, my mind working overtime. The sedatives would have brought welcome relief.

At breakfast I asked more questions.

'What makes you think that Adam and his father are bitter enemies? Couldn't this have just been a coincidence? Maybe Adam, like you, didn't know who owned the company? Perhaps he did care about the land. Believed in the fight, put his money where his mouth was?'

'The union did some digging, they didn't have to look far. His brother's wife spilled the beans, demanded money in return for information. She told us that it started when the old man was looking at buying up property in Melbourne. Old stuff, warehouses in the inner city, undervalued properties in a market that was about to explode. Turns out that Adam had the same idea and secretly went to the owner of a big old factory and made him an offer he couldn't refuse. Pulled the property right out from under his father's nose. Kicking out the long term tenant and redeveloping the site into a multi storey apartment block. Seems this is where all the rivalry started.'

'She said the two of them sparred like this all the time, playing games of one-upmanship, trying to outsmart each other. She was the one who told us it was always Adams intention to piss his father off by supporting the greenies. She told us that Graham Darcy threatened Adam. Told him to back off or he'd rip the whole lot out. Adam laughed at his father, didn't believe he'd take such drastic action. Adam didn't back off and when the court case was over Graham Darcy made good his threat and stripped the land. If it wasn't for Adam Darcy's pig headedness the forest would still be there. And if he felt so strongly about the environment, then why is he going to obliterate the site by mining it?'

I sat and stared blankly into my cup, even more confused than before.

'You didn't know any of this, did you?'

'No, but the man you describe is not the man I know,' I responded pathetically, hurt and somewhat defensive.

'I'm sorry to break the spell he had over you. I think you need to understand that men like him, his father, are just sociopaths that don't care who gets swept up in the games they play. They have no regard for the consequences of their behavior or for the people whose lives are incidental in their lust for power and wealth. At least Graham Darcy was honest about who he was, never sugar coating his intentions. Perhaps

Adam was just better at hiding it. Rich men like him can always pay some obsequious ass licker to do their dirty work, so that they come out looking squeaky clean.'

'His father did him a favour by bulldozing the forest. Originally Adam had wanted to buy the land but the father refused to sell it to him, sold it off to that other timber company instead. When they went broke, Adam Darcy would have been able to pick it up for next to nothing.'

'Sometimes I wonder if this was part of a very elaborate plan. That Darcy knew of the lands mining potential and worked out the best way to piss his father off, get him to make good his threat, so that no one would complain when Adam took over what had now become a worthless piece of land.'

I could barely take in what Moses was saying. That this was a well orchestrated scheme that would see Adam get the land all along. I had no comprehension of this type of thinking until I was reminded of the stories Paul and his friends would tell of Adams Machiavellian genius in business. They always spoke of how brilliantly he was able to out manoeuvre his competitors and pick up seemingly worthless businesses for a song. That he operated with a 'take no prisoners' ruthlessness that only a true sociopath could ever consider.'

The man Moses described fitted this description perfectly. The greenies, the loggers, the towns people were all just collateral damage.

'What I don't understand is why someone like you is with him? You're not one of them. What's the attraction? From what I've read, you're rich and successful. You're not after his money? What's the deal?'

I thought about what Moses had said and was wounded by his lecture. I hated that he had identified a weakness in me. The man Moses had just described wasn't the man I thought I loved. But there it was, the newspaper clipping and Moses story. The real Adam Darcy.

'I don't know now, I really don't,' I eventually replied

Perhaps Moses was not my kidnapper, but my saviour.

Confused

The cellar became my retreat. What was once my prison became my sanctuary. Moses had revealed so much. I didn't know what to think. I felt completely confused and lost. I was beaten and no longer wanted to be the unwitting player in these games of broken men.

Gone was the stoic wife, proud mother, business woman, survivor. I didn't give a fuck about anything, I didn't care.

Moses retreated too, leaving me alone to quietly sulk. My refuge breached only by offerings of food and water and the removal of the bucket. This was my choice. Moses didn't know what to make of this new situation.

'Christina, you hungry? Wanna cook something? I've got some new stuff I found in town. Thought you'd know what to do with it,' he would plead, hoping I would give up the indolence and return to be his friend and confidante.

I couldn't be bothered. Being here was not my choice, he was my captor, not my comrade.

After a few days of self enforced exile, I was woken by the sound of him walking up and down the steps, dragging something, moving things. Peeking out from under the covers I saw him carrying away the pelts, bundle after bundle, until the room was almost bare. He cleared all but my bed, which he dragged to the middle of the room. Using a broom he swept the cobwebs and dust from the walls and floor, then disappeared for awhile. I retreated back under the blankets like a sulking child.

It was the smell that disturbed me, new paint. He was whitewashing the walls. When he finished, he left me alone.

Power tools buzzed outside and I watched as he removed the vents and replaced some with new mesh and others with glass. Light and air flooded into my white room.

Still I remained a recluse.

Morning came and he dragged the bed back to its original position. I felt rather stupid pretending not to be affected by his strange manoeuvres, still hiding under the covers. More power tools saw cast iron hooks drilled into the walls near the sink, then armfuls of the dresses were hung neatly in rows. Clunk, clunk down the stairs, grunting with exertion as he wrestled a heavy old dresser to its position on the opposite wall. Next came a mirror and a small bedside table. I turned my back as if not to care and let him continue uninterrupted for the next few hours.

When he finally left, shutting the trap door, my curiosity got the better of me. I came out from under the covers to discover what all the activity had been about.

His truck drove off and eventually the distant sound of shooting told me he would be gone for the night.

I was free to explore.

It was bright. An electric light illuminated the room, the cord snaking its way from the floor above. He had filled the cellar with things to make it look homely and comfortable. It was feminine and I wondered whether the beautiful antique furniture had been originally collected for his own house, their home. A comfy high backed armchair sat next to a standard lamp. An elegant small table was set with fine china and fruit, beckoning me to sit and take tea. The dresser contained clean towels, linen and toiletries. The hard concrete floor was covered with a fine woollen rug. A bedside table, with a reading lamp, held my books. The cellar looked like a museum exhibit depicting the bedroom of a nineteenth century colonial lady.

I smiled at the genuine attempt to make amends and wept to discover the chains had been removed, only the ring remained around my ankle. I climbed the stairs and pushed the trap door, it was not locked, and I pushed it open.

It was strange to wander around the house without the sound of the chains following my every move, a pleasant quiet. So much had changed in the time since my capture. All the junk he'd been drowning in for the last few years had been removed. It still looked like a man's retreat, but gone was the dehumanising filth and clutter that had shocked me when I first looked upstairs.

A neat stack of papers remained, a recorded history of this man's life. The fight for the town and more recently the woman lost. They were openly laid out on the table, obviously meant for me to see.

He had kept all the clippings, the story of the search, familiar faces, disturbing reminders of the past. A stock photo of Adam, the caption described him as a 'friend' of the missing woman Christina Maxwell aka Chris Brown. I thought we were more than that?

The press didn't need to look far for a story. Fiona had become the spokesperson in the early days of the search.

'The Darcy family are saddened by the loss. We had become increasingly worried about Chris's behavior after her husband's death. We believe there was no romantic link between Adam and Chris and that she had spontaneously chosen to visit the site at Lands End Lagoon.'

The article implied almost stalkerish behavior, that I was somehow mentally unstable and that the police could not rule out suicide. Fiona was finally getting her revenge. I wondered how much she was being paid? The papers were having a field day.

As the weeks went on the story died down. The police concluded there were no suspicious circumstances and that my death was accidental.

A private memorial service was conducted, said the small paragraph, and with that I was gone.

A blurry picture of Margot, her arm around Kate, getting into a car.

I was furious. No one seemed to have spoken up in my defence. Adam's family closing ranks was no real surprise, I was only ever an interloper and my untimely demise would most likely have been celebrated. But Adam, Kate, Cindy, all my friends seemed to have kept silent, not a word in my defence.

I was hurt. Had I been so obsessed with my business that I'd failed to see just how much I'd neglected those around me? Could I no longer see what was real?

I kept turning the pages, a morbid fascination for the stories of my untimely demise. This wasn't healthy. I was about to stop, when I saw one last disturbing story.

The headline said, 'Mother and Daughter Estranged.' That nasty little shit Will, Kate's boyfriend, was interviewed. He spoke about how Kate and I could not agree on the way I had set up the business in Cambodia. That she and I had nothing to do with each other. Describing me as someone who put her business, making money, before anything else. I came across as someone not even I would like. Was there some truth in what he was saying?

Even before that disastrous meeting in Canberra, we had seen very little of each other. When home, Kate often chose to spend the time with her friends. And now she had found Will, he had filled the gap left by an absent mother.

What was the place she came back to? A soulless flat, with few of her possessions, most definitely not the family home she grew up in. By rejecting all those things from my past had I in fact rejected her?

Seeing her with Margot also brought home another confronting truth. She was not a copy of me. All those people whom I so deeply despised were in fact her people. She had gone to their schools, socialised with them, lived near them and would probably marry one of them. Not out of defiance, but because they were all she knew. She loved her father, he hadn't done anything to upset her. I had never told her the full story. Had I fantasised about some secret little pact we had? An 'us against the world' mentality, that was not her reality? My own insecurities about fitting in, being accepted, were my fears alone.

The photo clearly showed Margot embracing Kate, her demeanour one of care and affection. Had I missed Kate's need to be with her grandmother, a link to the father she loved, a man for whom she probably deeply grieved? Did she resent me for shipping her off to university in Canberra, rather than keeping her in Melbourne? Or now that I was gone, was Margot just claiming what was hers? Her grandchild, the daughter of her son.

Had I been so self obsessed that I didn't see my daughter slipping away from me?

Cindy too, had increasingly become frustrated at my micromanaging. She had sent me away because of it. I imagined that the sensationalism surrounding my disappearance would only boost traffic to the site and she would be working harder than ever. We had consciously put on more managers, writers and designers to ease my workload. The business could easily survive without me and, as the other main shareholder, Cindy would not let it slip through her fingers.

My mind started to fill with self doubt. Had I been delusional? Cindy and I had edited out the negative comments on the blog. 'I am great', was all we were letting the readers see. But was I just creating a lie, perpetuated to convince myself that all was ok?

Even my relationship with the Finestras had become strained. Fucking Raphael made me feel powerful. Being with him told the world that I was the choice of this desirable man. Nobody knew about the loveless, nihilistic sex. For God's sake, I had stooped so low as to allow his lover into my bed. What sort of a fucked up person lets this happen?

And the one man I had truly loved could not even make this declaration public, defending me against the nasty aspersions of that bitch Fiona and the stories in an increasingly hostile press.

Adam's and my relationship had only been able to survive in the most absurd situations, outside of the parameters of normality. His real life away, from the island, was one we'd never shared. And now, after what Moses had said and the clippings he'd left for me to read, I realised a life with Adam Darcy would never, ever work.

Anger started to overwhelm me.

What kind of fool had I been, lost in my own little world of make believe? What did I have to go home to? A big lonely house. A daughter who no longer needed me, despised what I did. And the man I'd so foolishly thought I could love, had already moved on.

The biggest wakeup call had been that picture of Adam. Climbing the stairs to his jet followed by a woman who supposedly meant nothing to him. The caption described him as the *'reclusive billionaire, leaving Melbourne with his girlfriend,* Georgina Snelling,' sister of Fiona.

No wonder Fiona's stories to the press had been so appalling. She had much more invested in that family than I had realised. Their bonds and loyalties were stronger than ever. The papers told me all I needed to know and now I needed to stop reading.

The warmth from the oven drew me towards it. I looked around the humble shack and felt a sense of peace. This place gave me an alternative, the option of a simpler life with someone who understood the real me. We had so much more in common, similar pasts, had both survived tragedy. Perhaps what I'd been looking for was here all along? I thought about the 'four commandments' of Aura and Henry and wondered whether the answers were here. Had I found someone to share the journey with? Somewhere safe to retreat to? Something away from my business?

I pulled up a chair and stared blankly at the embers. The table, set for one, invited me to eat. I lifted the lid of a pot of soup and was touched that Moses had thought to leave it for me. He had not forgotten.

He was a man I understood. No more pretending, he accepted me for who I was. To him, I had nothing to prove. My wealth and success had not filled the gap, perhaps it was here that I could find the peace and acceptance I had been looking for? The kidnapping just a serendipitous quirk of fate.

The door was unlocked, I walked outside. A bright full moon lit up the landscape. In the shed his guns were all laid out. I could take any one of them. He trusted me, I was free.

I returned to the house.

The hot bath washed away the smell of my week's withdrawal and, instead of retreating to my new boudoir, I went to Moses' vacant bed.

The Pact

He had tried to be quiet on his return, but I was already awake as the dawn light cast its greyness over the room, the bed, the sheets. I could see him through the open door of the bathroom. It took me some time to realise what he was doing. Clumps of hair fell from his face as the electric shaver did its work. A foggy image of a man began to appear in the mirror. He then took to his scalp buzzing away the mane that had kept him hidden for so long. He showered and washed away the blood of the night's kill and the last of the hair.

He did not dress, but walked naked to the bed and silently crawled in.

The beard had been a mask. He now looked angelic, boyish, vulnerable. I reached out and touched the soft virgin skin of his face and opened my palm to rub, sensuously, the rough stubble on his scalp. I held him close, feeling the need to cover and protect him.

I heard the sharp intake of air, his breath quickening, his cock stiffening against my stomach. I wanted him to savour this moment, control his response. I would work slowly.

Taking his hand I guided it to my mouth, delicately kissing, licking and biting each finger, stopping when I sensed him becoming overwhelmed, laying calmly against him till the moment passed. He knew what I was doing and responded by accepting the stillness. Calming himself by breathing slowly, fighting the longing that he was choosing to hold back.

I wanted him to touch me and again took his hand, letting him feel the exquisite sensation of my hardening nipples tickling his open palms. He repeated the gesture, teasing my other breast. I breathed deeply, my chest rising, my need building. He made his first assertive move and clasped both his hands around each breast, squeezing tightly, closing his eyes, groaning at the pleasure such a simple gesture offered. I let him twist the nipple between his fingers and delighted when he tugged firmly, beginning to awaken my entire body from its passionless sleep. I took his face in my hands, let my fingers trace the line of his jaw and kissed him, closing my mouth as his tongue delved impatiently. He retracted and I showed him how to bite playfully, his lips, his jaw, his neck.

He tentatively used his tongue to explore my mouth and I opened up to him, encouraging him, delighting in his now more decisive response. When he stopped to catch his breath, I played with his nipples. Running my hands across his chest, combing my fingers through the hair, then circling the sensitive areola. I followed the dark line down his flattened stomach and circled just above his pubic bone, then back up again. His back arched in response.

Unlike my first, short, seduction I did not need to fake arousal, taking his hand and letting him feel the hot, moist result of this slower foreplay. He tried to push deep inside, rushing with the unsophistication of his inexperience. Again I took his hand and guided it around the valley of my thighs, encouraging him to explore, groaning as he found my engorged clitoris, teaching him what I liked by proffering sighs of pleasure when he found the right place.

After relaxing into the delicate dance his fingers played, I sensed a greater confidence, and was curious to know, when he stopped, what would happen next.

Moses got up and opened the windows, the doors, letting the fresh air and bright morning sun fill the room.

He returned to the bed and assertively pulled the sheet away. He kneeled at my feet, then parted my legs, exposing my entire body. He sat and observed, almost awestruck by the beauty of his discovery and the boldness of his move. I watched as his eyes followed his hands, returning to my throbbing cunt, continuing the exploration. I bent my knee, opening up, inviting him in.

He let his fingers travel over my belly, leaving a glossy trail of wetness, circling my breast, then, leaning down, he placed his mouth over the rose tip and sucked hard until the nipple stood firm, sending electrifying signals throughout my body. I wanted more.

Almost apprehensively he raised his body above mine and I offered no resistance to his hard cock as it then forcefully parted my lips and slid easily into me. He paused, sucking in his breath, wanting to control his response, needing to delay his orgasm in order to truly appreciate the sensuousness of the act. He lay back down onto my body, slipping his hands under my head. He tilted my chin up, stared into my eyes and kissed me, while slowly pushing his cock deeper.

The fear and anger had left his eyes.

It was me who groaned, needing now to be fucked hard to release a pent up desire that had been building gradually over the last few days. I tilted my hips, begging him to move, and knowingly he slid his hands beneath my backside and gripped my cheeks giving him the traction needed to ram hard against my womb, pulling my clitoris firmly against his pubis, awakening the nerves tingling at the sensitive tip. And he held back no longer, slamming harder and harder, until his body exploded into a shattering orgasm, then falling limp, sated with satisfaction.

No sobbing this time, just the contented smile of a man gratified, replete.

Feeling his energy slip away, his arms relaxing, he fell asleep.

Soon he would learn how to satisfy me. I would be patient, give him time.

I had no need to stay in bed. I let him rest. I had heard him put his kill into the cool room this morning. It didn't take long, he must have had a meagre night. He wouldn't be going to town today. He would be out hunting again tonight.

The crumpled dress from the day before lay on the floor beside the bed. I slipped it over my head and walked outside.

Clear blue sky, warm summer's morning. My first whole day of freedom. My choice to be here. The beauty of the surroundings was breathtaking. I wandered about the place, looked at the half built house, thought of what could be created.

The lush green mountainous landscape looked so different to the barren drought stricken farm I'd grown up on. Could I possibly share it, stay here in this beautiful place, with someone who was more like me? Almost everything we wanted was here. And for the things the land could not provide, the hunting would give us all the money we needed. The garden was beginning to flourish, bright green lettuces were begging to be picked, the herbs were tantalising me with their fresh green tips, inspiring me to cook. Today it would be special, a slow cooked leg of wallaby, stuffed with garlic and rosemary. Baby potatoes, a crop sprouting from the compost, would only need a quick boiling. I would use what his land provided, show him just how little we needed from the outside world.

It was here in this simple garden, in this remote part of the world, I dreamed of what could be an uncomplicated life.

I remembered the formal ornate gardens of the big house and was embarrassed by their ostentation. They gave me no joy, with the never ending demands of watering, pruning, mowing, weeding. A frivolous fancy that was all for show.

In Fitzroy I had been convinced to build a house way beyond what I really needed. He had invited me to share his humble shack, cleaned it up, made it comfortable. Here I had taken pleasure in making do with what I had, realising I liked living simply. I felt a strange sense of freedom, no demands, no long working days, no confused relationships.

I could choose an unfettered life.

Moses had just made a stupid mistake, acted impulsively. I could forgive him, I didn't have to tell the truth, because that truth had changed.

I didn't want him to be punished.

He could take me into town. I could tell them he had found me. I had become hopelessly lost, lived by my wits. Saw the helicopters, but couldn't be seen. Couldn't believe my luck when I was finally rescued by the hunter. He would be hailed as a hero.

Surely they'd believe me, when I would tell them just how difficult the past eighteen months had been. That I hadn't truly grieved for my husband and all that had been taken when he had died. That I needed some time out to recover, to think about what my future would hold. I would tell them I wanted to stay here. I liked where the hunter lived. It was a place of sanctuary. He would tell them he was happy for me to remain.

Eventually Kate would understand. I had fought for her financial security, she was now a strong independent woman. Being here did not mean abandonment, she could come and visit, see the beauty that had lured me in, understand my need for a simpler life.

I knew what it was like to live a lie, it was easy to deceive. I could make it work.

He surprised me, I hadn't heard his quiet hunter's footsteps. He held me from behind and ran his hand over my breasts, down my stomach, feeling my body, naked beneath the flimsy cotton.

'What are you doing?' he whispered.

'Looking at how beautiful it is up here.'

He pulled me closer and I felt shielded in his embrace. We stood silently together, without words to describe what was happening. Both aware that things had changed.

Moses lifted the dress, wanting to touch the skin the fabric had shielded. He wore only pants and I breathed deeply as I felt the warmth of his hard body against my nakedness. An erect nipple, a tangle of hair and a moist cunt, gave in to his touch. His hard cock spoke the language of his body, and he lifted my dress off in response. He picked me up and carried me to the soft grass under the bay tree and, reverently, laid me down. He unbuttoned his worn khaki pants, kicked them aside and joined me. His cock stood proud and rigid, his pale body looked vulnerable, only the skin of his arms had seen sun. Without the need for the foreplay of the morning's first tentative encounter, I rolled onto his body and lifted my hips to allow his hard cock straight into me. I sat upright, feeling the slight agony at such deep penetration and groaned at the pleasure of this erotic pain. His back arched and he gasped for breath trying to control his primal response. He came quickly, and again, I would wait have to wait patiently as he learned to become a more adept lover, to give me sexual release. For now it didn't matter.

His eyes were no longer filled with melancholy, but showed me something new, something real, something that was, quite simply, life.

Serenaded by the summer cicadas, I looked at him. Calm, relaxed, dreaming of a future together.

Trip to Town

As I cooked, I told him of my plan and he was silent in his contemplation. He answered by getting up from the table, kissing me deeply, confirming my ideas. I happily finished preparing the evening meal and delighted as he wolfed down the food, wiping his chin with the back of his hand, smiling in praise.

I knew he loved the way I looked after this most primitive need.

'Come over here woman,' he said, slapping his belly and opening his arms, gesturing for me to come and sit on his lap.

'No, no, you need to get out and fill your quota.'

'It can wait,' he said unconvincingly.

'But I can't, the sooner you get into town, the sooner I get you back into my bed.'

'You are a devious bitch,' he said, smiling back wickedly.

He packed up his gear, kissed me farewell and drove off, with an eagerness my proposition had created.

The warm, still night was ideal for hunting and Moses had a full load way before sunrise. If he left now he would be back before lunch.

'Do you need anything?' he asked.

'Surprise me, bring me back a treat, something unexpected,' I replied.

'God, I think I've just about bought everything possible from that place, you make it difficult for me woman!'

'Chocolate, bring me chocolate, I will melt it and pour it over parts of your body I would like to lick clean. That's what I want.'

'Don't talk like that, or I'll never leave.'

Before he drove off, he told me it was Friday and that the guy who picks up the carcasses didn't work on weekends. Small snippets of information slowly bringing me in touch with the outside world. We could spend the whole weekend together, he wouldn't need to hunt. He wanted to be with me.

Moses said that he would to take me out into the forest, show me some of the magical places further away. That we could pack some food, sleep under the stars, get away for a few days, away from the hut, do things together.

He left smiling, window down, waving goodbye as the truck disappeared down the road. I waved back and when I could no longer see him, went inside, my head full of the things I would cook to satisfy his hunger.

I felt like the good country wife.

There was so much I wanted to get done. I didn't want to linger around the house. I wanted it to all be ready, so that we could set off as soon as he returned.

Time is a strange thing. I remembered the long drawn out days, weeks, of my early incarceration, a stark contrast to the urgency I now felt trying to have things ready and perfect for our trip into the forest.

Deadlines had recently taken over. I rarely had time for anything but work, a life filled to avoid thinking about the reality of my lonely existence.

I think I had finally found peace.

The food was ready. I didn't want to pack too much stuff, Moses lived simply and would have his way of spending time in the bush, knowing what to take.

I would leave that up to him.

My heart raced as I heard him speed up the track. The sight of a cloud of dust created as he pulled up abruptly right in front of door, told me his excitement and urgency were as great as mine.

The car door slammed and I was startled as he kicked the wooden door to the hut open, almost knocking it off its hinges.

'You scheming fuckin' cunt, you planned this all along,' gobs of spit coming from his mouth as he yelled, his face contorted with rage.

And before I could react to his madness I felt the searing pain of his fist hitting the side of my face. As I staggered to the table to steady myself, I felt a second, a third, a fourth blow taking me down, falling heavily to the hard concrete floor. My face smashed and broken, the taste of blood in my mouth. He didn't stop. A hard boot in my gut, winding me, causing me to gulp for breath, panting in short fearful bursts. Before I could get up he'd roughly tied my arms, re-chained my legs, then yanked me to my feet, pulling the ropes so hard, I thought he would dislocate my shoulders. He frog marched me to the truck, brutally forcing me into the back, hitting me with the butt of a gun till I laid down flat, covering me in hessian sacks. The indignity continued as I felt him toss his armoury of guns on top of me, bruising my head and legs.

'You fuckin' women are all the same!' he screamed, as he slammed the tailgate shut.

Moses tore furiously down the road, my body tossed around, the pain excruciating as I hit the hard metal sides of the vehicle.

Where was he going? What had changed? Who was this Jeckyll and Hyde man?

A familiar sound, helicopters above, sirens wailing.

The truck screamed to a halt, throwing my body hard against the cabin.

'Moses, you need to get out of the truck, we just want to talk,' said the voice, amplified by a loud hailer.

I heard the click, click of weapons loading. The deafening sound of gunshot rang out. They returned fire, my ears ringing at the assault.

It seemed to go on forever, voices imploring Moses to stop. The sound of him reversing, then the truck madly swerving, changing direction, tumbling me mercilessly around. My aching body tossed violently as we drove on even more bumpy terrain.

A sudden burning in my shoulder, told me I'd been hit, the pain excruciating. Another shot, the explosion of shattering glass, then nothing. We had stopped, the engine was dead.

Warm blood seeped under me. My head reeled at the thought that I may be dying.

Then silence.

I was losing consciousness.

Then nothing.

Follow Christina on her adventures with the final book in the trilogy.

Finding the Lost Woman
(book three in the lost woman trilogy)

Christina returns to her family and friends after her ordeal in Tasmania. She tries to convince herself that all will be well and that the voices in her head can be silenced.

Originally Christina created her blog to tell the truth, but now feels disconnected to the massive empire she has created. After her lies are exposed she seeks a simpler life.

Christina discovers the truth about her family's past.

How do you break down the protective emotional barriers you have built up over the years and confront what is truth?

Will she find sanctuary, a place where she can be her true self. Can she ever find lasting love?

Available by order from most book shops, buy on-line at Amazon, Book Depository, Barnes & Noble and other retailers, or as an eBook from Amazon, Google Books, Kobo and iBooks.

For more information go to annabuckley.com

www.ingramcontent.com/pod-product-compliance
Lightning Source LLC
Chambersburg PA
CBHW061515020726
47502CB00006B/2081

* 9 780992 478117 *